Writers
**FRED VAN LENTE, TODD DEZAGO,
CHRISTOPHER YOST,
BRANDON AUMAN & J**

P9-BZH-722

Pencilers
**MATTEO LOLLI, DEREC DONOVAN,
SCOTT KOBLISH, VICENTE CIFUENTES,
SCOTT WEGENER & WES CRAIG**

Inkers
**CHRISTIAN VECCHIA, DEREC DONOVAN,
SCOTT KOBLISH, VICENTE CIFUENTES,
SCOTT WEGENER & WES CRAIG**

Colorists
**GURU-eFX, CHRIS SOTOMAYOR &
JEAN-FRANCOIS BEAULIEU**

Letterer
DAVE SHARPE

Cover Art
**CLAYTON HENRY & GURU-eFX,
STEPHEN SEGOVIA AND CHRISTOPHER JONES**

Editors
**NATHAN COSBY, MICHAEL HOROWITZ,
TOM BRENNAN, STEPHEN WACKER &
SEBASTIAN GIRNER**

Collection Editor: Alex Starbuck **Assistant Editor:** Sarah Brunstad
Editors, Special Projects: Jennifer Grünwald & Mark D. Beazley
Senior Editor, Special Projects: Jeff Youngquist **SVP Print, Sales & Marketing:** David Gabriel

Editor in Chief: Axel Alonso **Chief Creative Officer:** Joe Quesada
Publisher: Dan Buckley **Executive Producer:** Alan Fine

MARVEL UNIVERSE ANT-MAN DIGEST. Contains material originally published in magazine form as MARVEL ADVENTURES SUPER HEROES #6 and 10, MARVEL UNIVERSE AVENGERS EARTH'S MIGHTIEST HEROES #17, AVENGERS: EARTH'S MIGHTIEST HEROES #2, and SUPER HEROES #19. First printing 2015. ISBN# 978-0-7851-9747-8. Published by MARVEL WORLDWIDE, INC., a subsidiary of MARVEL ENTERTAINMENT, LLC. OFFICE OF PUBLICATION: 135 West 50th Street, New York, NY 10020. Copyright © 2015 MARVEL No similarity between any of the names, characters, persons, and/or institutions in this magazine with those of any living or dead person or institution is intended, and any such similarity which may exist is purely coincidental. **Printed in the U.S.A.** ALAN FINE, President, Marvel Entertainment; DAN BUCKLEY, President, TV, Publishing and Brand Management; JOE QUESADA, Chief Creative Officer; TOM BREVOORT, SVP of Publishing; DAVID BOGART, SVP of Operations & Procurement, Publishing; C.B. CEBULSKI, VP of International Development & Brand Management; DAVID GABRIEL, SVP Print, Sales & Marketing; JIM O'KEEFE, VP of Operations & Logistics; DAN CARR, Executive Director of Publishing Technology; SUSAN CRESPI, Editorial Operations Manager; ALEX MORALES, Publishing Operations Manager; STAN LEE, Chairman Emeritus. For information regarding advertising in Marvel Comics or on Marvel.com, please contact Jonathan Rheingold, VP of Custom Solutions & Ad Sales, at jrheingold@marvel.com. For Marvel subscription inquiries, please call 800-217-9158. **Manufactured between 4/10/2015 and 5/18/2015 by SHERIDAN BOOKS, INC., CHELSEA, MI, USA.**

10 9 8 7 6 5 4 3 2 1

BRILLIANT-IF-MISUNDERSTOOD DOCTOR HENRY "HANK" PYM, THE AVENGERS' RESIDENT SCIENTIST, CREATED TECHNOLOGIES THAT ALLOW HIM TO TALK TO ANTS AND SHRINK DOWN TO THEIR LEVEL! HE'S A LITTLE GUY FIGHTING BIG CRIME AS...ANT-MAN!

WHEN HANK PYM, THE ORIGINAL ANT-MAN, RETIRED FROM THE JOB, ANOTHER MAN ROSE TO THE OCCASION (ERR, STOLE THE COSTUME) — NONE OTHER THAN SCOTT LANG! HIS SOMEWHAT SORDID PAST BEHIND HIM, SCOTT TOOK ON THE SIZE-CHANGING, ANT-COMMUNICATING ABILITIES OF ANT-MAN!

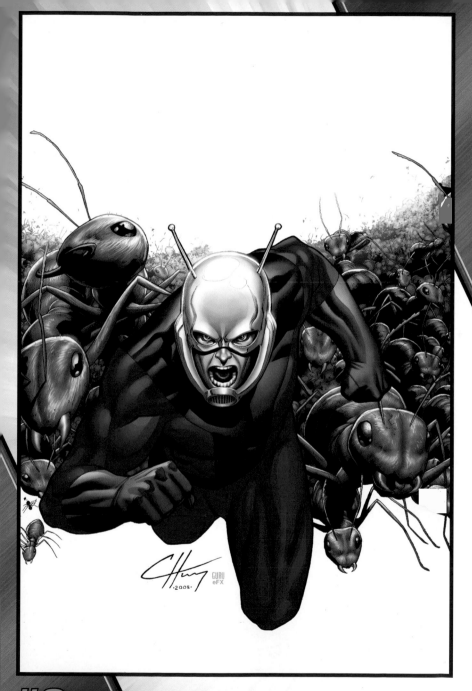

#6 MARVEL ADVENTURES SUPER HEROES

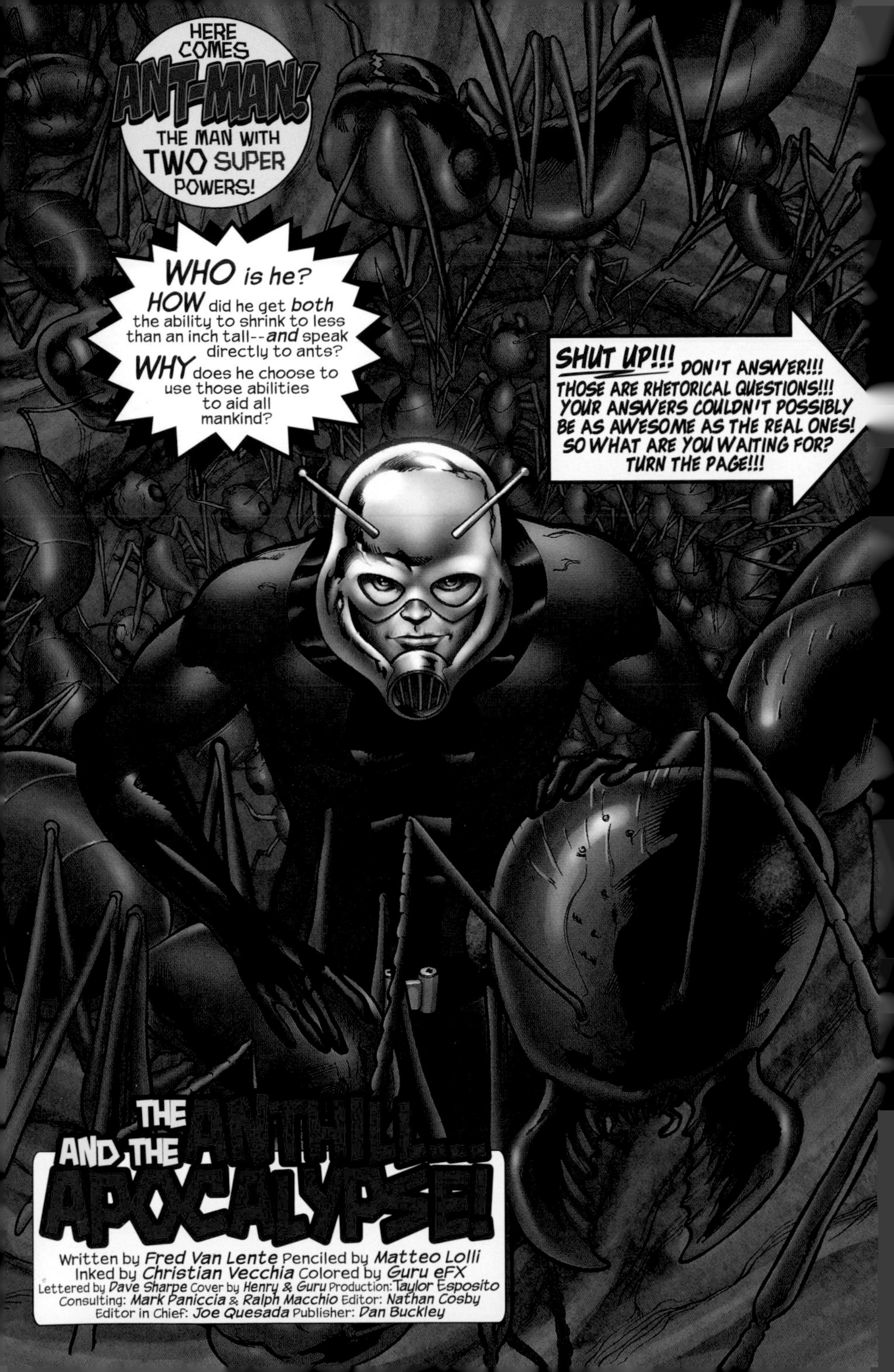

HERE COMES ANT-MAN! THE MAN WITH TWO SUPER POWERS!
WHO is he? HOW did he get both the ability to shrink to less than an inch tall--and speak directly to ants? WHY does he choose to use those abilities to aid all mankind?
SHUT UP!!! DON'T ANSWER!!! THOSE ARE RHETORICAL QUESTIONS!!! YOUR ANSWERS COULDN'T POSSIBLY BE AS AWESOME AS THE REAL ONES! SO WHAT ARE YOU WAITING FOR? TURN THE PAGE!!!
THE ANTHILL... AND THE APOCALYPSE!
Written by Fred Van Lente Penciled by Matteo Lolli
Inked by Christian Vecchia Colored by Guru eFX
Lettered by Dave Sharpe Cover by Henry & Guru Production: Taylor Esposito
Consulting: Mark Paniccia & Ralph Macchio Editor: Nathan Cosby
Editor in Chief: Joe Quesada Publisher: Dan Buckley

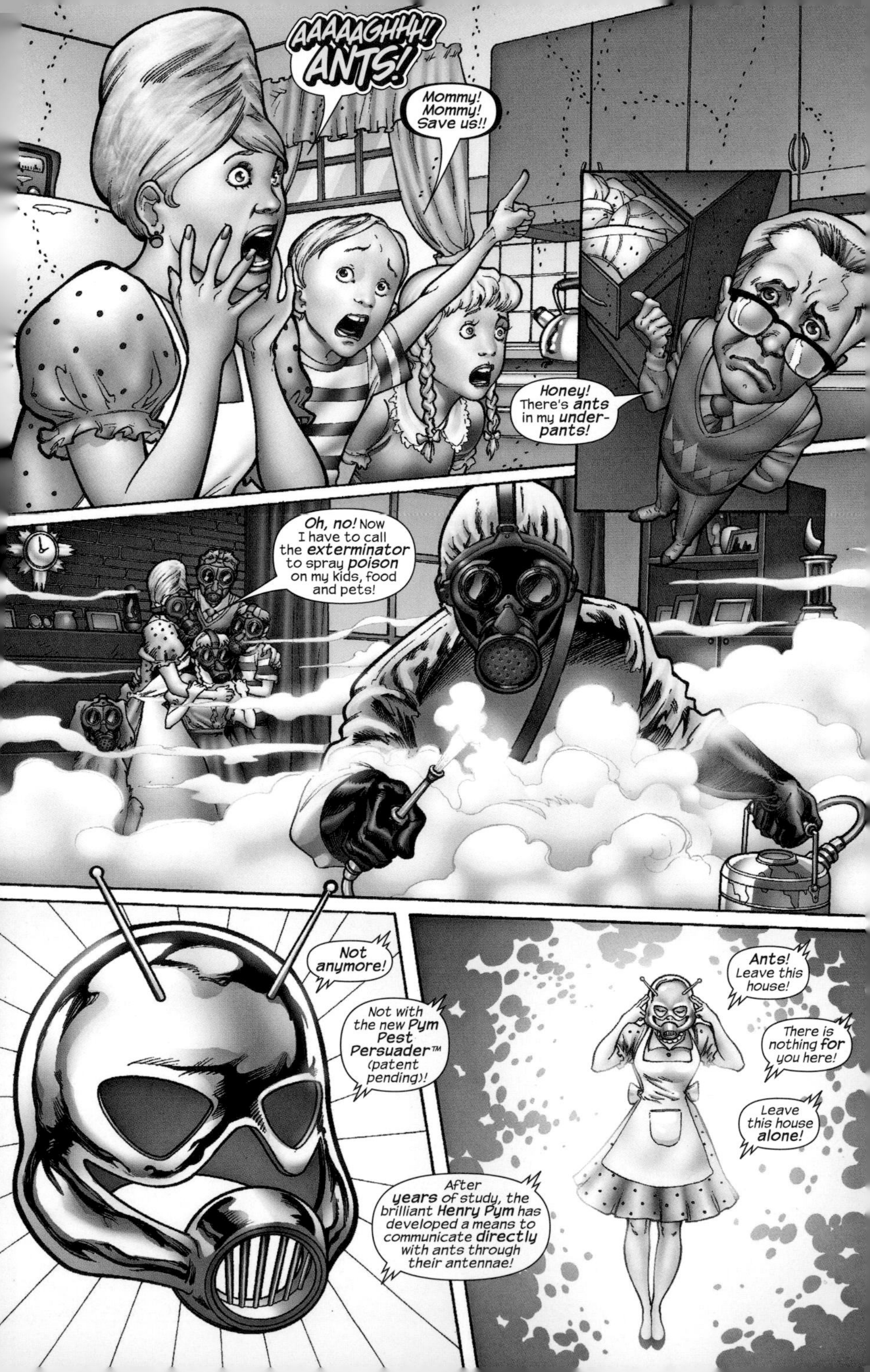
AAAAAGHHH! ANTS!
Mommy! Mommy! Save us!!
Honey! There's ants in my underpants!
Oh, no! Now I have to call the exterminator to spray poison on my kids, food and pets!
Not anymore!
Not with the new Pym Pest Persuader™ (patent pending)!
After years of study, the brilliant Henry Pym has developed a means to communicate directly with ants through their antennae!
Ants! Leave this house!
There is nothing for you here!
Leave this house alone!

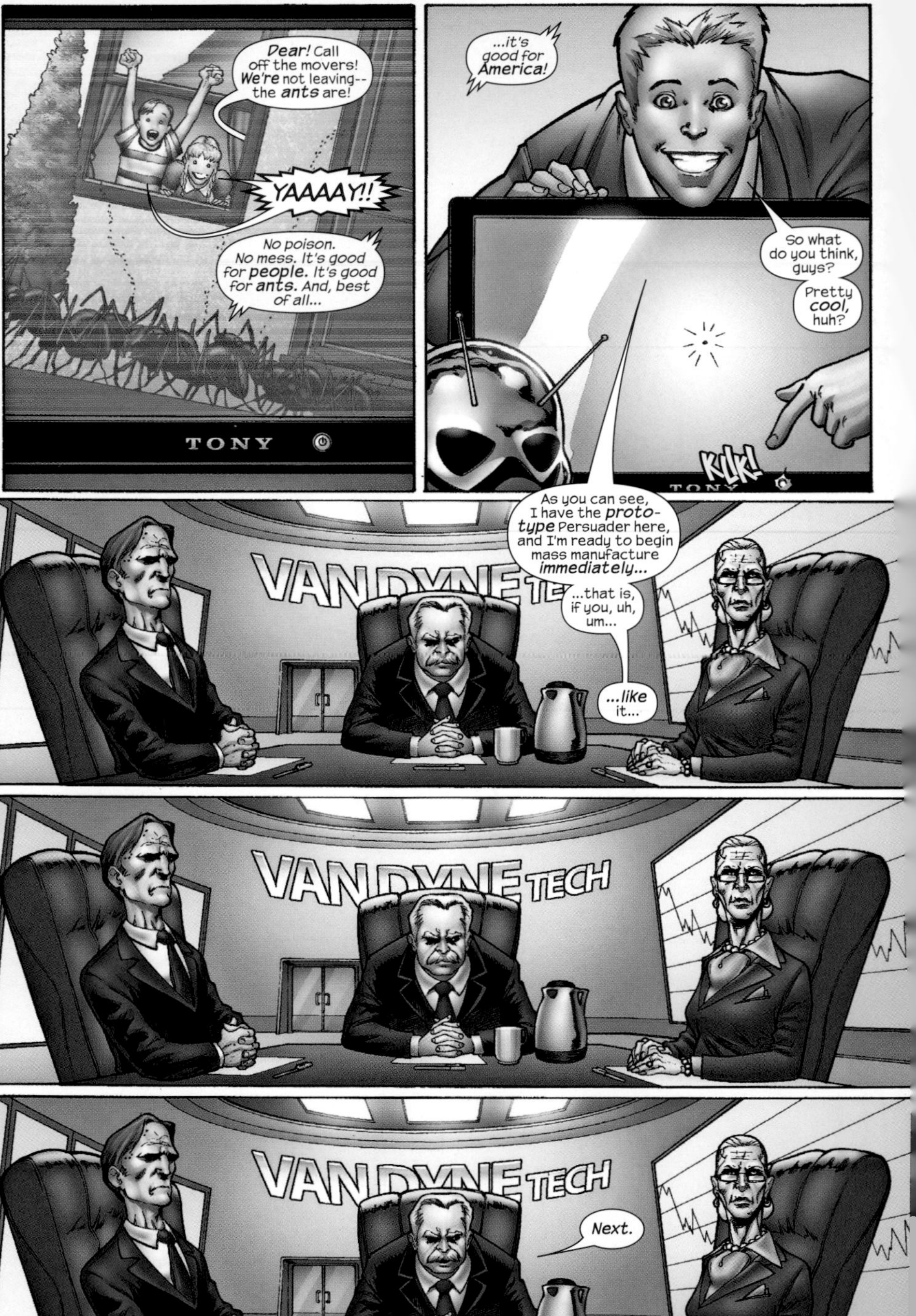
Dear! Call off the movers! We're not leaving-- the ants are!
YAAAAY!!
No poison. No mess. It's good for people. It's good for ants. And, best of all...
TONY
...it's good for America!
So what do you think, guys?
Pretty cool, huh?
KLIK!
TONY
As you can see, I have the proto-type Persuader here, and I'm ready to begin mass manufacture immediately...
...that is, if you, uh, um...
...like it...
VAN DYNE TECH
VAN DYNE TECH
VAN DYNE TECH
Next.

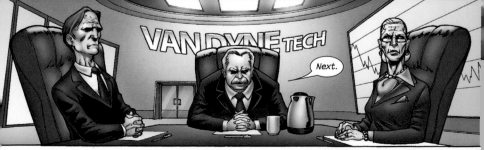

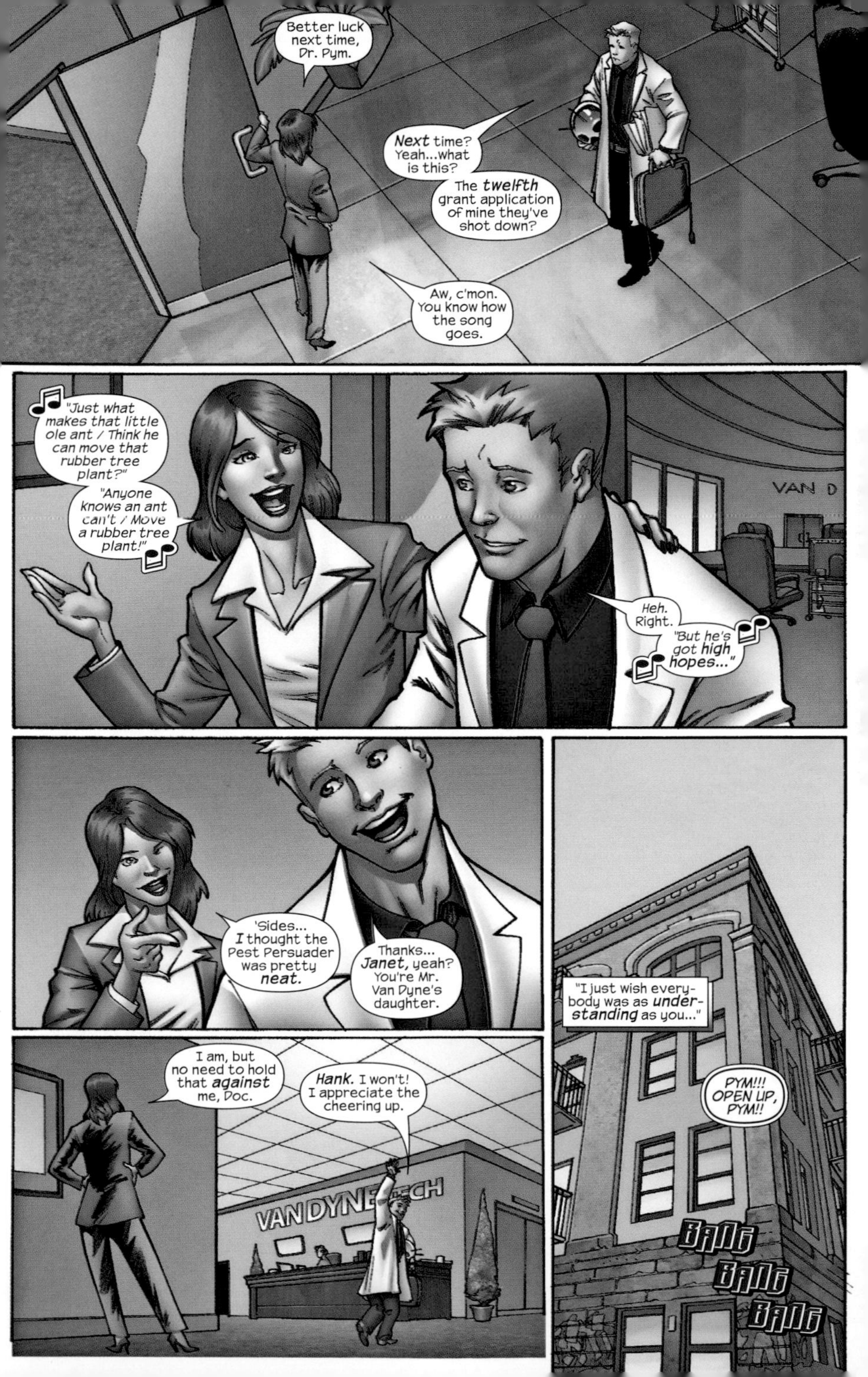
Better luck next time, Dr. Pym.
Next time? Yeah...what is this?
The twelfth grant application of mine they've shot down?
Aw, c'mon. You know how the song goes.
"Just what makes that little ole ant / Think he can move that rubber tree plant?"
"Anyone knows an ant can't / Move a rubber tree plant!"
VAN D
Heh. Right.
"But he's got high hopes..."
'Sides... I thought the Pest Persuader was pretty neat.
Thanks... Janet, yeah? You're Mr. Van Dyne's daughter.
"I just wish every-body was as under-standing as you..."
I am, but no need to hold that against me, Doc.
Hank. I won't! I appreciate the cheering up.
PYM!!! OPEN UP, PYM!!
BANG
BANG
BANG

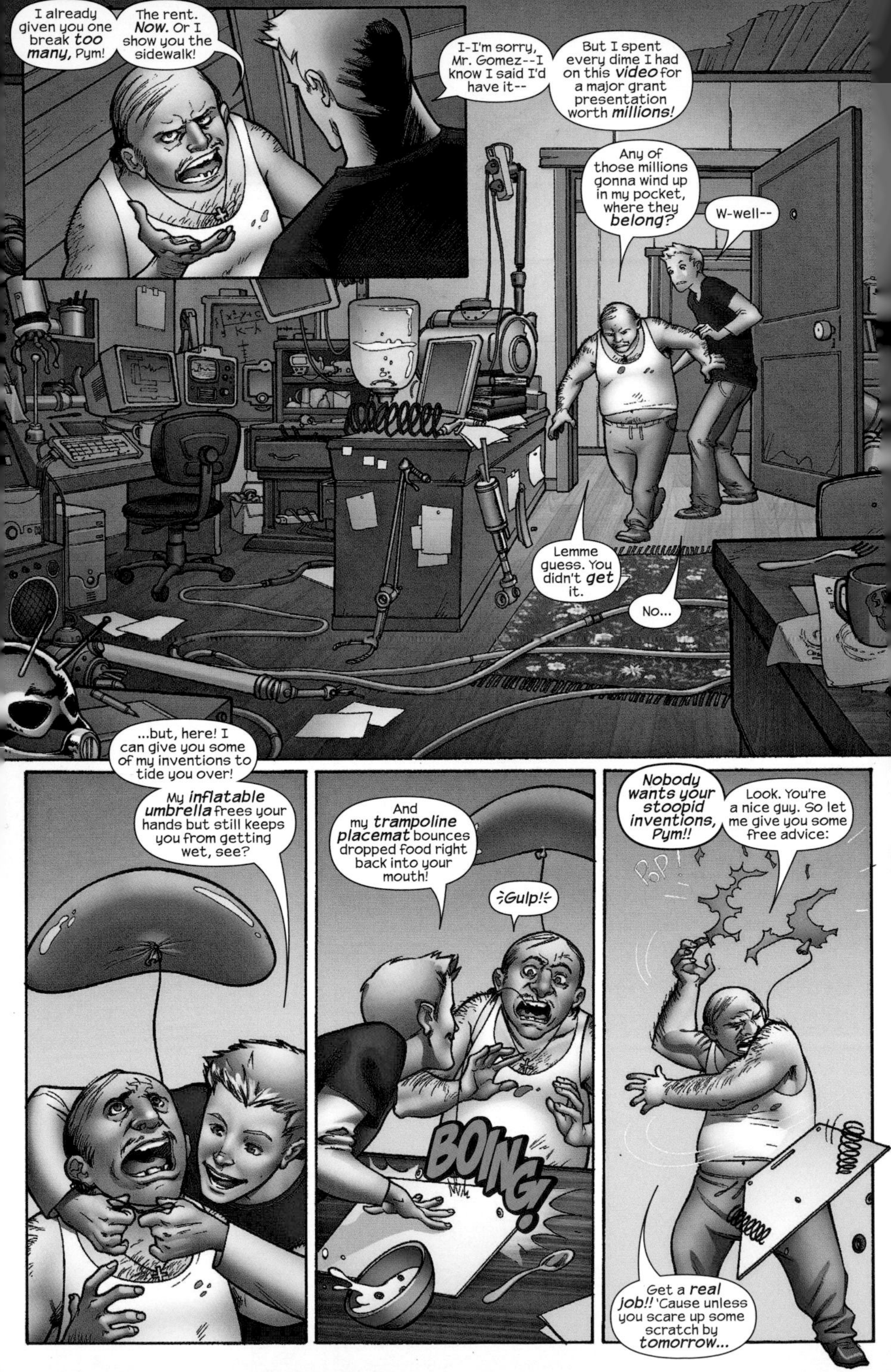
I already given you one break too many, Pym!
The rent. Now. Or I show you the sidewalk!
I-I'm sorry, Mr. Gomez--I know I said I'd have it--
But I spent every dime I had on this video for a major grant presentation worth millions!
Any of those millions gonna wind up in my pocket, where they belong?
W-well--
Lemme guess. You didn't get it.
No...
...but, here! I can give you some of my inventions to tide you over!
My inflatable umbrella frees your hands but still keeps you from getting wet, see?
And my trampoline placemat bounces dropped food right back into your mouth!
Gulp!
BOING!
Nobody wants your stoopid inventions, Pym!!
Look. You're a nice guy. So let me give you some free advice:
POP!
Get a real job!! 'Cause unless you scare up some scratch by tomorrow...

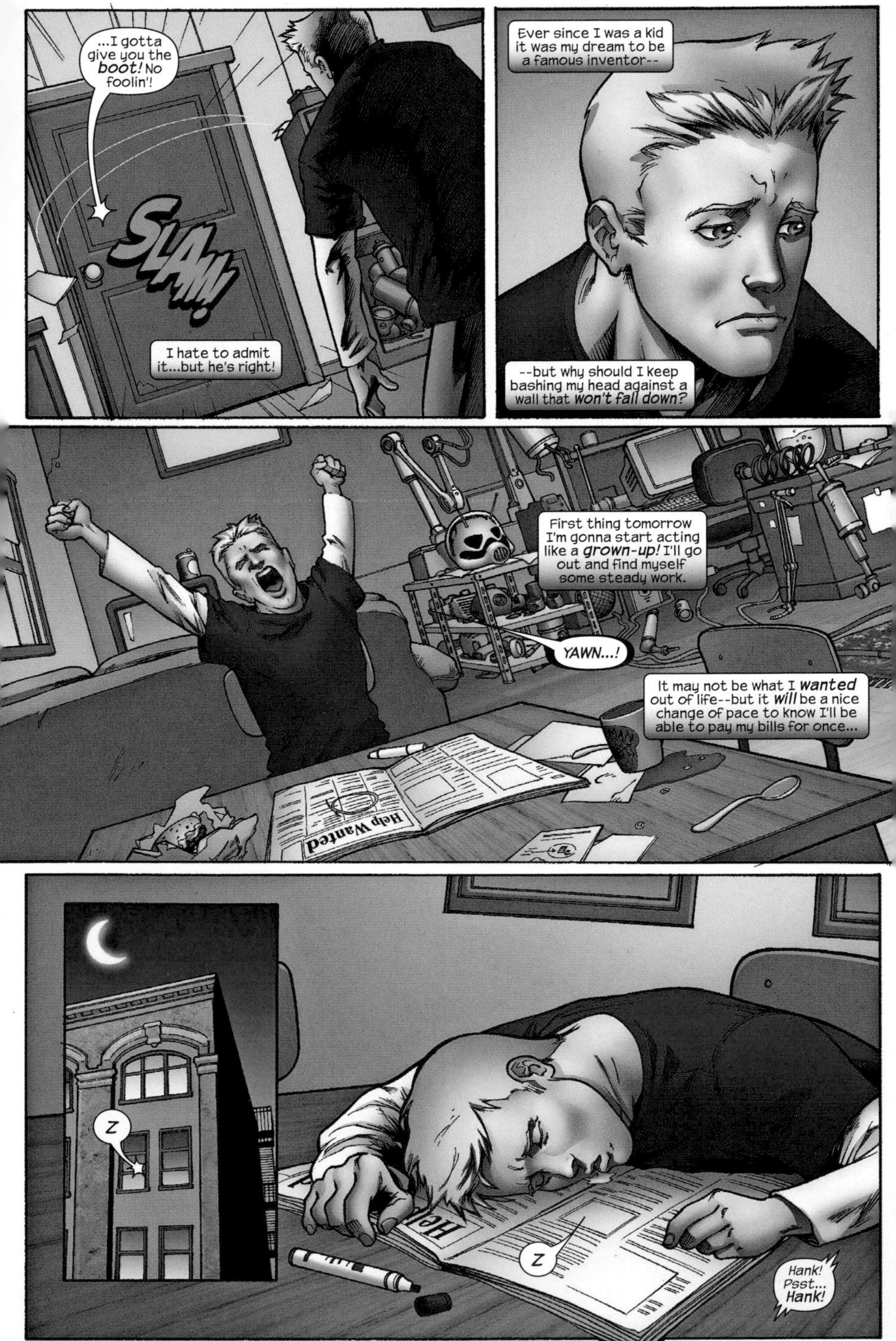
...I gotta give you the *boot!* No foolin'!
SLAM!
I hate to admit it...but he's right!
Ever since I was a kid it was my dream to be a famous inventor--
--but why should I keep bashing my head against a wall that *won't fall down?*
First thing tomorrow I'm gonna start acting like a *grown-up!* I'll go out and find myself some steady work.
YAWN...!
It may not be what I *wanted* out of life--but it *will* be a nice change of pace to know I'll be able to pay my bills for once...
Help Wanted
Z
Z
Hank! Psst... Hank!

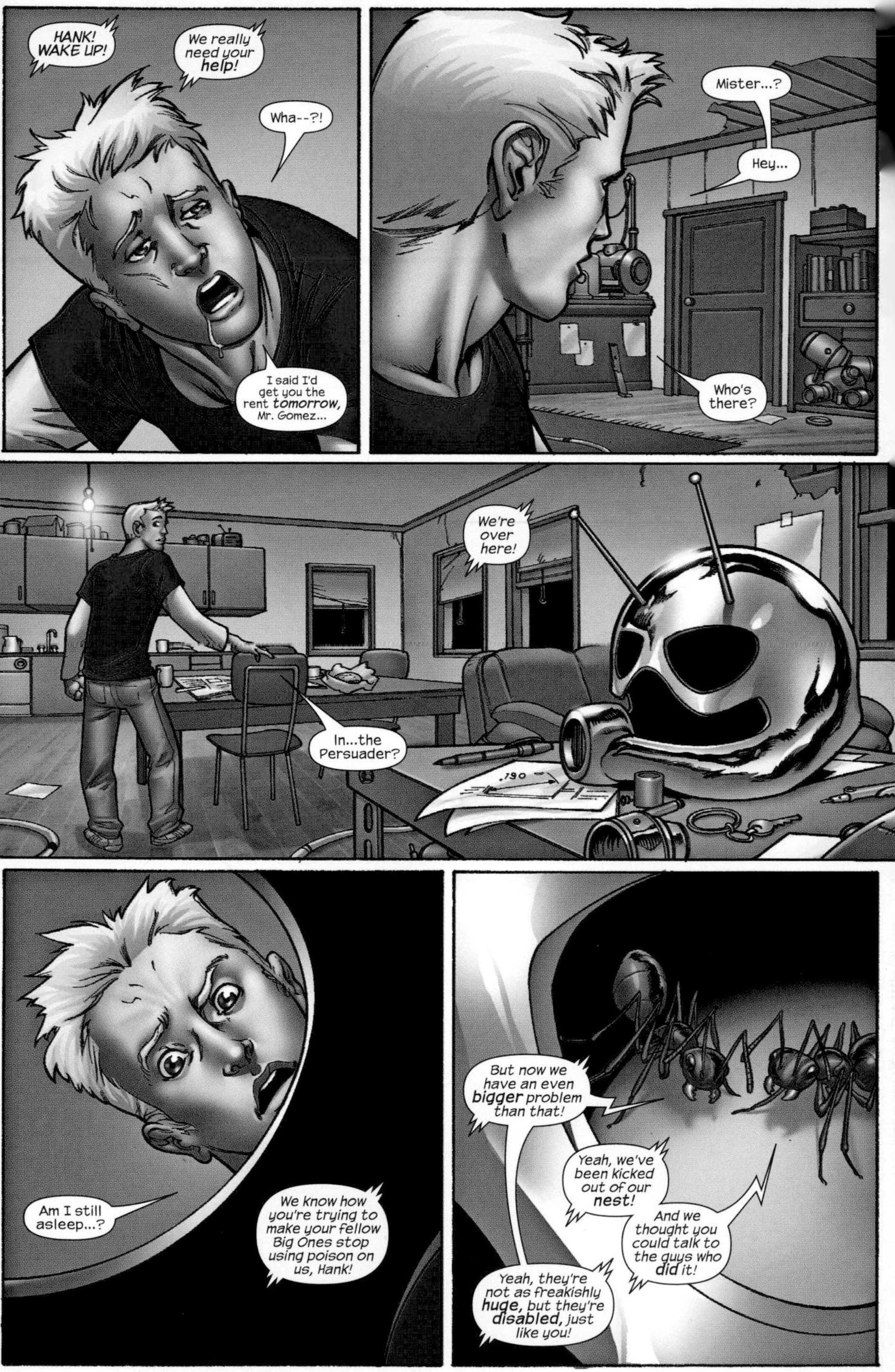

HANK! WAKE UP!
We really need your help!
Wha--?!
I said I'd get you the rent tomorrow, Mr. Gomez...
Mister...?
Hey...
Who's there?
We're over here!
In...the Persuader?
Am I still asleep...?
We know how you're trying to make your fellow Big Ones stop using poison on us, Hank!
But now we have an even bigger problem than that!
Yeah, we've been kicked out of our nest!
And we thought you could talk to the guys who did it!
Yeah, they're not as freakishly huge, but they're disabled, just like you!

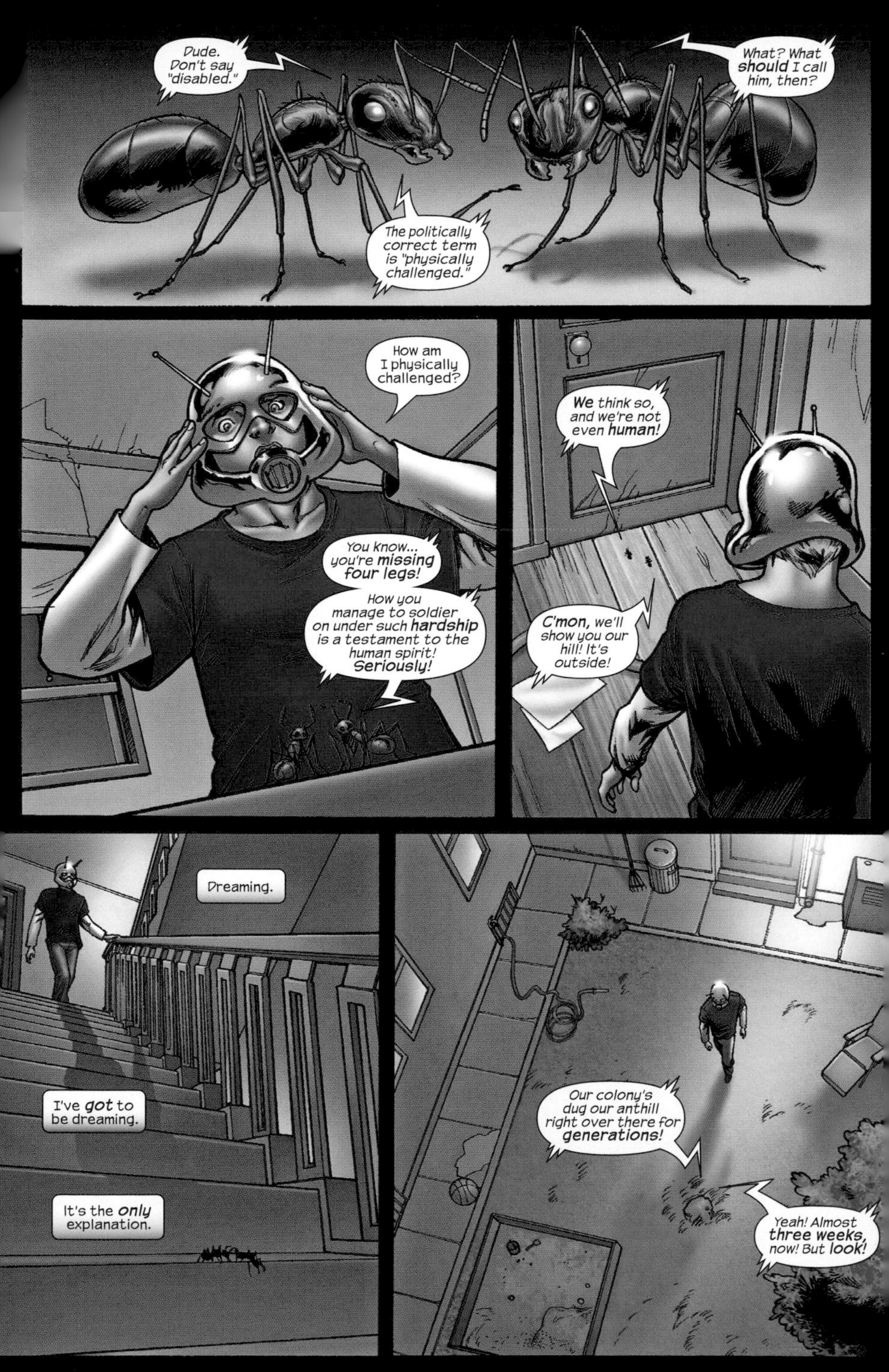

Dude. Don't say "disabled."
What? What should I call him, then?
The politically correct term is "physically challenged."
How am I physically challenged?
You know... you're missing four legs!
How you manage to soldier on under such hardship is a testament to the human spirit! Seriously!
We think so, and we're not even human!
C'mon, we'll show you our hill! It's outside!
Dreaming.
I've got to be dreaming.
It's the only explanation.
Our colony's dug our anthill right over there for generations!
Yeah! Almost three weeks, now! But look!

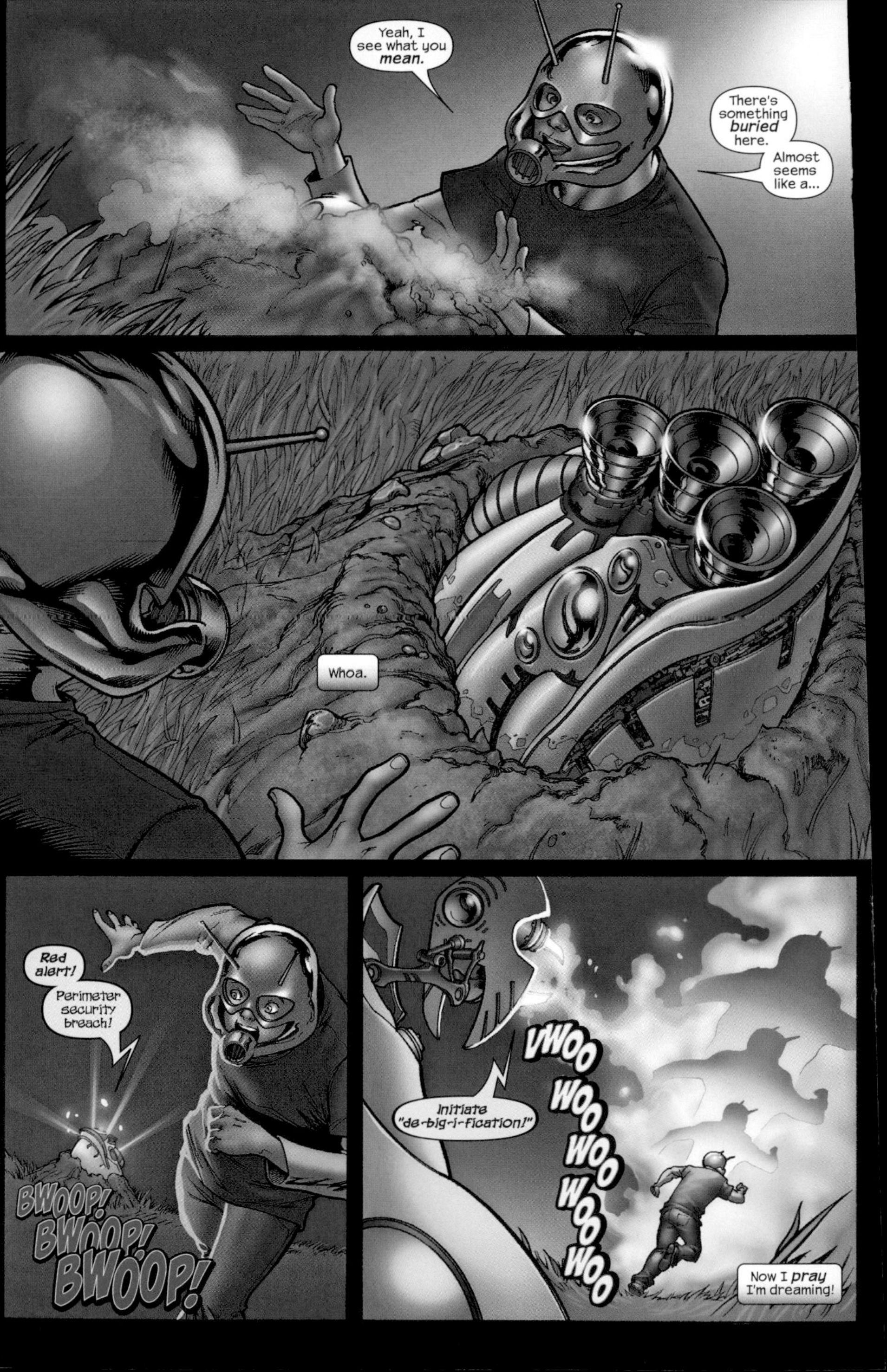
Yeah, I see what you *mean.*
There's something *buried* here.
Almost seems like a...
Whoa.
Red alert!
Perimeter security breach!
BWOOP! BWOOP! BWOOP!
Initiate "de-big-i-fication!"
VWOO WOO WOO WOO WOO WOO
Now I *pray* I'm dreaming!

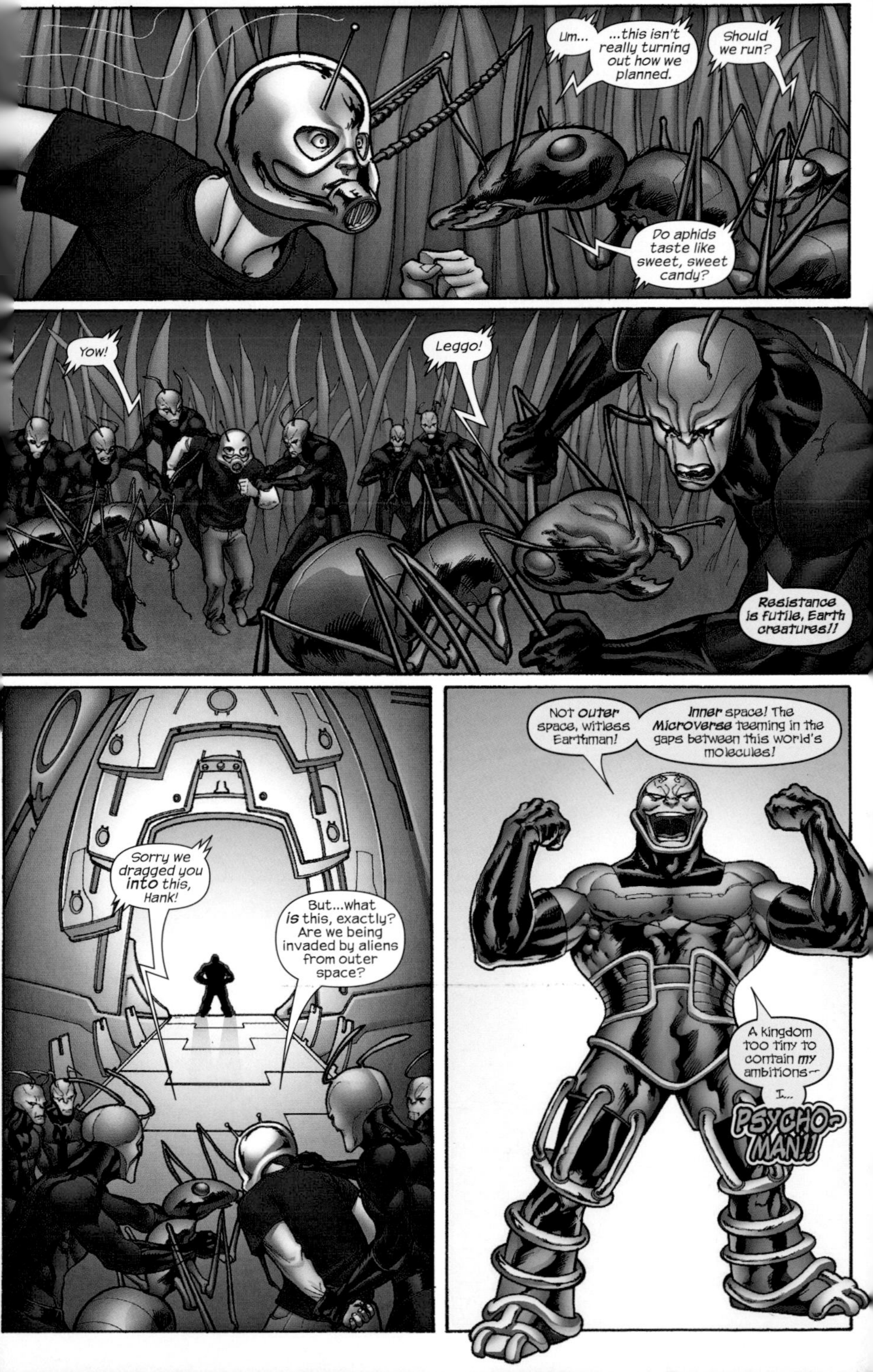
Um...
...this isn't really turning out how we planned.
Should we run?
Do aphids taste like sweet, sweet candy?
Yow!
Leggo!
Resistance is futile, Earth creatures!!
Sorry we dragged you into this, Hank!
But...what is this, exactly? Are we being invaded by aliens from outer space?
Not outer space, witless Earthman!
Inner space! The Microverse teeming in the gaps between this world's molecules!
A kingdom too tiny to contain my ambitions--
I...
PSYCHO-MAN!!

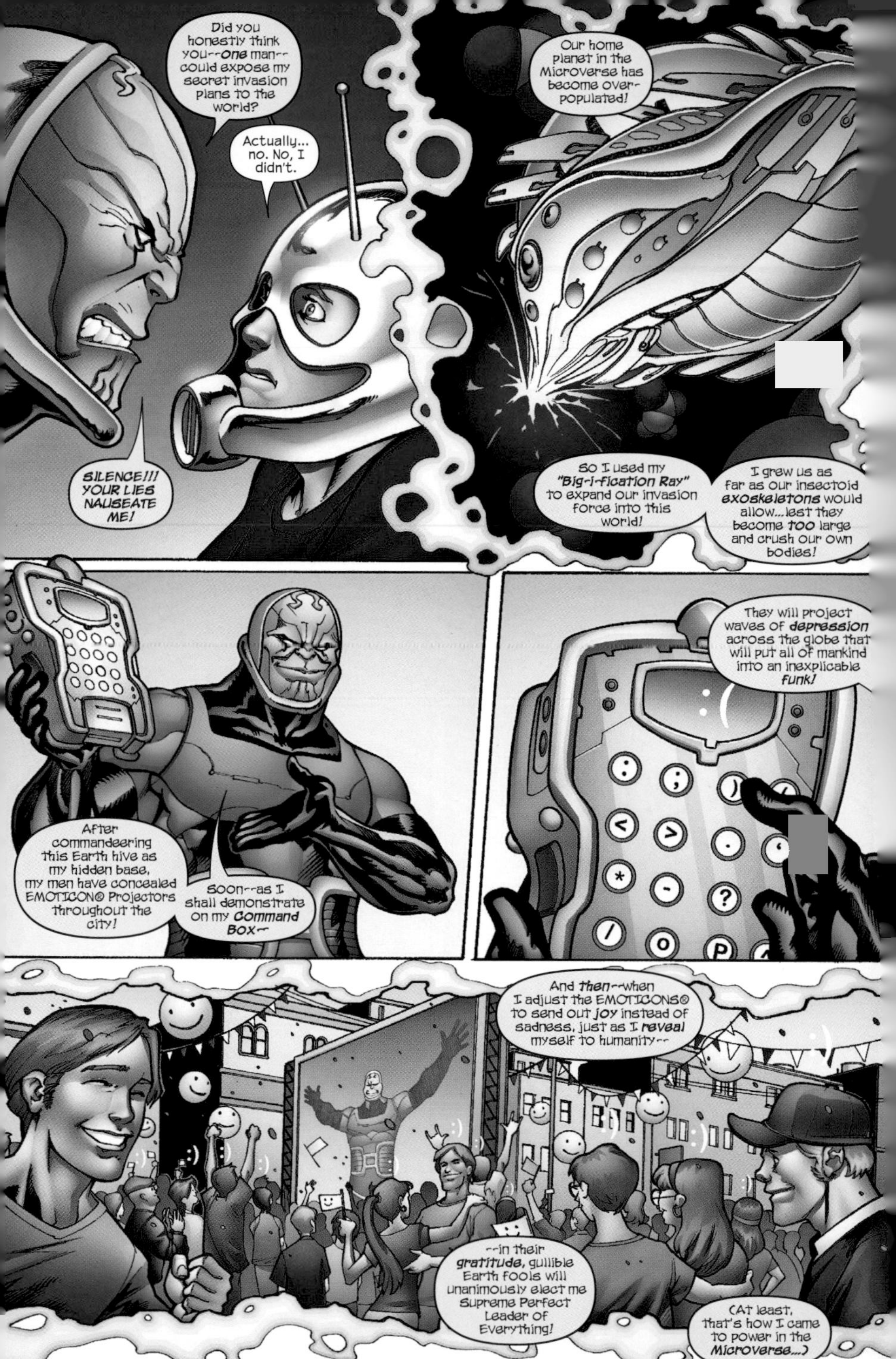

Did you honestly think you--one man--could expose my secret invasion plans to the world?
Actually... no. No, I didn't.
Our home planet in the Microverse has become over-populated!
SILENCE!!! YOUR LIES NAUSEATE ME!
So I used my "Big-i-fication Ray" to expand our invasion force into this world!
I grew us as far as our insectoid exoskeletons would allow...lest they become TOO large and crush our own bodies!
After commandeering this Earth hive as my hidden base, my men have concealed EMOTICON® Projectors throughout the city!
Soon--as I shall demonstrate on my Command Box--
They will project waves of depression across the globe that will put all of mankind into an inexplicable funk!
And then--when I adjust the EMOTICONS® to send out joy instead of sadness, just as I reveal myself to humanity--
--in their gratitude, gullible Earth fools will unanimously elect me Supreme Perfect Leader of Everything!
(At least, that's how I came to power in the Microverse...)

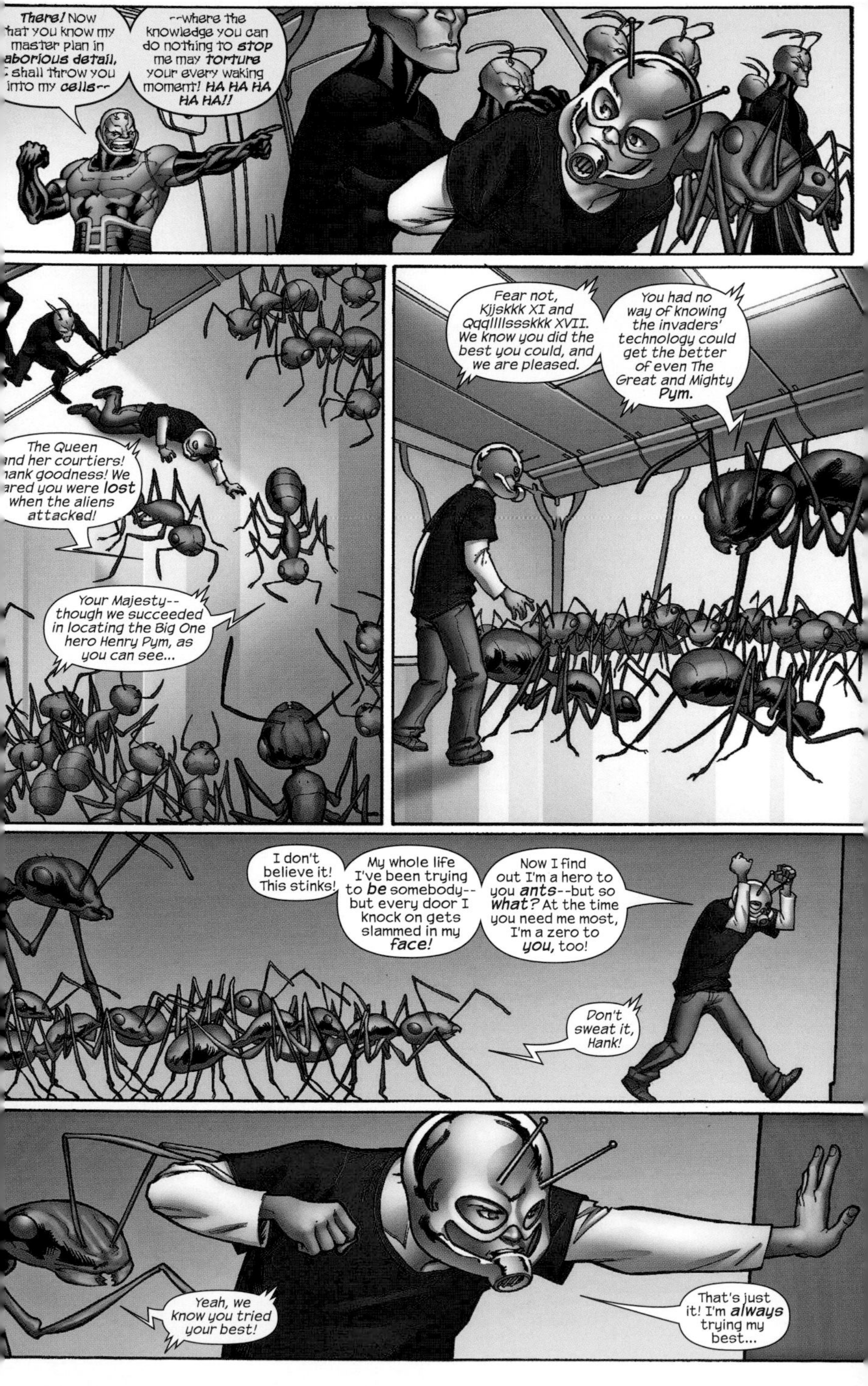

There! Now
hat you know my master plan in
aborious detail,
shall throw you into my cells--
--where the knowledge you can do nothing to stop me may torture your every waking moment! HA HA HA HA HA!!
The Queen
nd her courtiers!
hank goodness! We
ared you were lost when the aliens attacked!
Your Majesty-- though we succeeded in locating the Big One hero Henry Pym, as you can see...
Fear not, Kjjskkk XI and Qqqlllllsssskkk XVII. We know you did the best you could, and we are pleased.
You had no way of knowing the invaders' technology could get the better of even The Great and Mighty Pym.
I don't believe it! This stinks!
My whole life I've been trying to be somebody-- but every door I knock on gets slammed in my face!
Now I find out I'm a hero to you ants--but so what? At the time you need me most, I'm a zero to you, too!
Don't sweat it, Hank!
Yeah, we know you tried your best!
That's just it! I'm always trying my best...

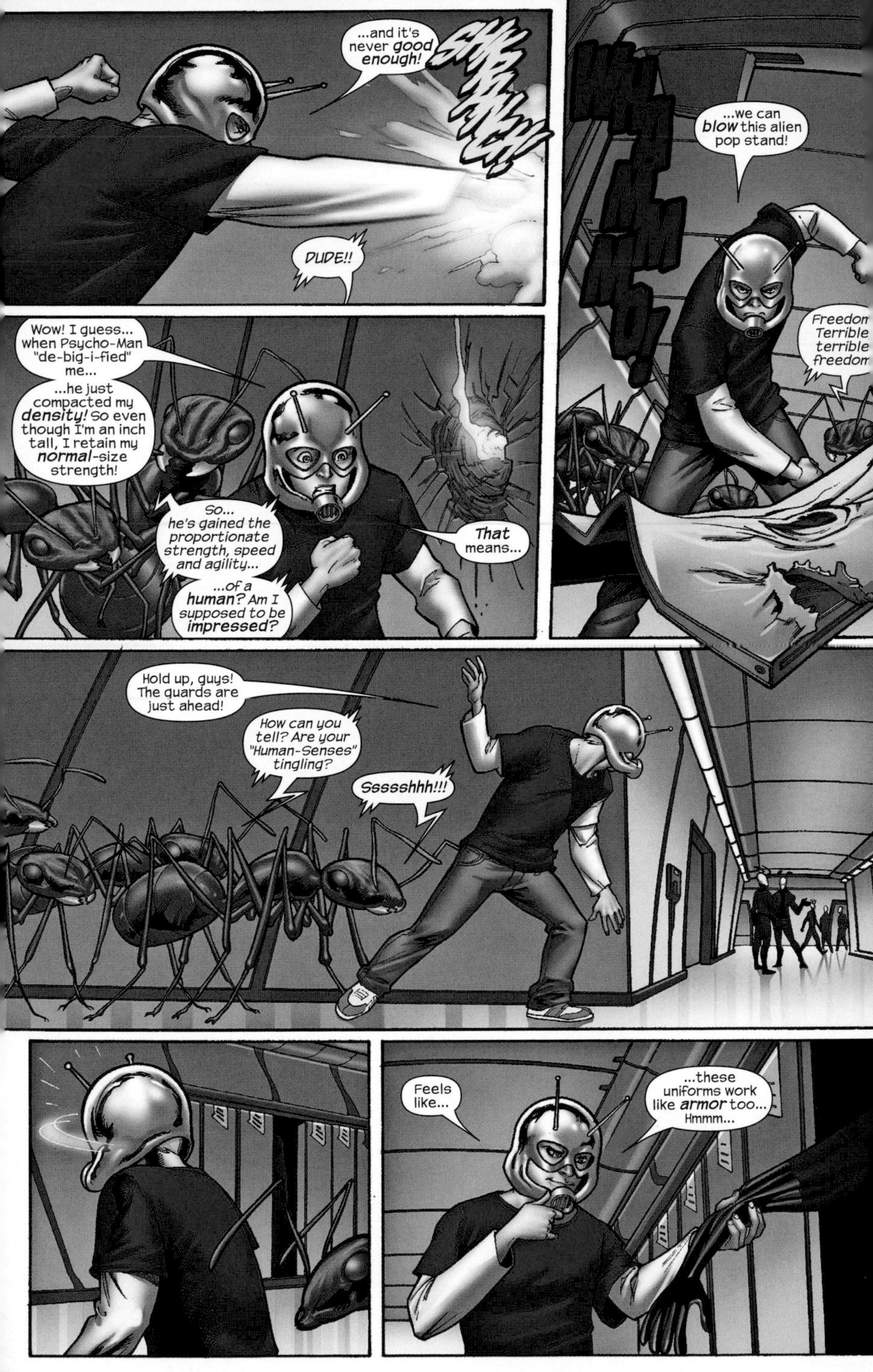
...and it's never good enough!
DUDE!!
...we can blow this alien pop stand!
Wow! I guess... when Psycho-Man "de-big-i-fied" me...
...he just compacted my density! So even though I'm an inch tall, I retain my normal-size strength!
So... he's gained the proportionate strength, speed and agility...
That means...
...of a human? Am I supposed to be impressed?
Freedom Terrible terrible freedom
Hold up, guys! The guards are just ahead!
How can you tell? Are your "Human-Senses" tingling?
Ssssshhh!!!
Feels like...
...these uniforms work like armor too... Hmmm...

AND SO...

C'mon, guys! That psycho *Psycho-Man's* command center is *this* way!

You lead, we'll *follow*, Hank!

FIZAK

Incredible! Even accounting for the armor, their ray blasts aren't affecting me at *all!*

...not to mention making me *equally* good at dishing it *out!*

POW!

Shrunk down like this, my greater *density* must make me unusually resistant to *injury...*

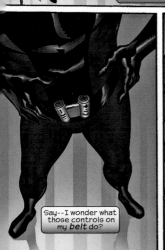

Say--I wonder what those controls on my *belt* do?

But I have no time to *tinker!* Gotta stay *focused!*

Everything is going *exactly* as I planned-- as *usual!*

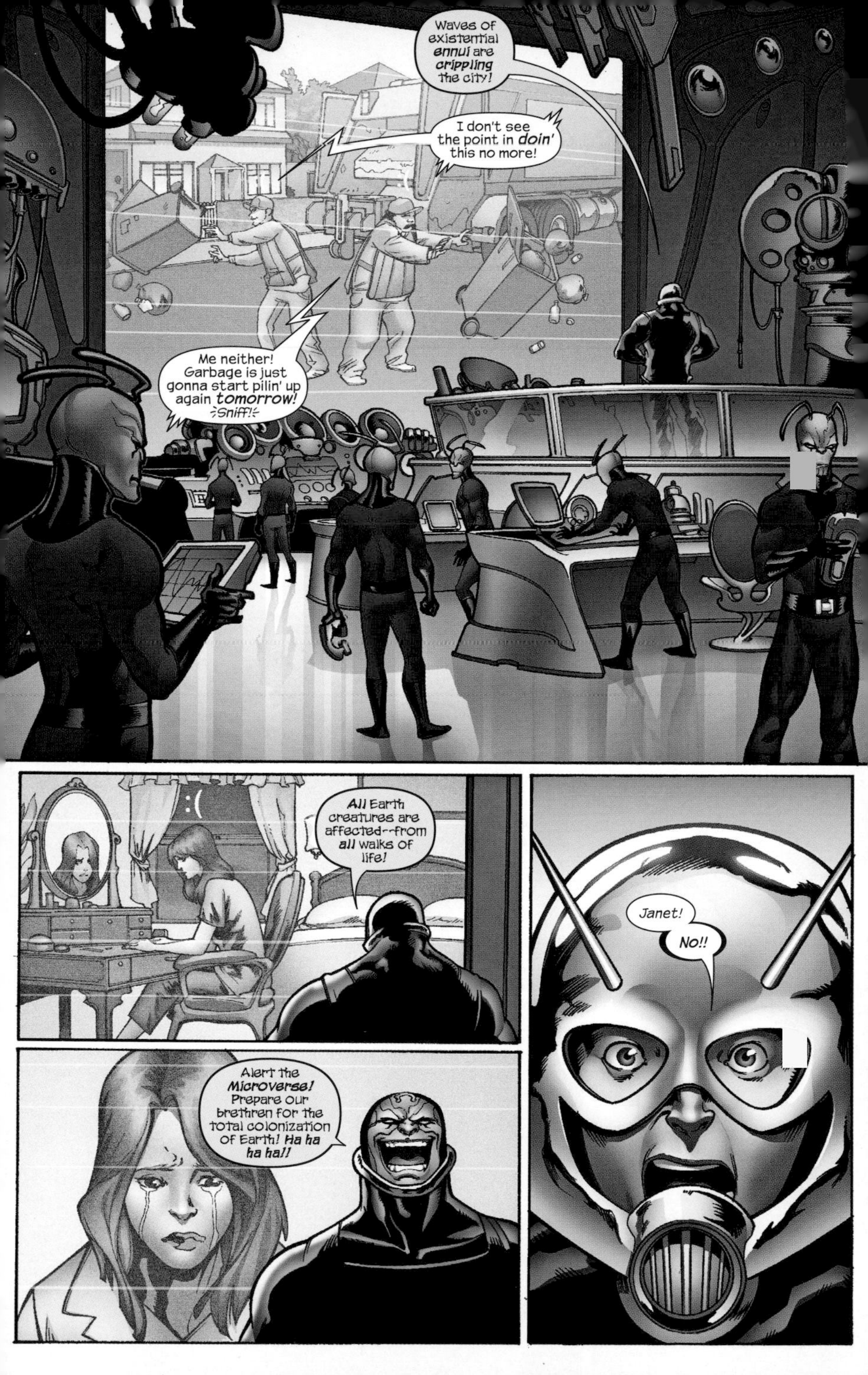
Waves of existential ennui are crippling the city!
I don't see the point in doin' this no more!
Me neither! Garbage is just gonna start pilin' up again tomorrow!
Sniff!
:(
All Earth creatures are affected--from all walks of life!
Alert the Microverse! Prepare our brethren for the total colonization of Earth! Ha ha ha ha!!
Janet!
No!!

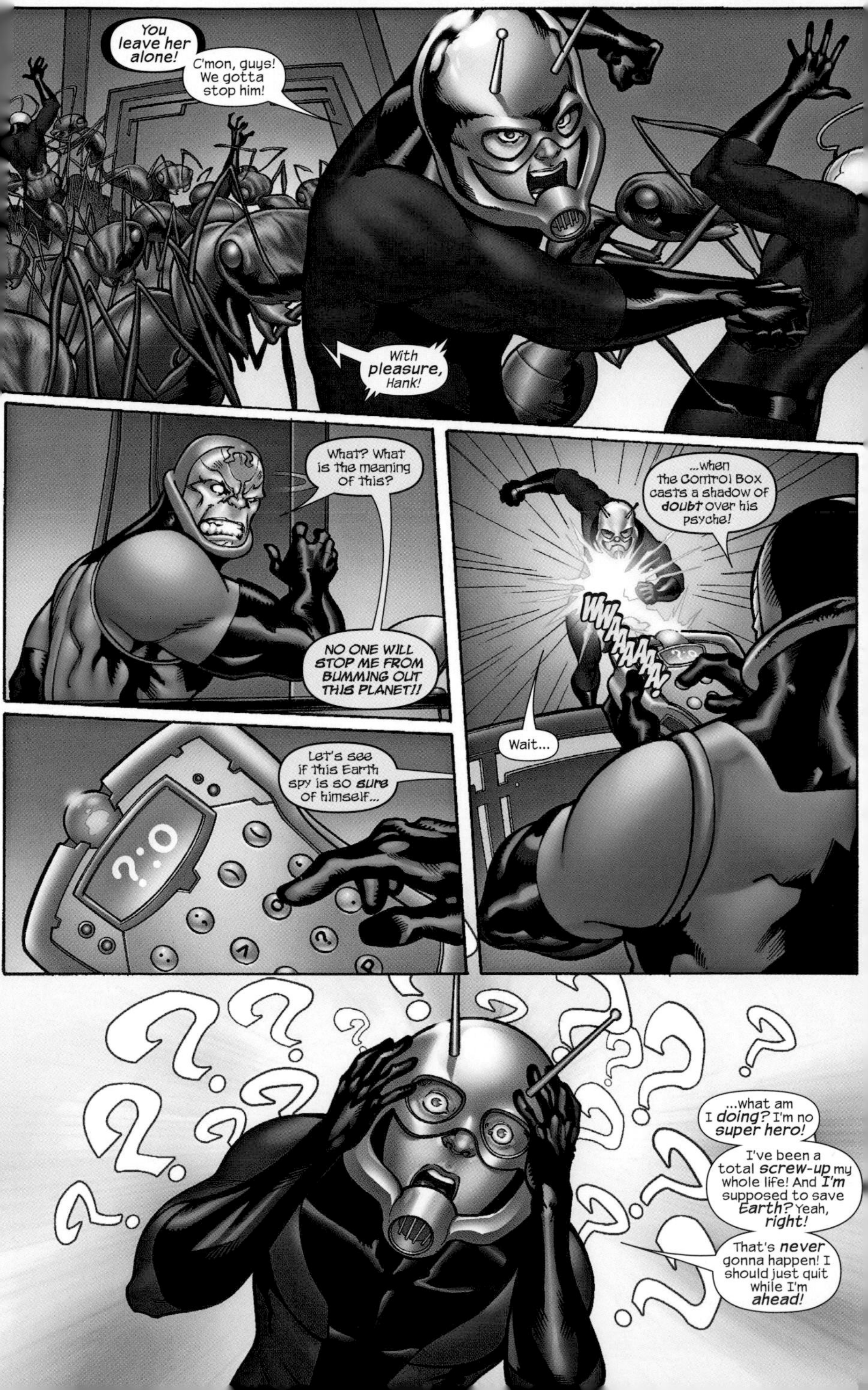
You leave her alone!
C'mon, guys! We gotta stop him!
With pleasure, Hank!
What? What is the meaning of this?
NO ONE WILL STOP ME FROM BUMMING OUT THIS PLANET!!
...when the Control Box casts a shadow of doubt over his psyche!
WWAAAAAAA!
Wait...
Let's see if this Earth spy is so sure of himself...
?:0
...what am I doing? I'm no super hero!
I've been a total screw-up my whole life! And I'm supposed to save Earth? Yeah, right!
That's never gonna happen! I should just quit while I'm ahead!

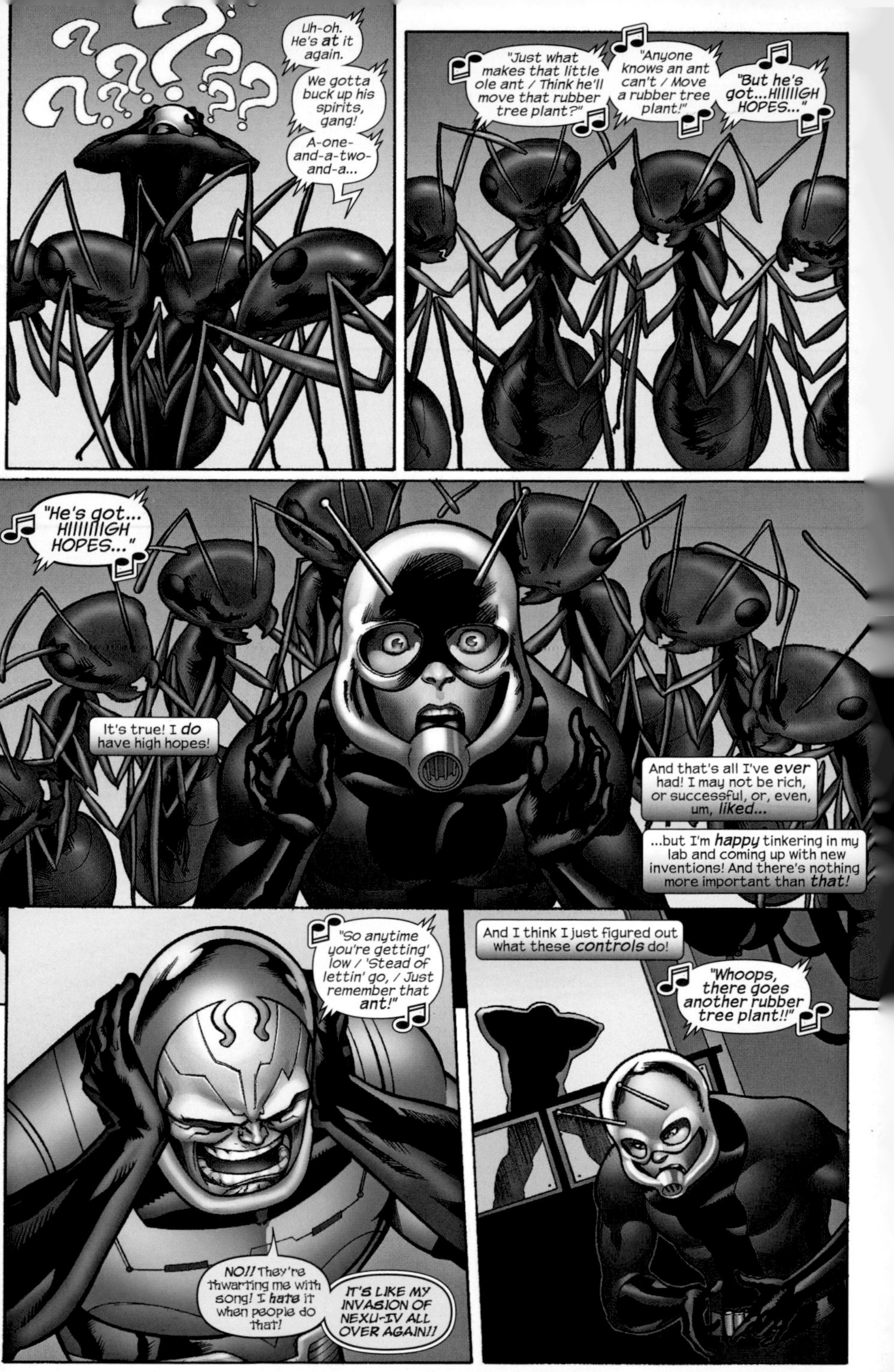
Uh-oh. He's at it again.
We gotta buck up his spirits, gang!
A-one-and-a-two-and-a...
"Just what makes that little ole ant / Think he'll move that rubber tree plant?"
"Anyone knows an ant can't / Move a rubber tree plant!"
"But he's got...HIIIIIGH HOPES..."
"He's got... HIIIIIGH HOPES..."
It's true! I do have high hopes!
And that's all I've ever had! I may not be rich, or successful, or, even, um, liked...
...but I'm happy tinkering in my lab and coming up with new inventions! And there's nothing more important than that!
"So anytime you're getting' low / 'Stead of lettin' go, / Just remember that ant!"
NO!! They're thwarting me with song! I hate it when people do that!
IT'S LIKE MY INVASION OF NEXU-IV ALL OVER AGAIN!!
And I think I just figured out what these controls do!
"Whoops, there goes another rubber tree plant!!"

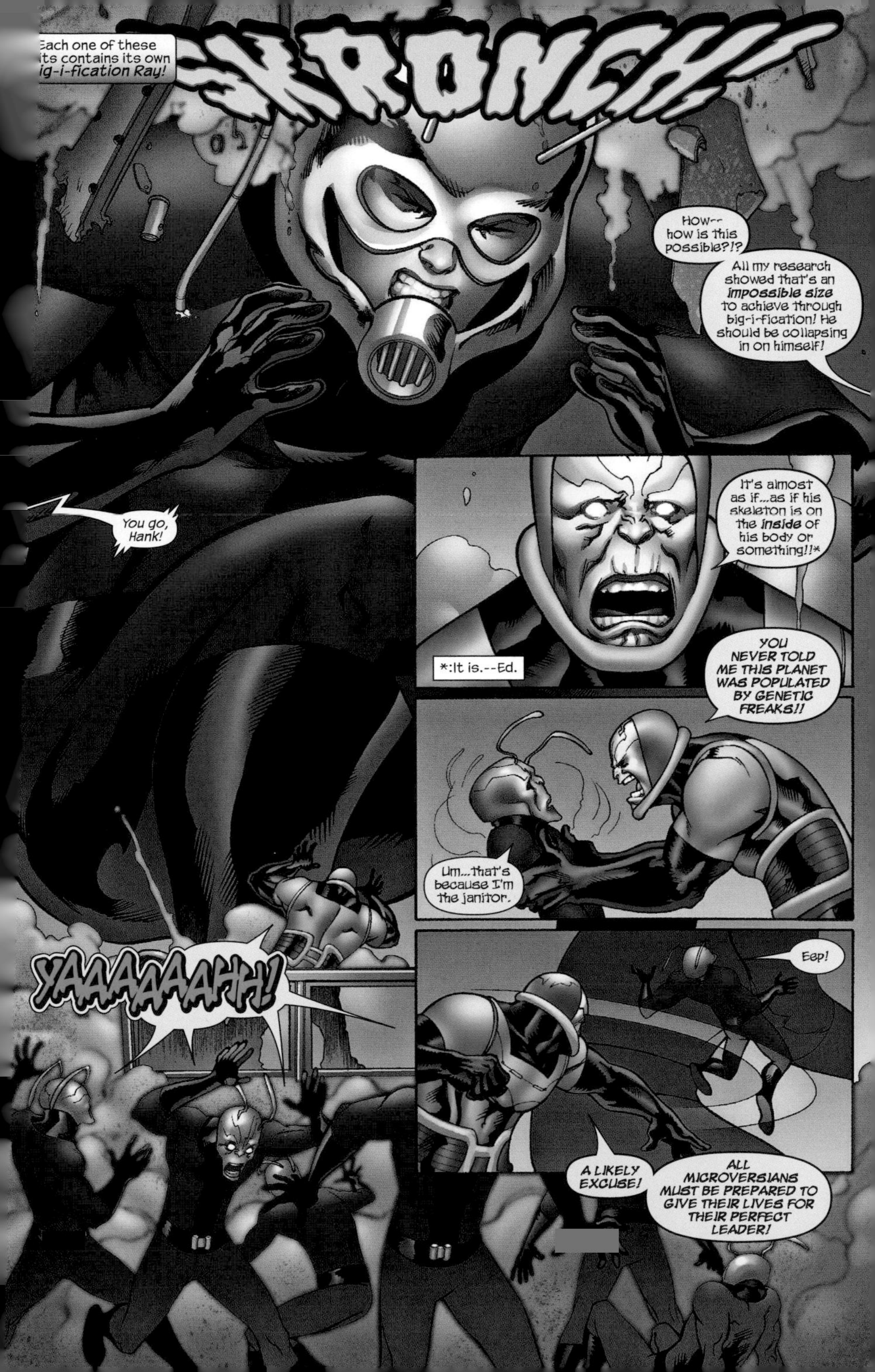

Each one of these
its contains its own
ig-i-fication Ray!
SKRONCH!!
How-- how is this possible?!?
All my research showed that's an **impossible size** to achieve through big-i-fication! He should be collapsing in on himself!
You go, Hank!
It's almost as if...as if his skeleton is on the **inside** of his body or something!!*
*:It is.--Ed.
YOU NEVER TOLD ME THIS PLANET WAS POPULATED BY GENETIC FREAKS!!
Um...that's because I'm the janitor.
YAAAAAAHH!
Eep!
A LIKELY EXCUSE!
ALL MICROVERSIANS MUST BE PREPARED TO GIVE THEIR LIVES FOR THEIR PERFECT LEADER!

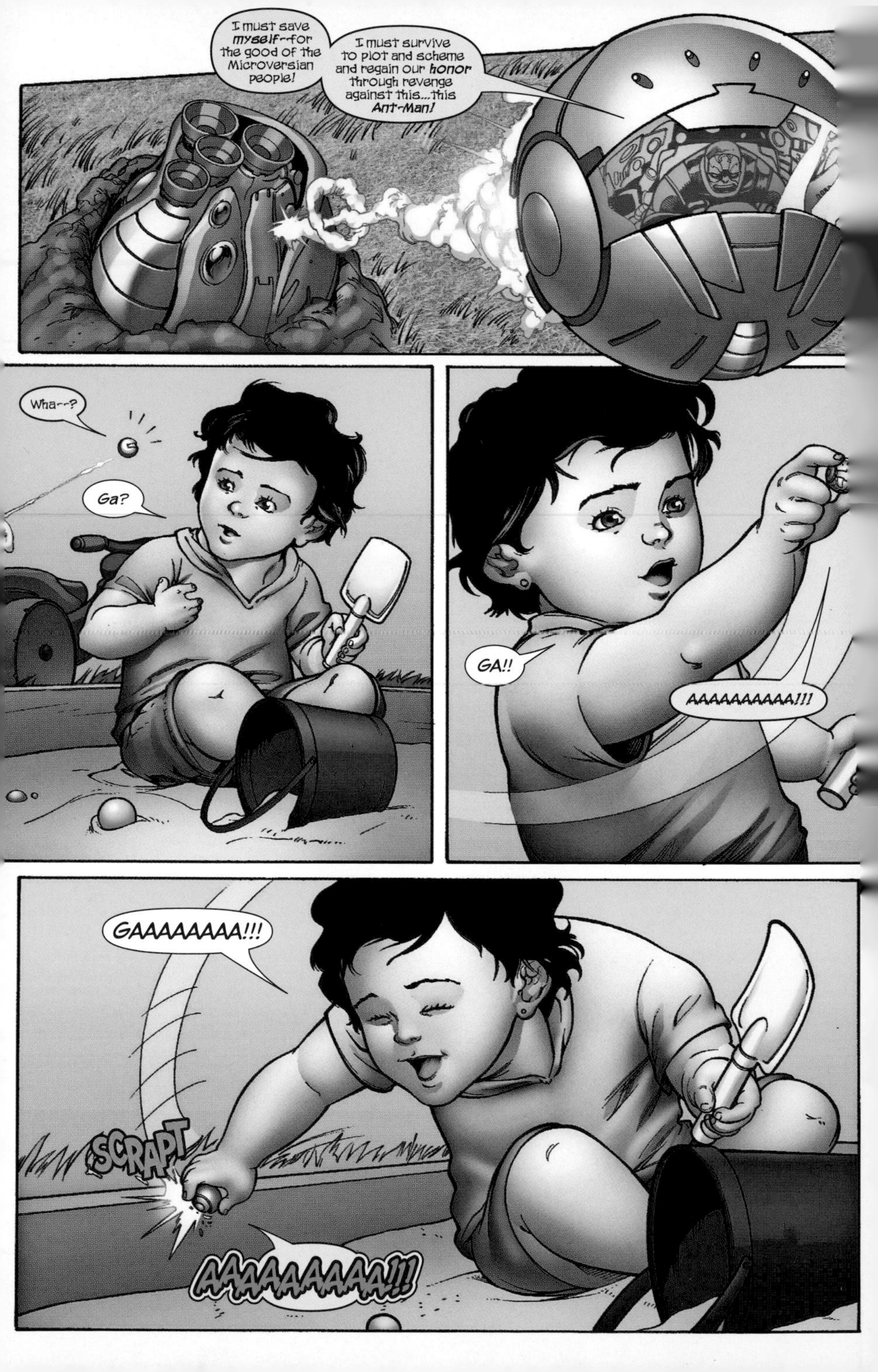
I must save myself--for the good of the Microversian people!
I must survive to plot and scheme and regain our honor through revenge against this...this Ant-Man!
Wha--?
Ga?
GA!!
AAAAAAAAAA!!!
GAAAAAAAA!!!
SCRAPT
AAAAAAAAA!!!

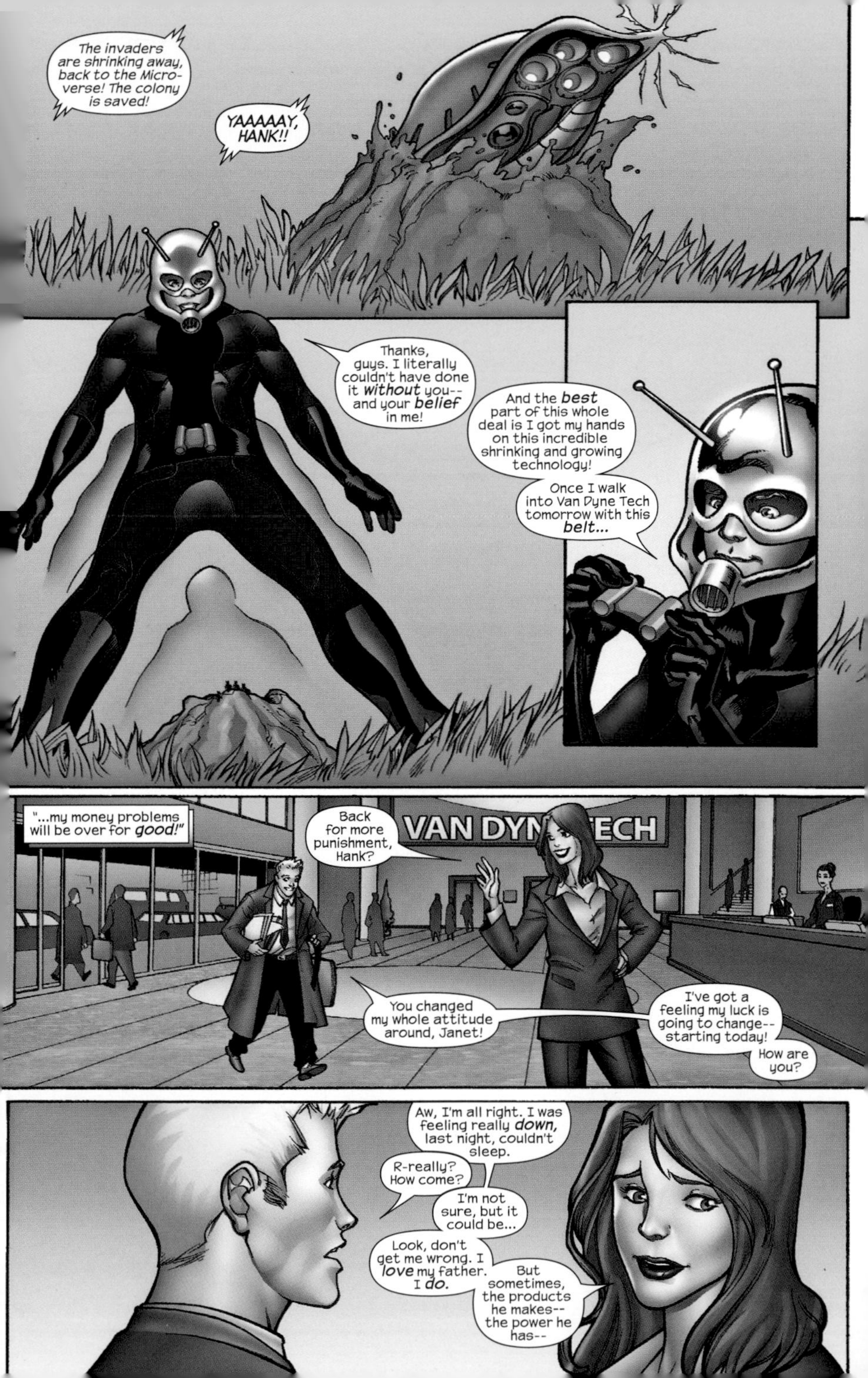
The invaders are shrinking away, back to the Micro-verse! The colony is saved!
YAAAAAY, HANK!!
Thanks, guys. I literally couldn't have done it *without* you--and your *belief* in me!
And the *best* part of this whole deal is I got my hands on this incredible shrinking and growing technology!
Once I walk into Van Dyne Tech tomorrow with this *belt...*
"...my money problems will be over for *good!*"
VAN DYN TECH
Back for more punishment, Hank?
You changed my whole attitude around, Janet!
I've got a feeling my luck is going to change--starting today!
How are you?
Aw, I'm all right. I was feeling really *down,* last night, couldn't sleep.
R-really? How come?
I'm not sure, but it could be...
Look, don't get me wrong. I *love* my father. I *do.*
But sometimes, the products he makes--the power he has--

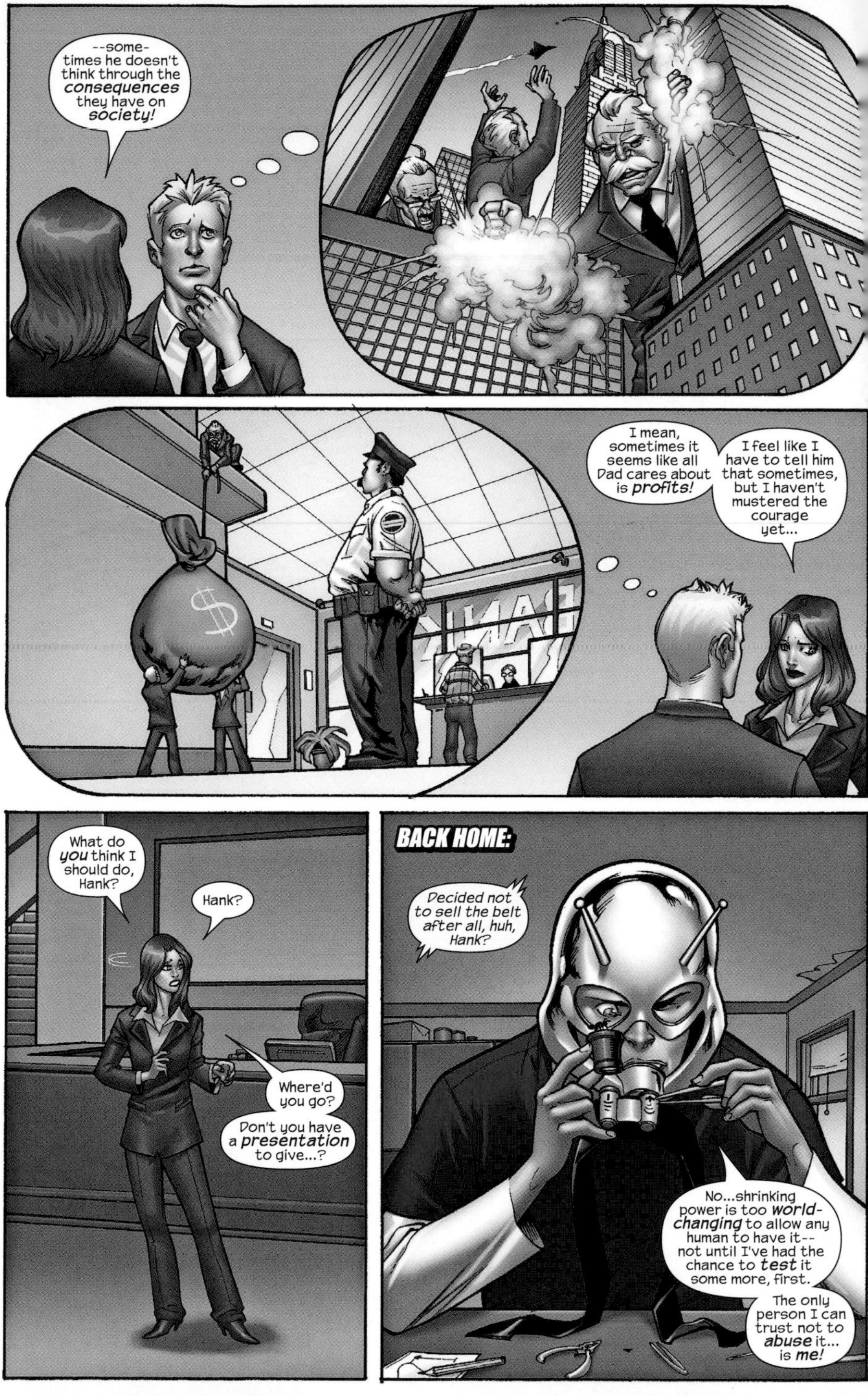
--some- times he doesn't think through the consequences they have on society!
I mean, sometimes it seems like all Dad cares about is profits!
I feel like I have to tell him that sometimes, but I haven't mustered the courage yet...
What do you think I should do, Hank?
Hank?
Where'd you go?
Don't you have a presentation to give...?
BACK HOME:
Decided not to sell the belt after all, huh, Hank?
No...shrinking power is too world-changing to allow any human to have it-- not until I've had the chance to test it some more, first.
The only person I can trust not to abuse it... is me!

I can keep on **helping** people with the power, though!

If only I could think of a good **hero name** to call myself...

But you guys are going to have to make room for me and my equipment in your **anthill!** I don't have the rent, so Mr. Gomez is gonna kick me out on the street!

What if you gave him **this?**

What is it?

We found it buried out in the courtyard a while ago. **We** don't have any use for it, but we know you Big Ones have some **strange** customs!

It's filled with old silver dollars! Some miser must have buried it **decades** ago!

This will cover my rent-- and **then** some! Thanks, guys!

It's the **least** we could do for saving our nest, Hank!

And if you shrink down, our Queen has another surprise for you!

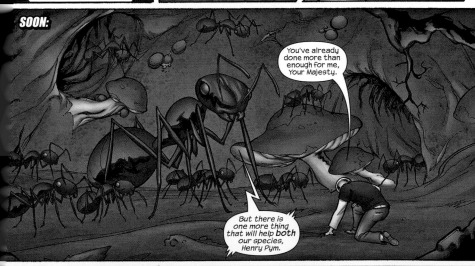

SOON:

You've already done more than enough for me, Your Majesty.

But there is one more thing that will help **both** our species, Henry Pym.

You would honor us by accepting the hand of our **daughter,** Princess Kkkrrkkkikk, in **marriage!**

IIII wuuuvvv yooouu, Henreee Pyyyym...

GAK!

By which I mean, uh... **Thanks,** Your Highness...

...but I'll just take the money...

A HERO IS BORN!

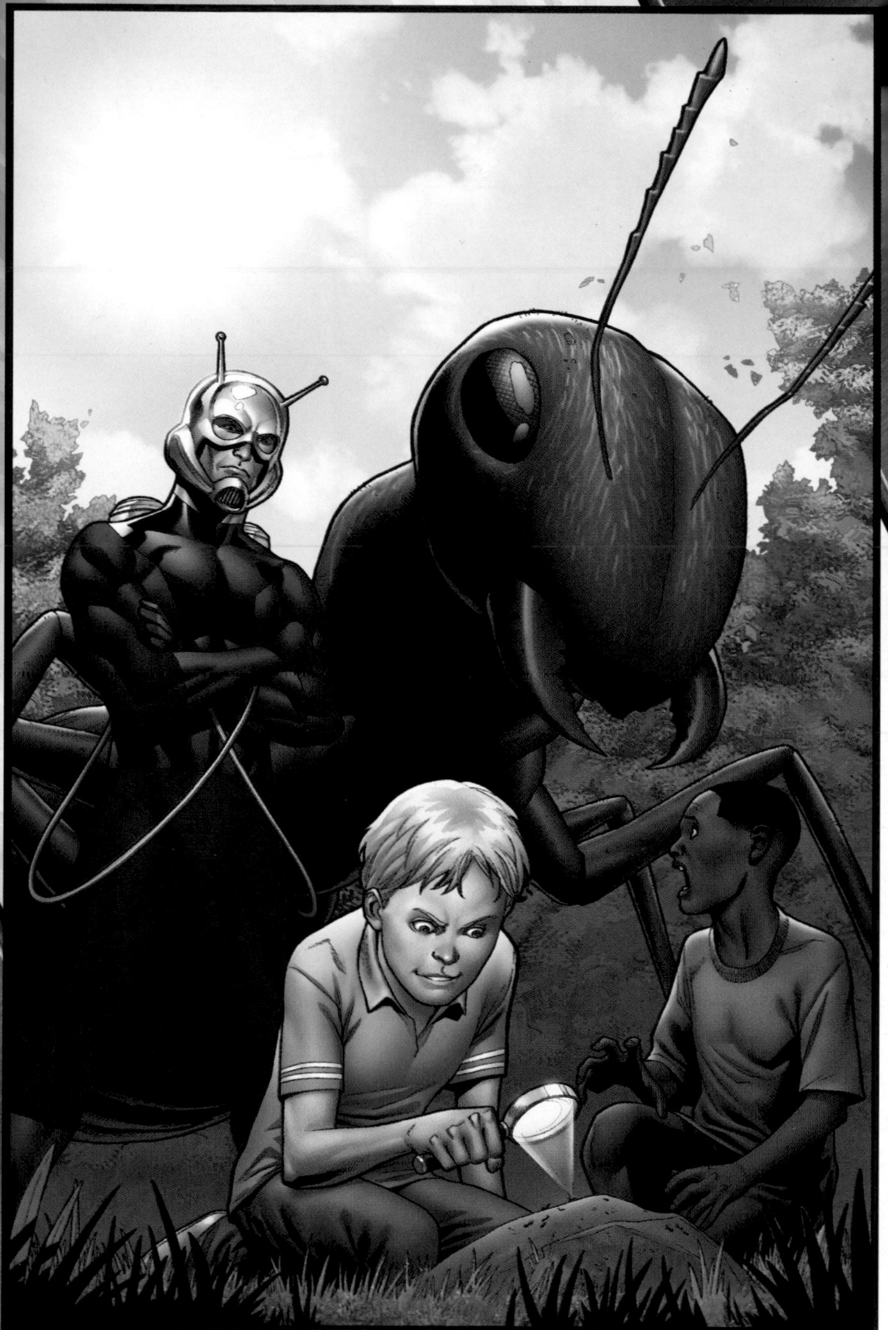

#10 MARVEL ADVENTURES SUPER HEROES

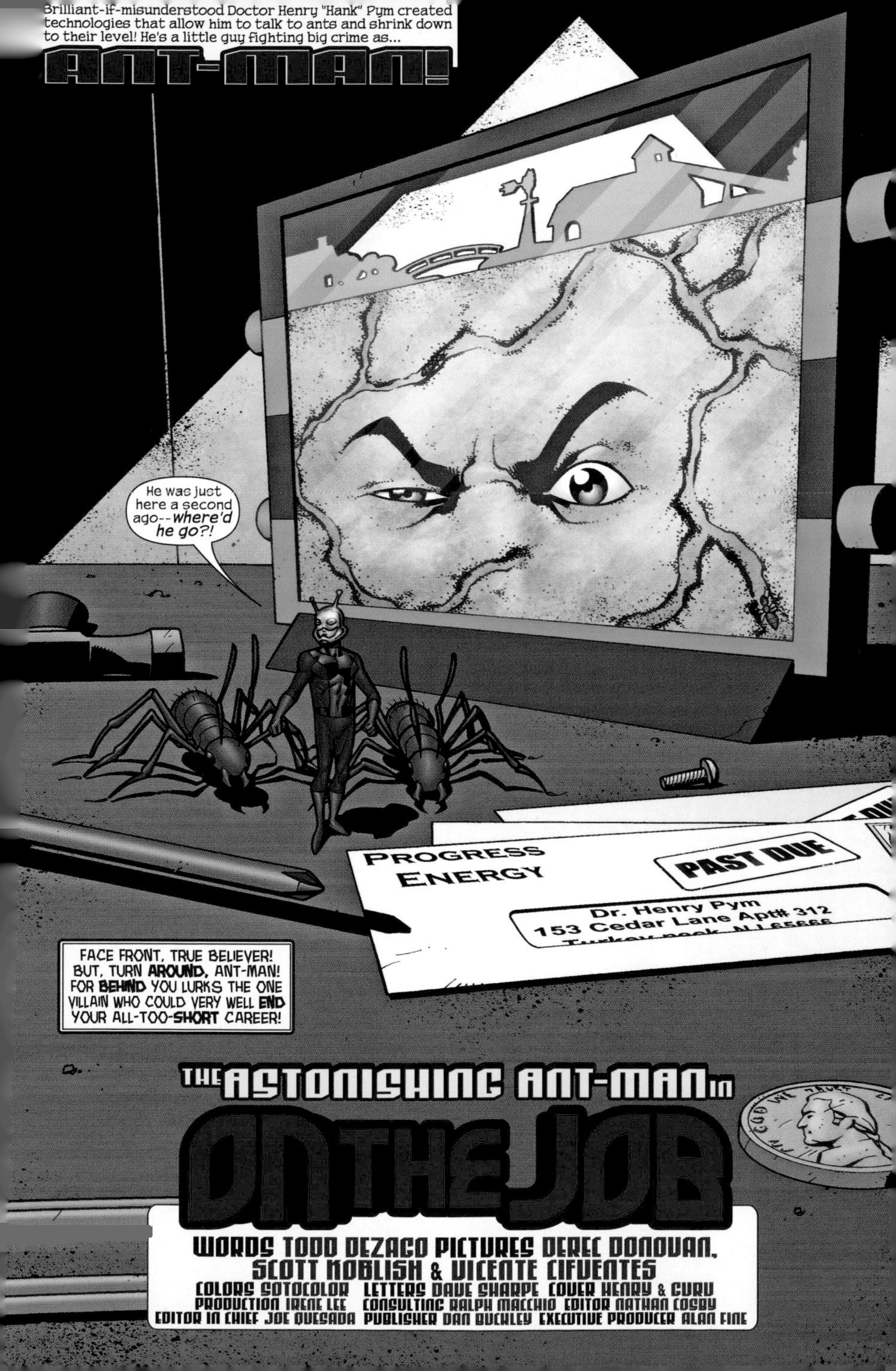

Brilliant-if-misunderstood Doctor Henry "Hank" Pym created technologies that allow him to talk to ants and shrink down to their level! He's a little guy fighting big crime as...
ANT-MAN!
He was just here a second ago--where'd he go?!
PROGRESS ENERGY
PAST DUE
Dr. Henry Pym
153 Cedar Lane Apt# 312
FACE FRONT, TRUE BELIEVER! BUT, TURN AROUND, ANT-MAN! FOR BEHIND YOU LURKS THE ONE VILLAIN WHO COULD VERY WELL END YOUR ALL-TOO-SHORT CAREER!
THE ASTONISHING ANT-MAN in
ON THE JOB
WORDS TODD DEZAGO PICTURES DEREC DONOVAN, SCOTT KOBLISH & VICENTE CIFUENTES
COLORS SOTOCOLOR LETTERS DAVE SHARPE COVER HENRY & GURU
PRODUCTION IRENE LEE CONSULTING RALPH MACCHIO EDITOR NATHAN COSBY
EDITOR IN CHIEF JOE QUESADA PUBLISHER DAN BUCKLEY EXECUTIVE PRODUCER ALAN FINE

New Jersey.

...sorry, fellas--I hate this part of the job.

Seein' as I only got *one position* on the loading dock to fill and the three'a *you* applyin' for it, I gotta make a choice.

VAN DYNE TECHNOLOGIES

KEEP OUT

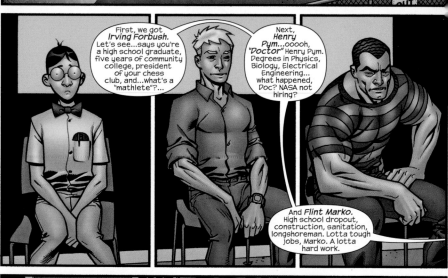

First, we got *Irving Forbush.* Let's see...says you're a high school graduate, five years of community college, president of your chess club, and...what's a "mathlete"?...

Next, *Henry Pym*...ooooh, *"Doctor"* Henry Pym. Degrees in Physics, Biology, Electrical Engineering... what happened, Doc? NASA not hiring?

And *Flint Marko.* High school dropout, construction, sanitation, longshoreman. Lotta tough jobs, Marko. A lotta hard work.

But *this* job is a lotta hard work too and I gotta pick the guy I think is gonna work the hardest. So I pick...

...*Irving*, ya got the job.

Wha--?

Huh?

Me?

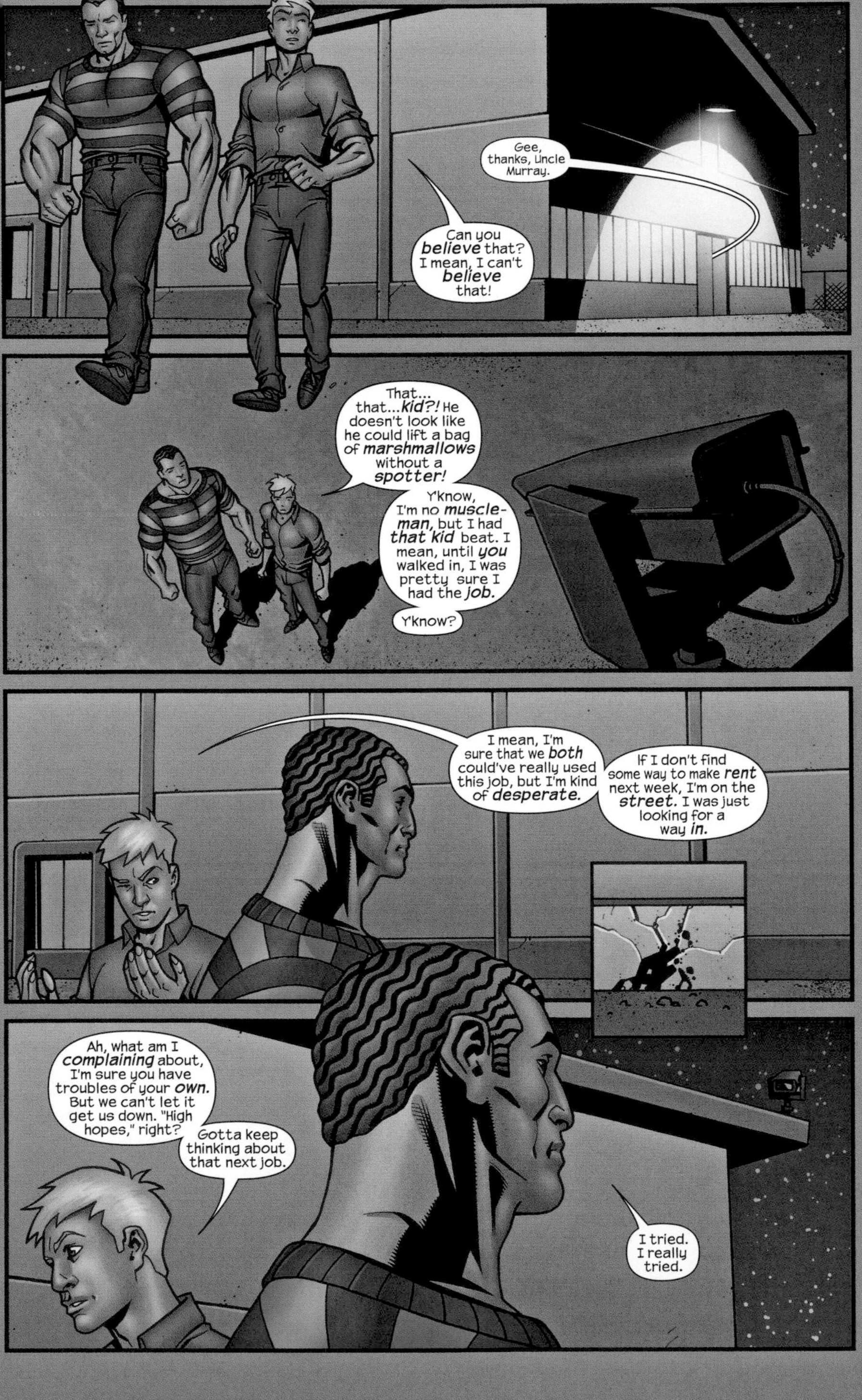
Gee, thanks, Uncle Murray.
Can you *believe* that? I mean, I can't *believe* that!
That... that...*kid?!* He doesn't look like he could lift a bag of *marshmallows* without a *spotter!*
Y'know, I'm no *muscle-man,* but I had *that kid* beat. I mean, until *you* walked in, I was pretty sure I had the *job.*
Y'know?
I mean, I'm sure that we *both* could've really used this job, but I'm kind of *desperate.*
If I don't find some way to make *rent* next week, I'm on the *street.* I was just looking for a way *in.*
Ah, what am I *complaining* about, I'm sure you have troubles of your *own.* But we can't let it get us down. "High hopes," right?
Gotta keep thinking about that next job.
I tried. I really tried.

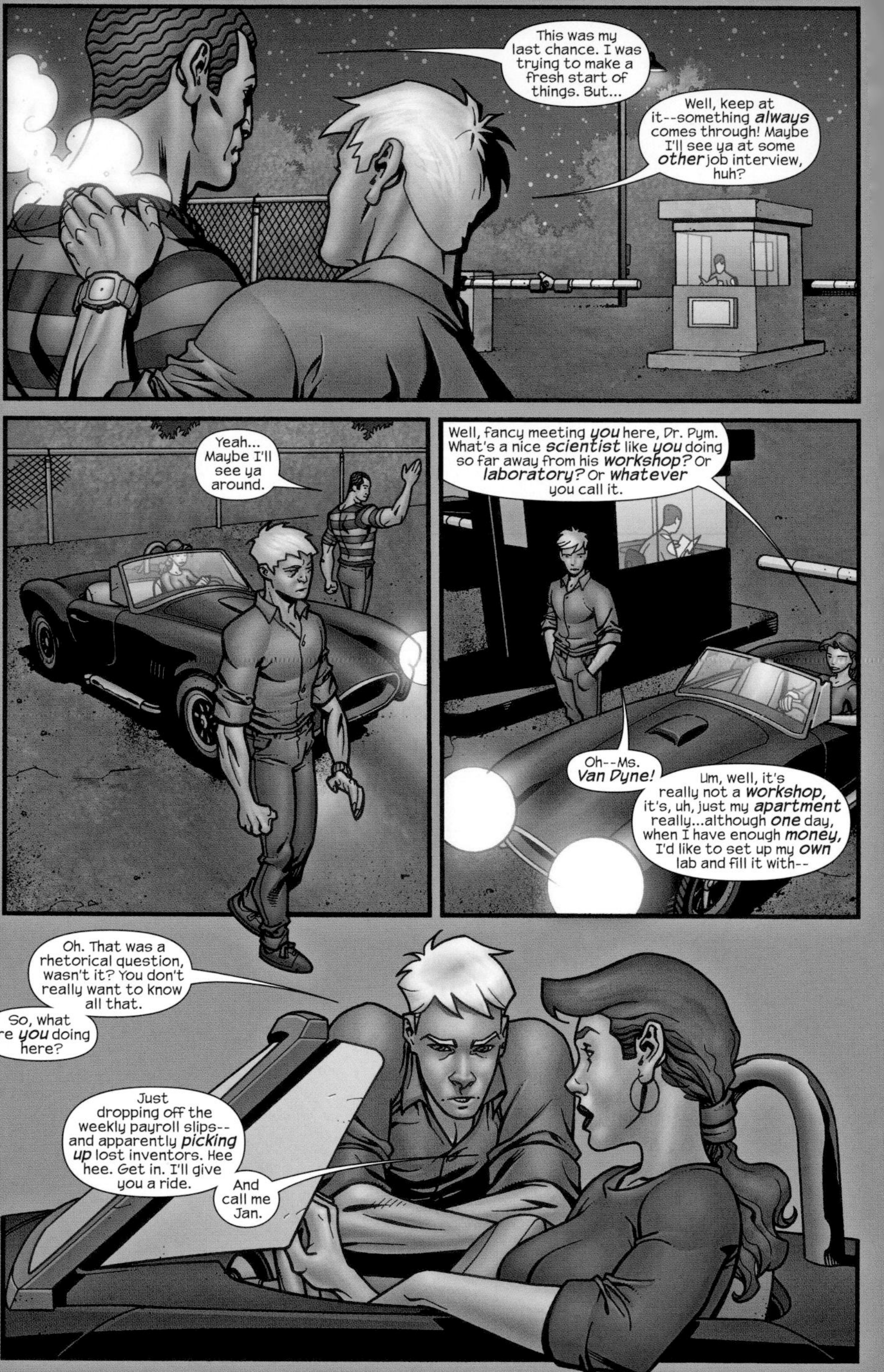
This was my last chance. I was trying to make a fresh start of things. But...
Well, keep at it--something always comes through! Maybe I'll see ya at some other job interview, huh?
Yeah... Maybe I'll see ya around.
Well, fancy meeting you here, Dr. Pym. What's a nice scientist like you doing so far away from his workshop? Or laboratory? Or whatever you call it.
Oh--Ms. Van Dyne!
Um, well, it's really not a workshop, it's, uh, just my apartment really...although one day, when I have enough money, I'd like to set up my own lab and fill it with--
Oh. That was a rhetorical question, wasn't it? You don't really want to know all that.
So, what are you doing here?
Just dropping off the weekly payroll slips--and apparently picking up lost inventors. Hee hee. Get in. I'll give you a ride.
And call me Jan.

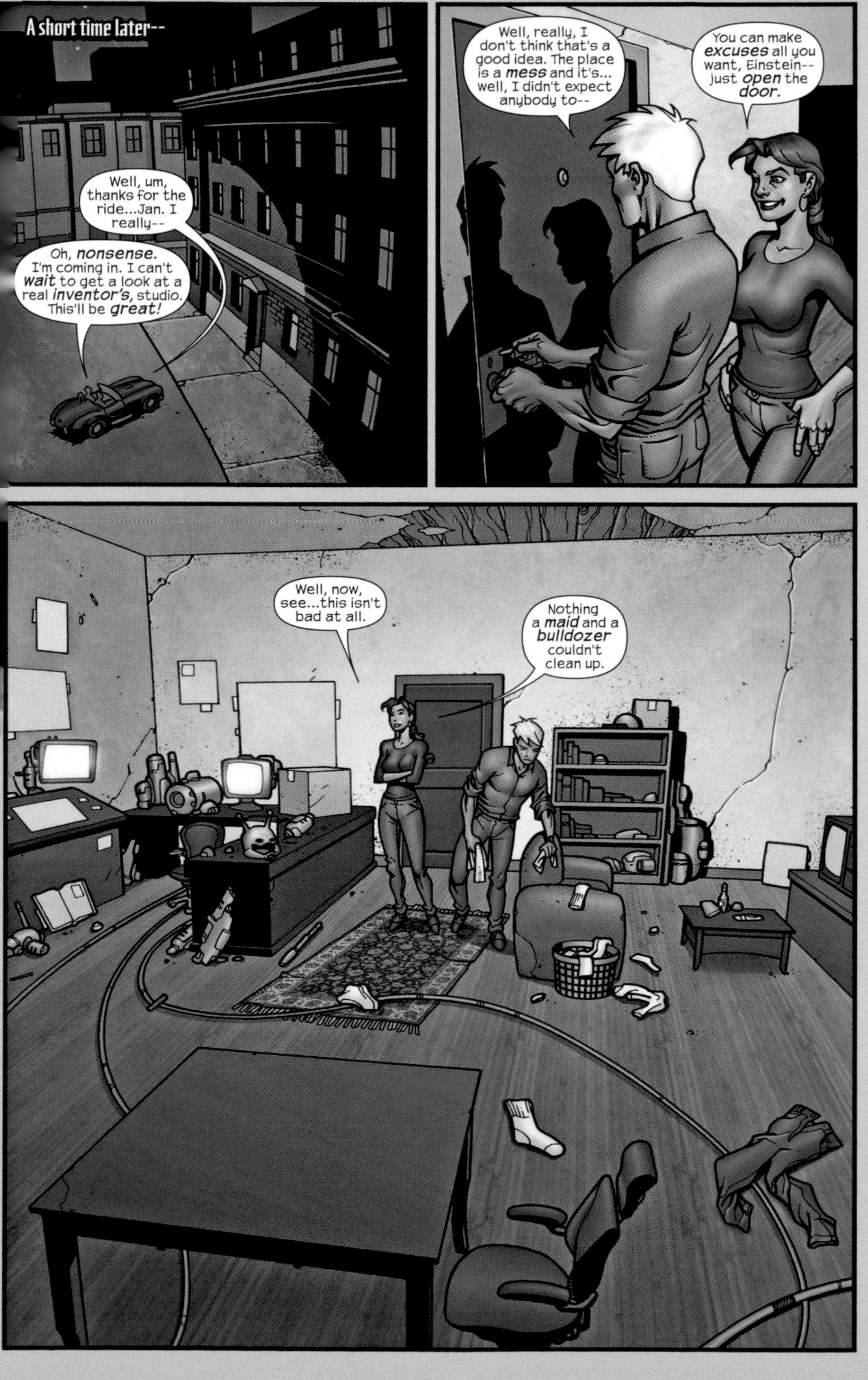
A short time later--
Well, um, thanks for the ride...Jan. I really--
Oh, nonsense. I'm coming in. I can't wait to get a look at a real inventor's, studio. This'll be great!
Well, really, I don't think that's a good idea. The place is a mess and it's... well, I didn't expect anybody to--
You can make excuses all you want, Einstein-- just open the door.
Well, now, see...this isn't bad at all.
Nothing a maid and a bulldozer couldn't clean up.

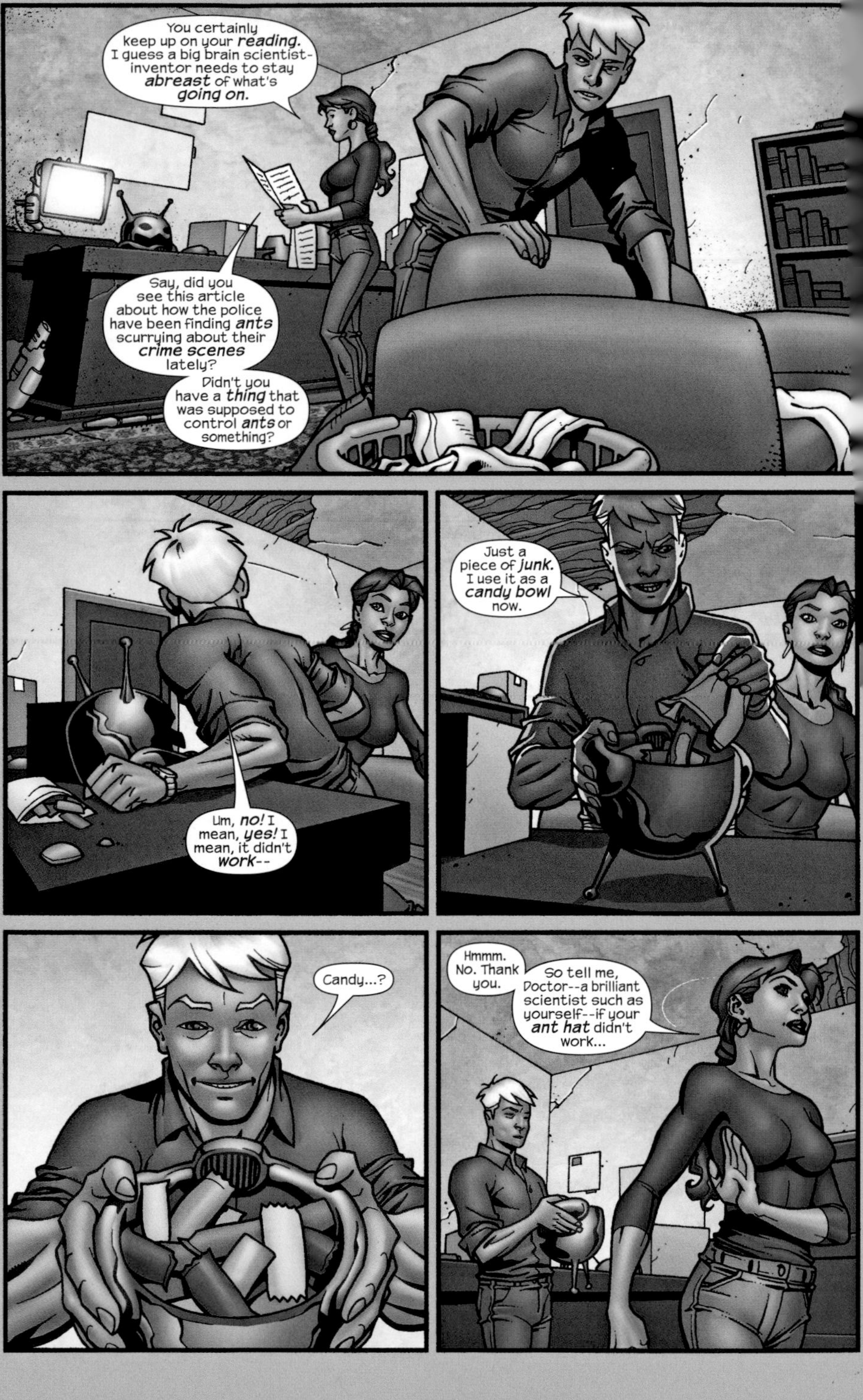

You certainly keep up on your reading. I guess a big brain scientist-inventor needs to stay abreast of what's going on.
Say, did you see this article about how the police have been finding ants scurrying about their crime scenes lately?
Didn't you have a thing that was supposed to control ants or something?
Um, no! I mean, yes! I mean, it didn't work--
Just a piece of junk. I use it as a candy bowl now.
Candy...?
Hmmm. No. Thank you.
So tell me, Doctor--a brilliant scientist such as yourself--if your ant hat didn't work...

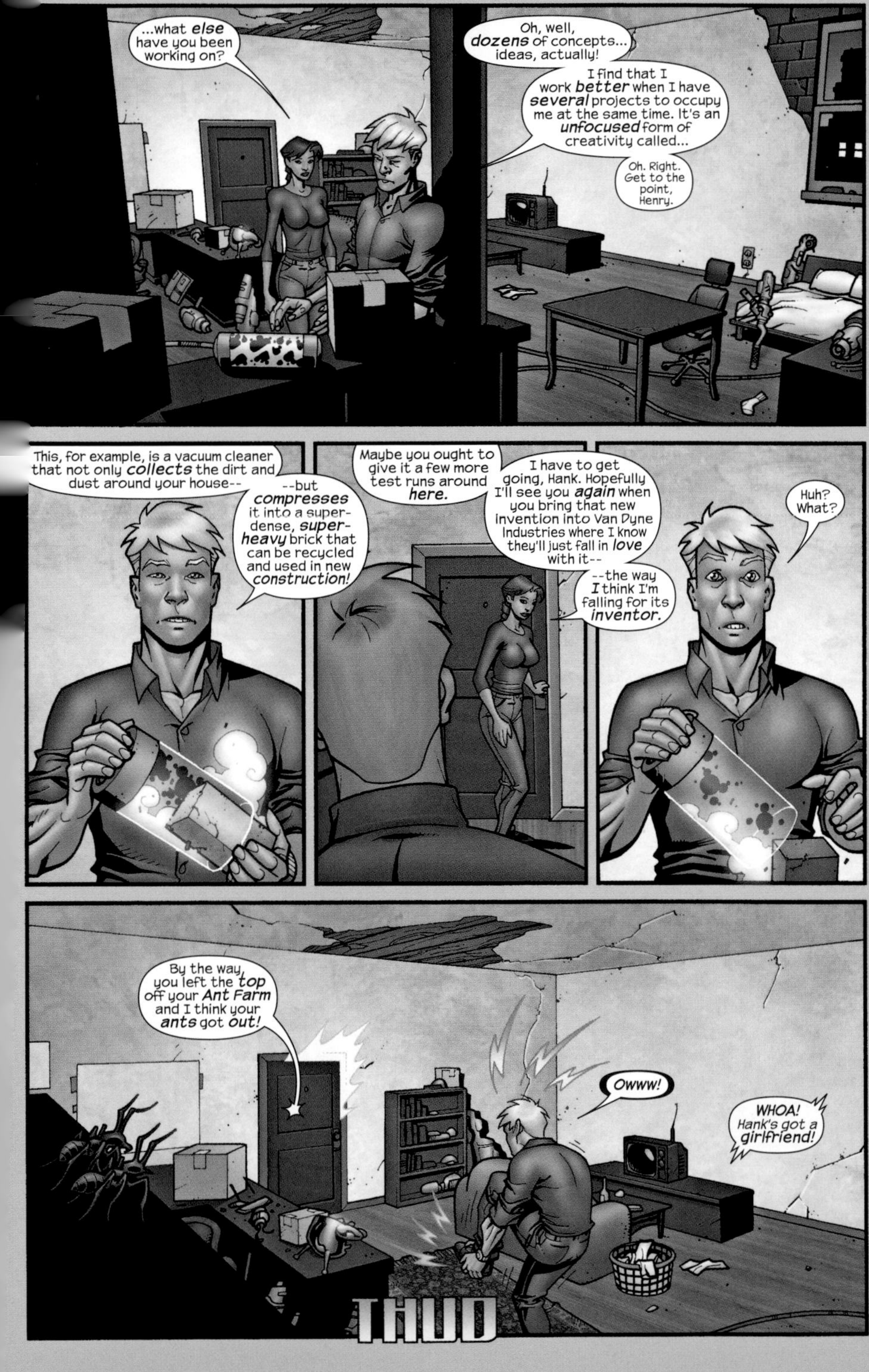
...what else have you been working on?
Oh, well, dozens of concepts... ideas, actually!
I find that I work better when I have several projects to occupy me at the same time. It's an unfocused form of creativity called...
Oh. Right. Get to the point, Henry.
This, for example, is a vacuum cleaner that not only collects the dirt and dust around your house--
--but compresses it into a super-dense, super-heavy brick that can be recycled and used in new construction!
Maybe you ought to give it a few more test runs around here.
I have to get going, Hank. Hopefully I'll see you again when you bring that new invention into Van Dyne Industries where I know they'll just fall in love with it--
--the way I think I'm falling for its inventor.
Huh? What?
By the way, you left the top off your Ant Farm and I think your ants got out!
Owww!
WHOA! Hank's got a girlfriend!
THUD

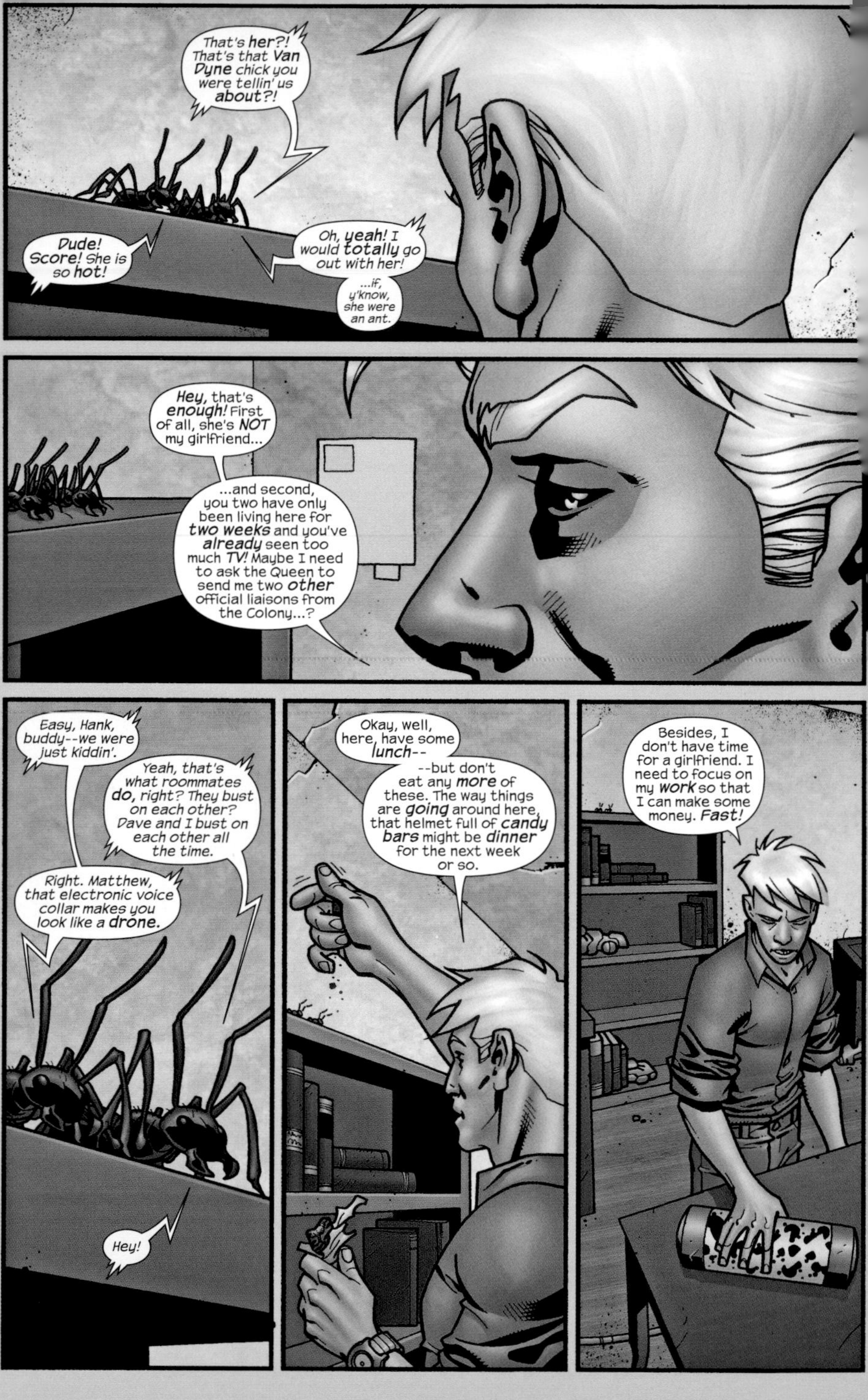
That's her?! That's that Van Dyne chick you were tellin' us about?!
Dude! Score! She is so hot!
Oh, yeah! I would totally go out with her!
...if, y'know, she were an ant.
Hey, that's enough! First of all, she's NOT my girlfriend...
...and second, you two have only been living here for two weeks and you've already seen too much TV! Maybe I need to ask the Queen to send me two other official liaisons from the Colony...?
Easy, Hank, buddy--we were just kiddin'.
Yeah, that's what roommates do, right? They bust on each other? Dave and I bust on each other all the time.
Right. Matthew, that electronic voice collar makes you look like a drone.
Hey!
Okay, well, here, have some lunch--
--but don't eat any more of these. The way things are going around here, that helmet full of candy bars might be dinner for the next week or so.
Besides, I don't have time for a girlfriend. I need to focus on my work so that I can make some money. Fast!

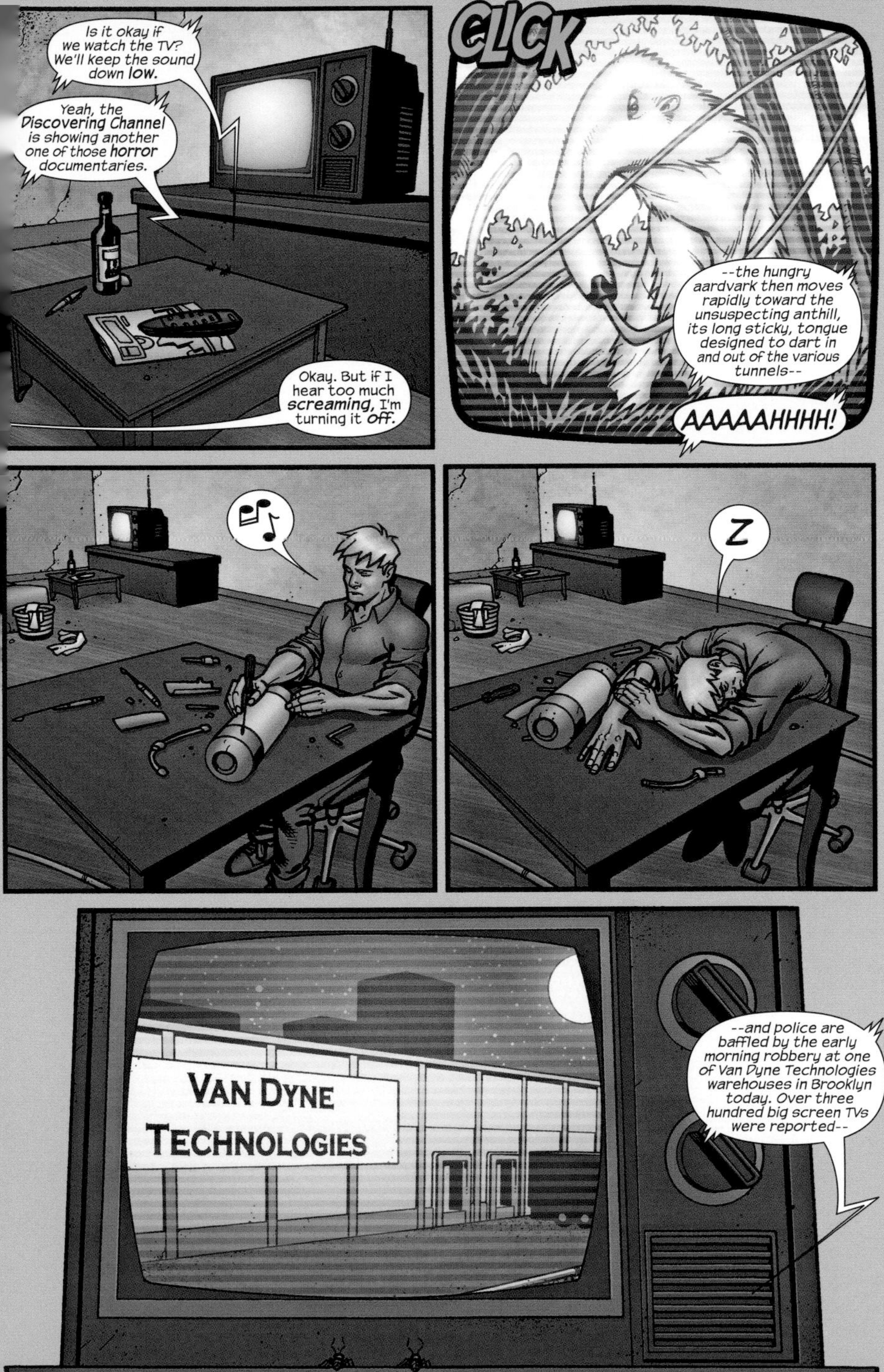
Is it okay if we watch the TV? We'll keep the sound down low.
Yeah, the Discovering Channel is showing another one of those horror documentaries.
Okay. But if I hear too much screaming, I'm turning it off.
CLICK
--the hungry aardvark then moves rapidly toward the unsuspecting anthill, its long sticky, tongue designed to dart in and out of the various tunnels--
AAAAAHHHH!
Z
VAN DYNE TECHNOLOGIES
--and police are baffled by the early morning robbery at one of Van Dyne Technologies warehouses in Brooklyn today. Over three hundred big screen TVs were reported--

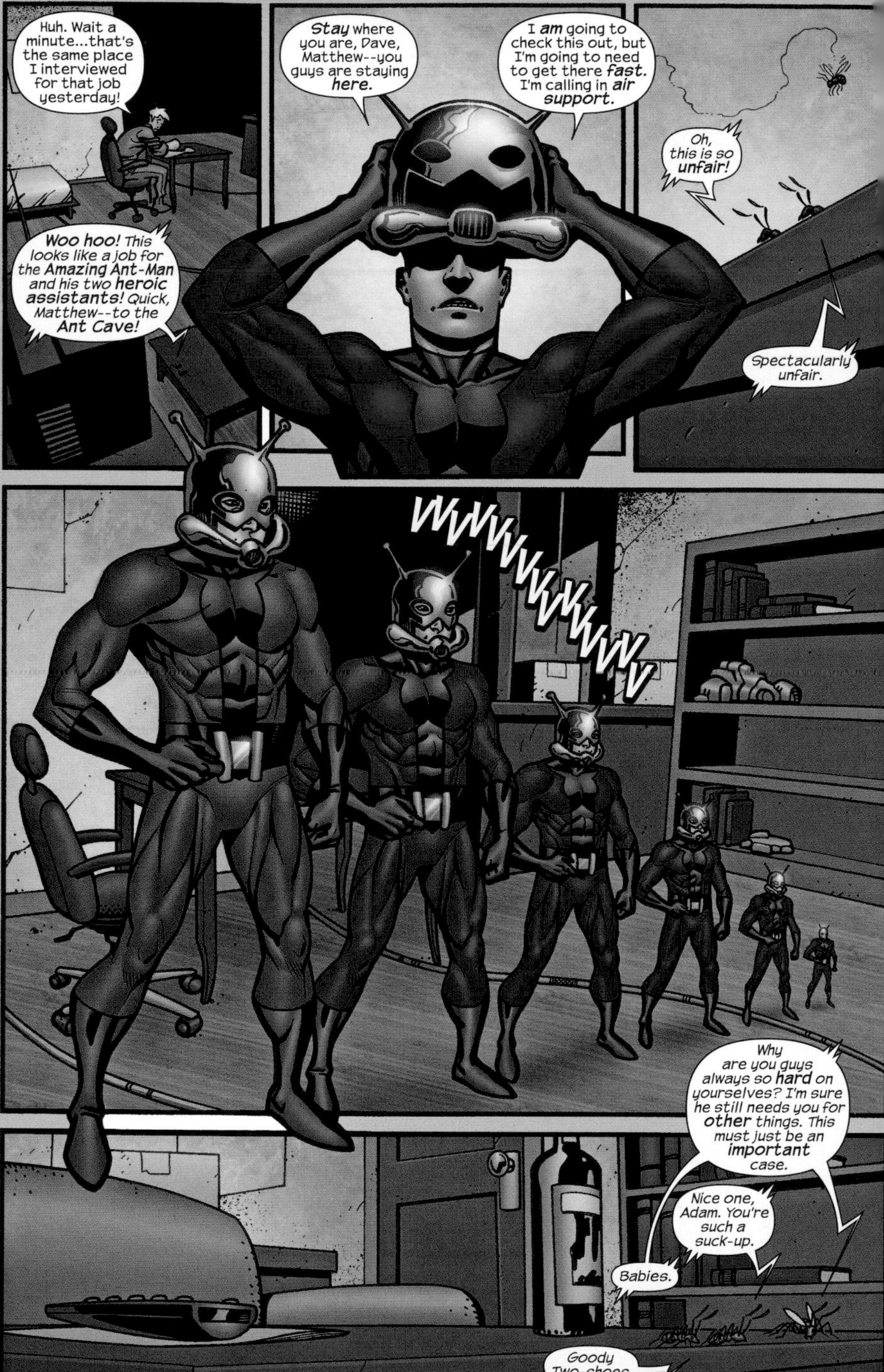

Huh. Wait a minute...that's the same place I interviewed for that job yesterday!
Woo hoo! This looks like a job for the Amazing Ant-Man and his two heroic assistants! Quick, Matthew--to the Ant Cave!
Stay where you are, Dave, Matthew--you guys are staying here.
I am going to check this out, but I'm going to need to get there fast. I'm calling in air support.
Oh, this is so unfair!
Spectacularly unfair.
VVVVVVVVVVVVVVVVV
Why are you guys always so hard on yourselves? I'm sure he still needs you for other things. This must just be an important case.
Nice one, Adam. You're such a suck-up.
Babies.
Goody Two-shoes.

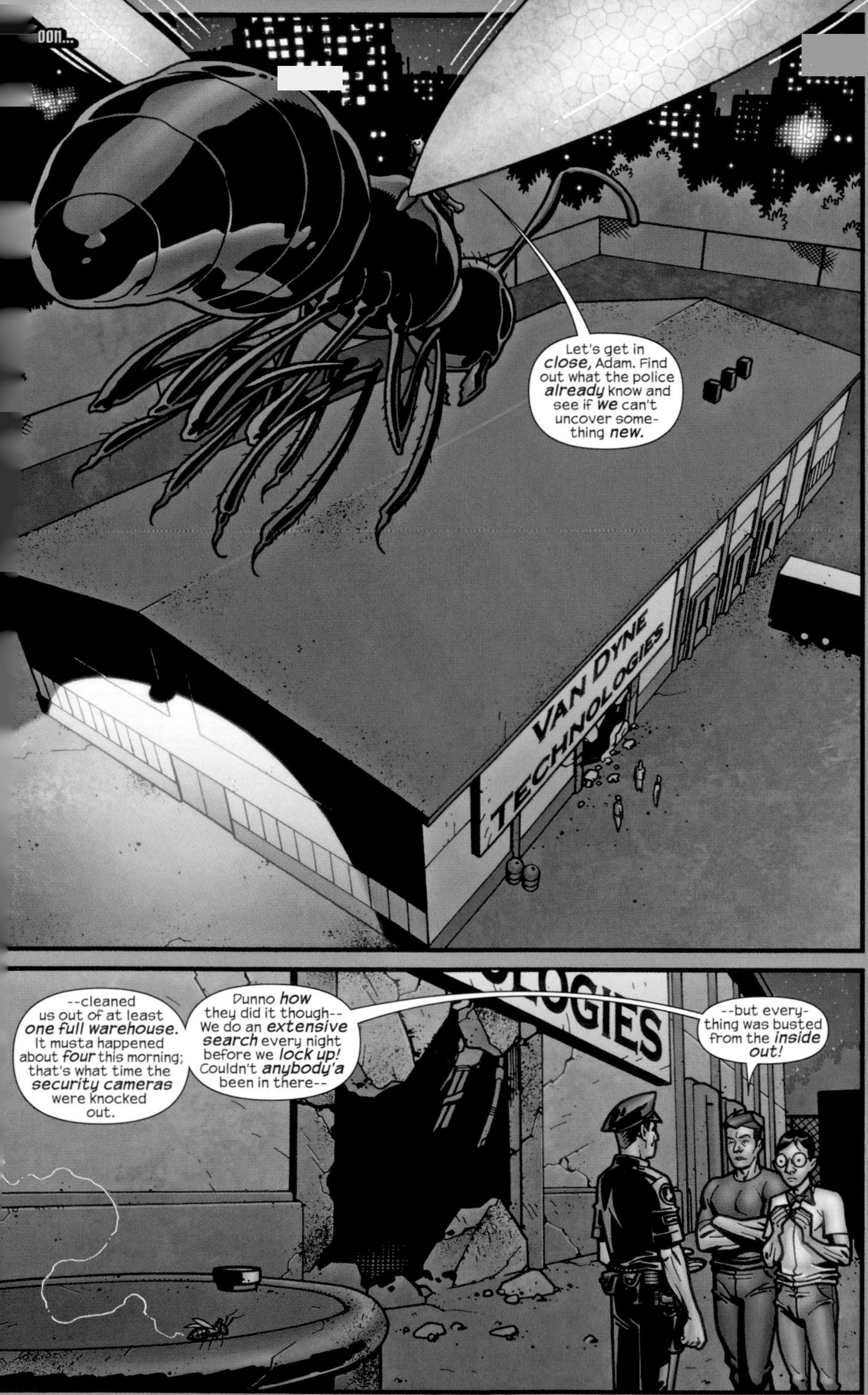
oon...
Let's get in close, Adam. Find out what the police already know and see if we can't uncover something new.
VAN DYNE TECHNOLOGIES
--cleaned us out of at least one full warehouse. It musta happened about four this morning; that's what time the security cameras were knocked out.
Dunno how they did it though-- We do an extensive search every night before we lock up! Couldn't anybody'a been in there--
--but everything was busted from the inside out!

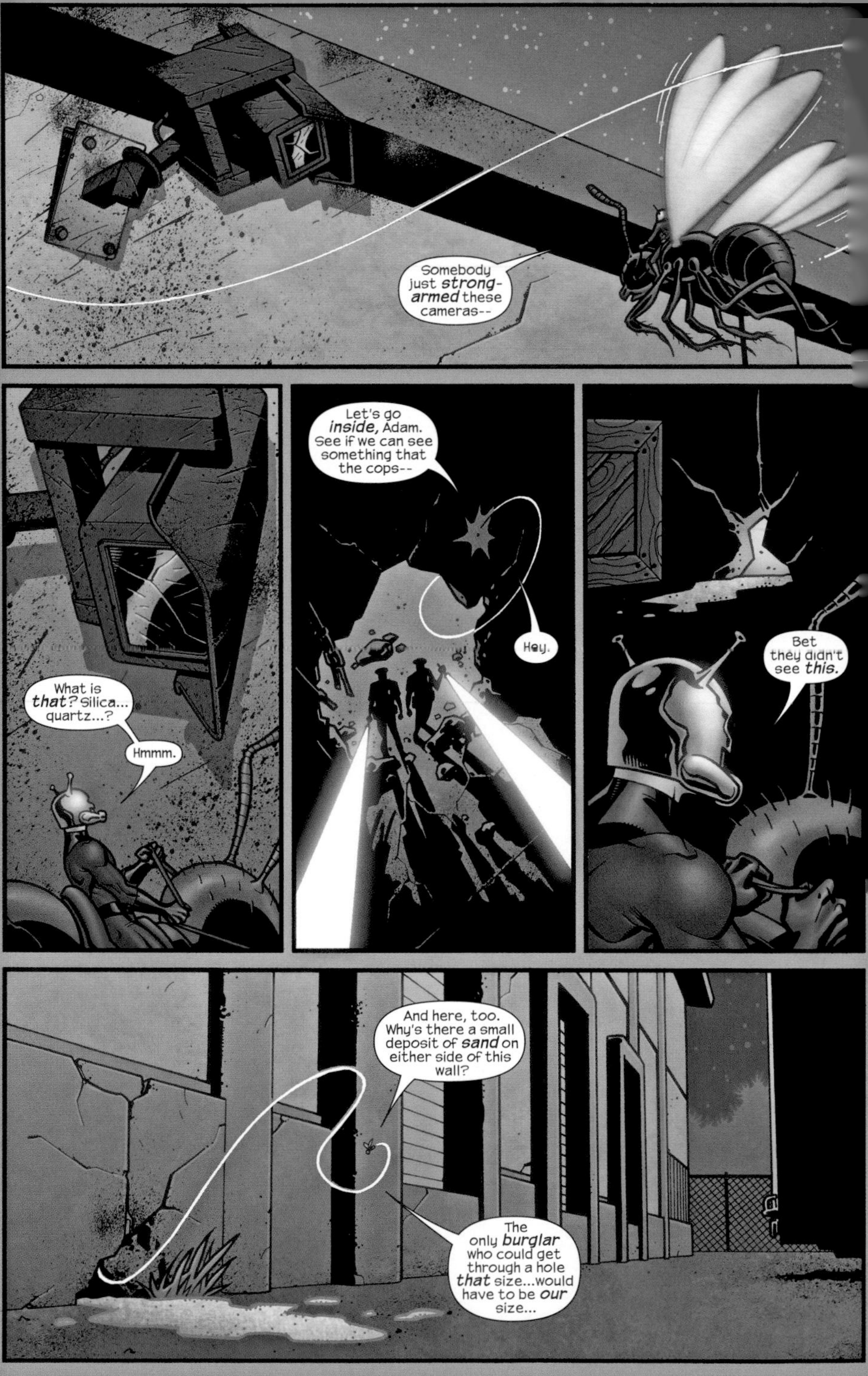

Somebody just strong-armed these cameras--
What is that? Silica... quartz...?
Hmmm.
Let's go inside, Adam. See if we can see something that the cops--
Hey.
Bet they didn't see this.
And here, too. Why's there a small deposit of sand on either side of this wall?
The only burglar who could get through a hole that size...would have to be our size...

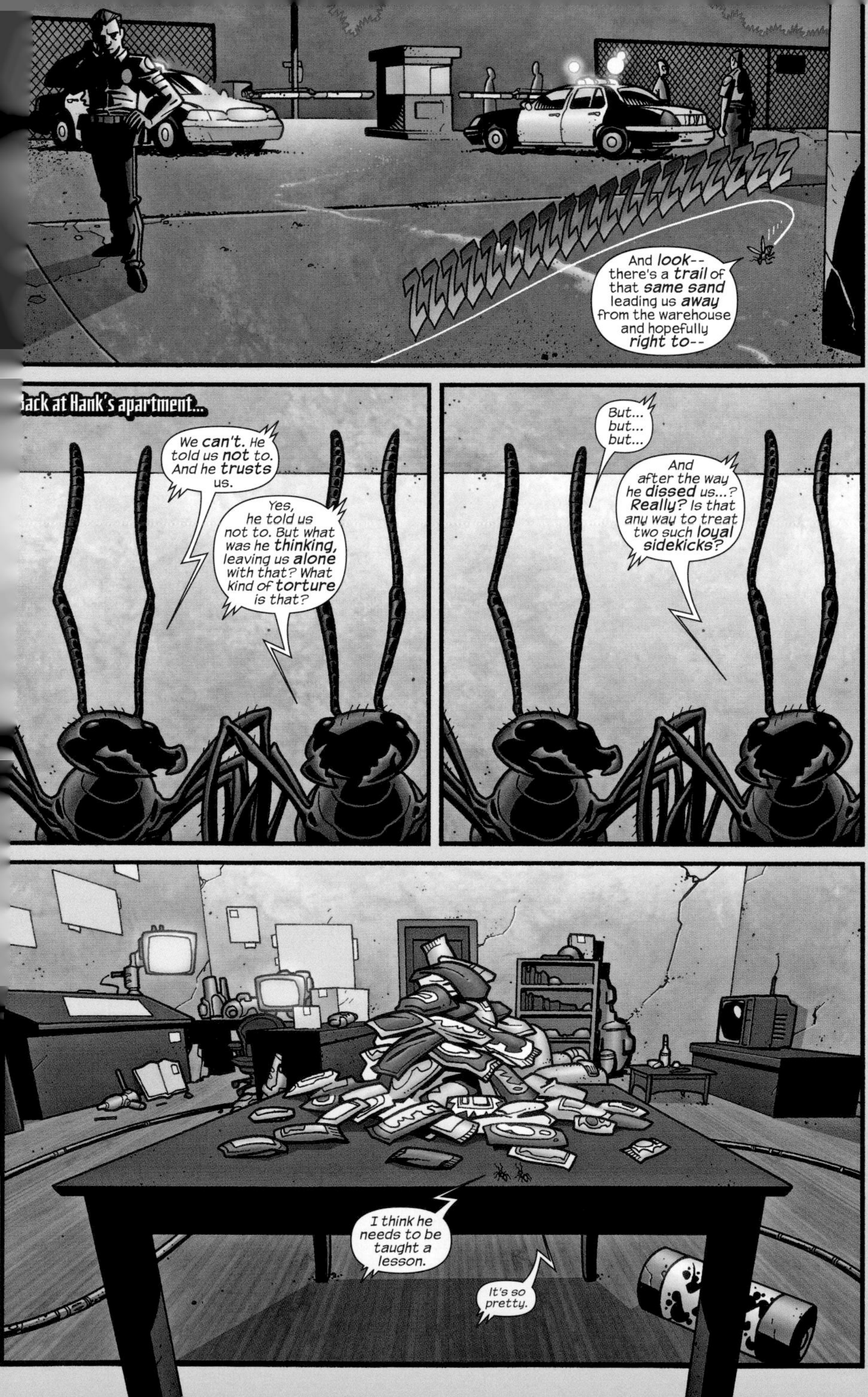

ZZZZZZZZZZZZZZZZZZZZZZZZZZZZ
And look-- there's a trail of that same sand leading us away from the warehouse and hopefully right to--
Back at Hank's apartment...
We can't. He told us not to. And he trusts us.
Yes, he told us not to. But what was he thinking, leaving us alone with that? What kind of torture is that?
But... but... but...
And after the way he dissed us...? Really? Is that any way to treat two such loyal sidekicks?
I think he needs to be taught a lesson.
It's so pretty.

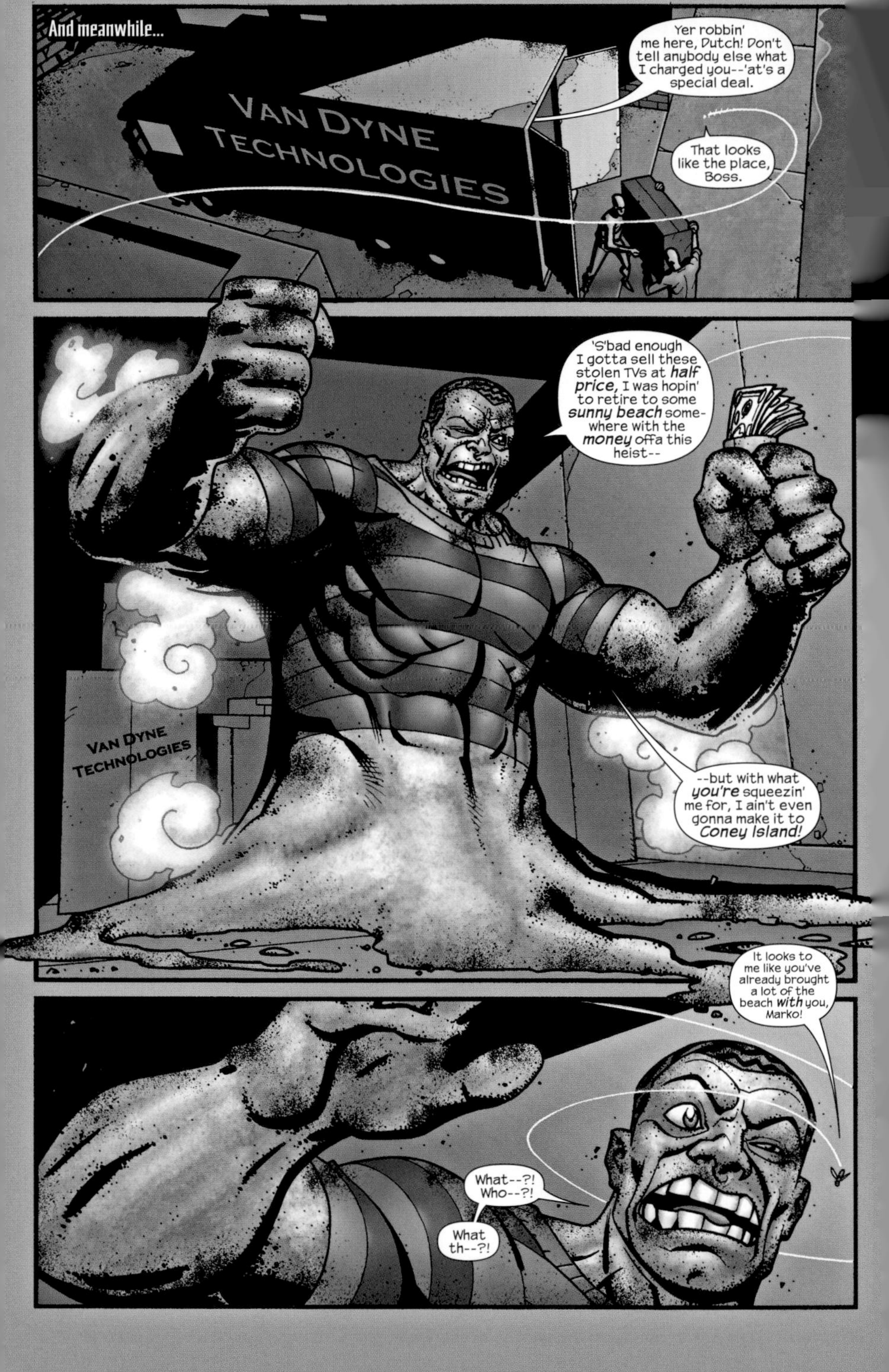
And meanwhile...
VAN DYNE TECHNOLOGIES
Yer robbin' me here, Dutch! Don't tell anybody else what I charged you--'at's a special deal.
That looks like the place, Boss.
'S'bad enough I gotta sell these stolen TVs at *half price*, I was hopin' to retire to some *sunny beach* somewhere with the *money* offa this heist--
VAN DYNE TECHNOLOGIES
--but with what *you're* squeezin' me for, I ain't even gonna make it to *Coney Island!*
It looks to me like you've already brought a lot of the beach *with* you, Marko!
What--?! Who--?!
What th--?!

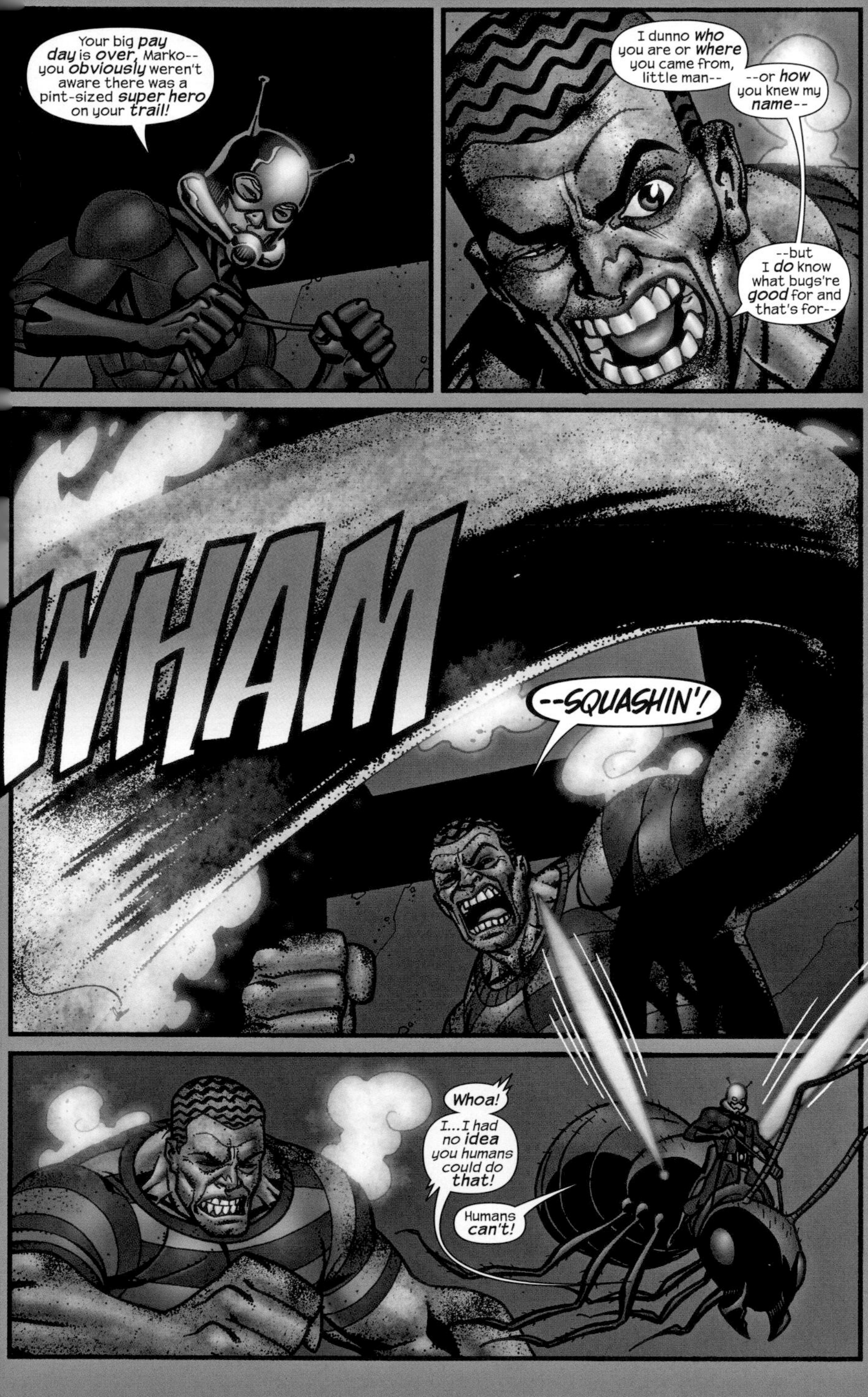

Your big pay day is over, Marko-- you obviously weren't aware there was a pint-sized super hero on your trail!
I dunno who you are or where you came from, little man--
--or how you knew my name--
--but I do know what bugs're good for and that's for--
WHAM
--SQUASHIN'!
Whoa!
I...I had no idea you humans could do that!
Humans can't!

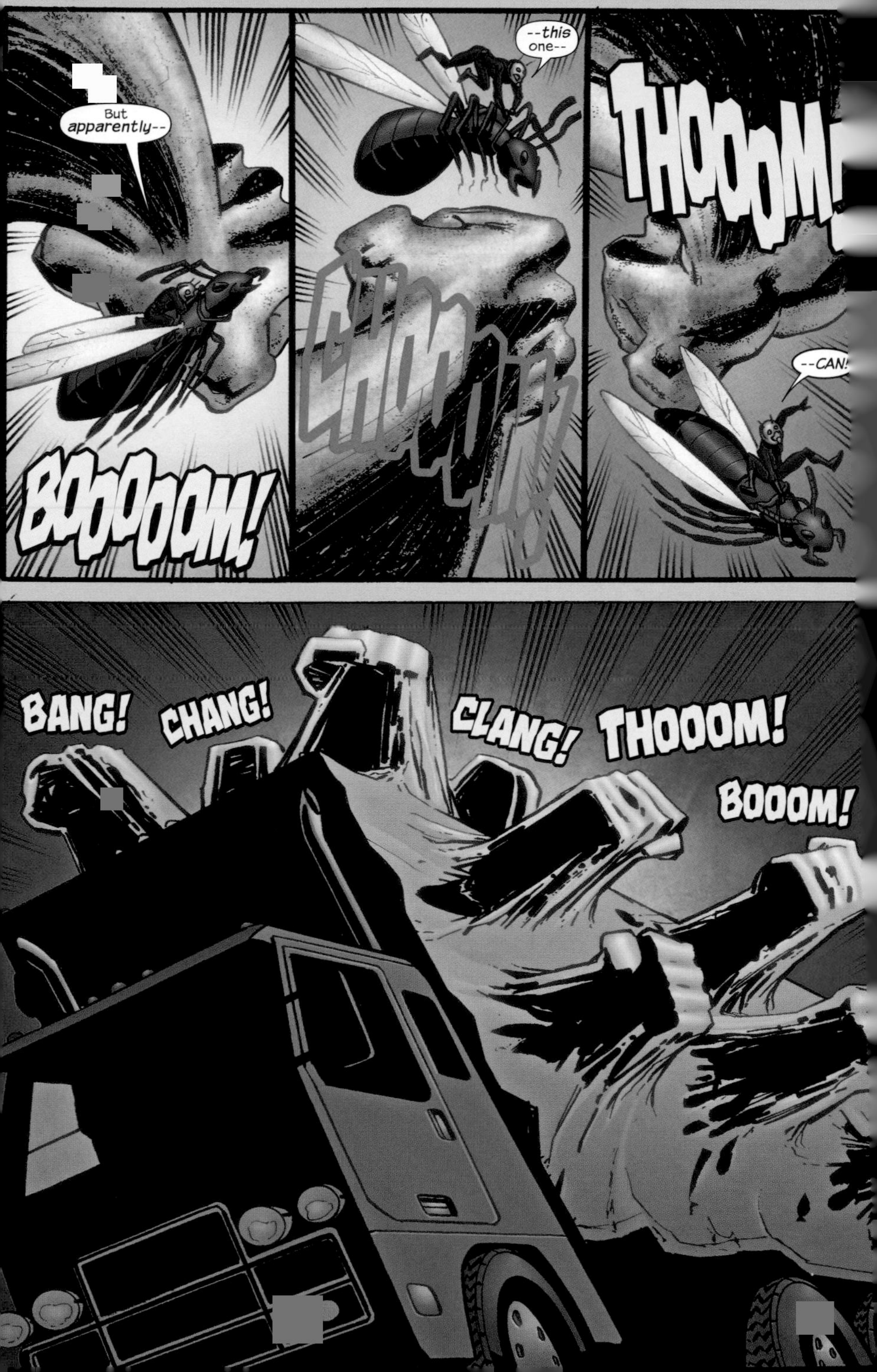
But apparently--
BOOOOOM!
--this one--
THOOOM!
--CAN!
BANG!
CHANG!
CLANG!
THOOOM!
BOOOM!

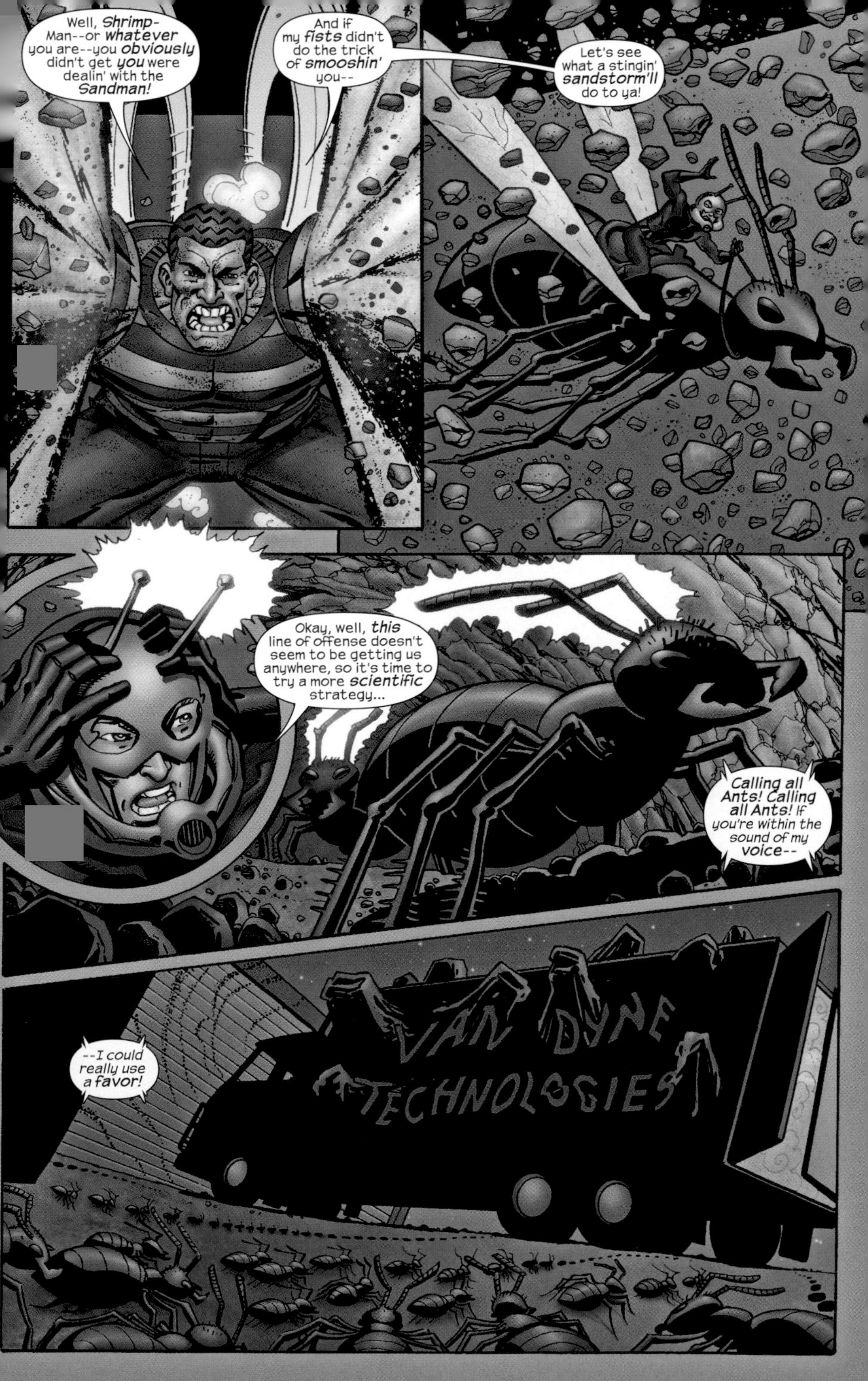
Well, Shrimp-Man--or whatever you are--you obviously didn't get you were dealin' with the Sandman!
And if my fists didn't do the trick of smooshin' you--
Let's see what a stingin' sandstorm'll do to ya!
Okay, well, this line of offense doesn't seem to be getting us anywhere, so it's time to try a more scientific strategy...
Calling all Ants! Calling all Ants! If you're within the sound of my voice--
VAN DYNE TECHNOLOGIES
--I could really use a favor!

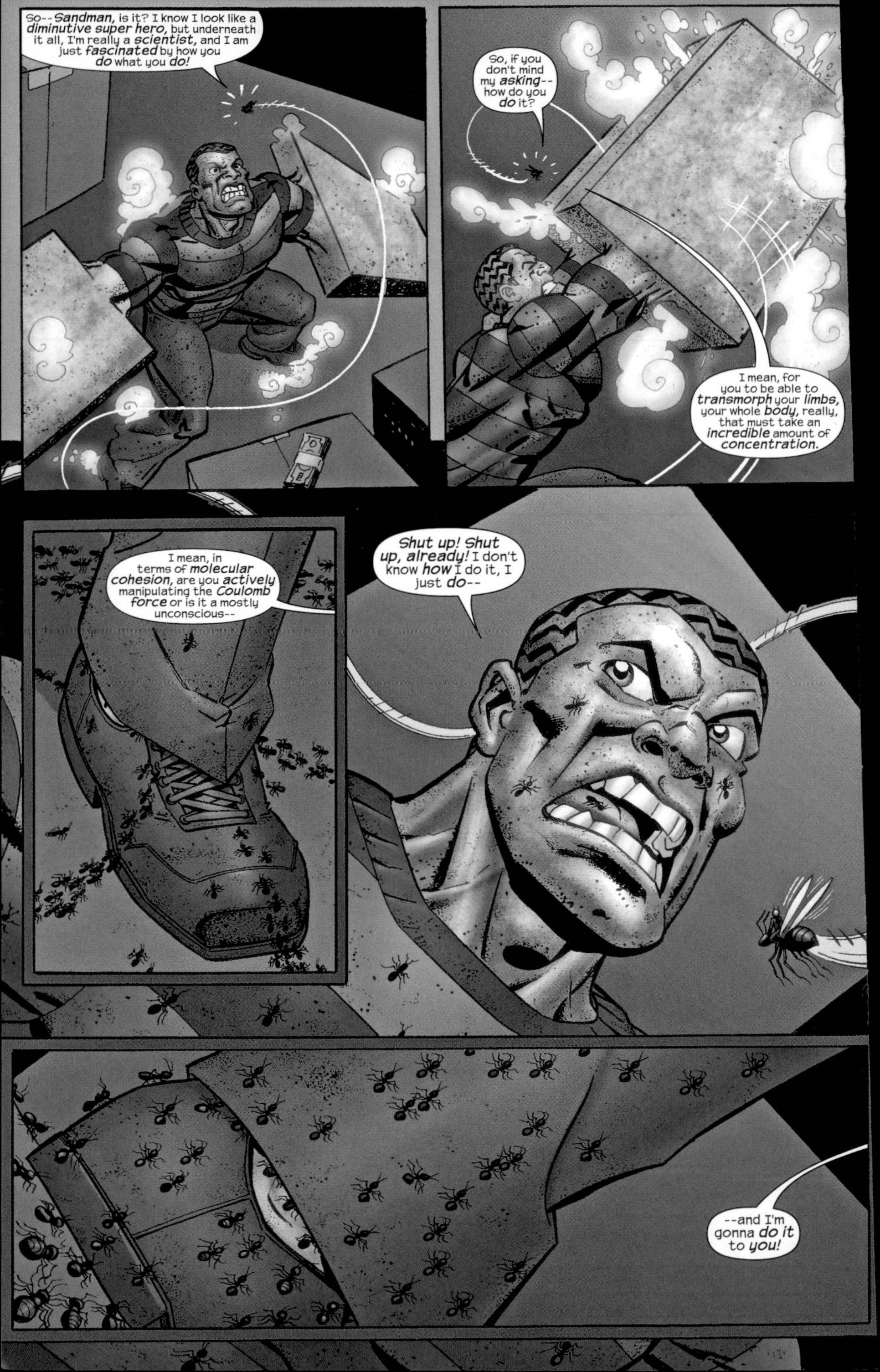
So--Sandman, is it? I know I look like a diminutive super hero, but underneath it all, I'm really a scientist, and I am just fascinated by how you do what you do!
So, if you don't mind my asking--how do you do it?
I mean, for you to be able to transmorph your limbs, your whole body, really, that must take an incredible amount of concentration.
I mean, in terms of molecular cohesion, are you actively manipulating the Coulomb force or is it a mostly unconscious--
Shut up! Shut up, already! I don't know how I do it, I just do--
--and I'm gonna do it to you!

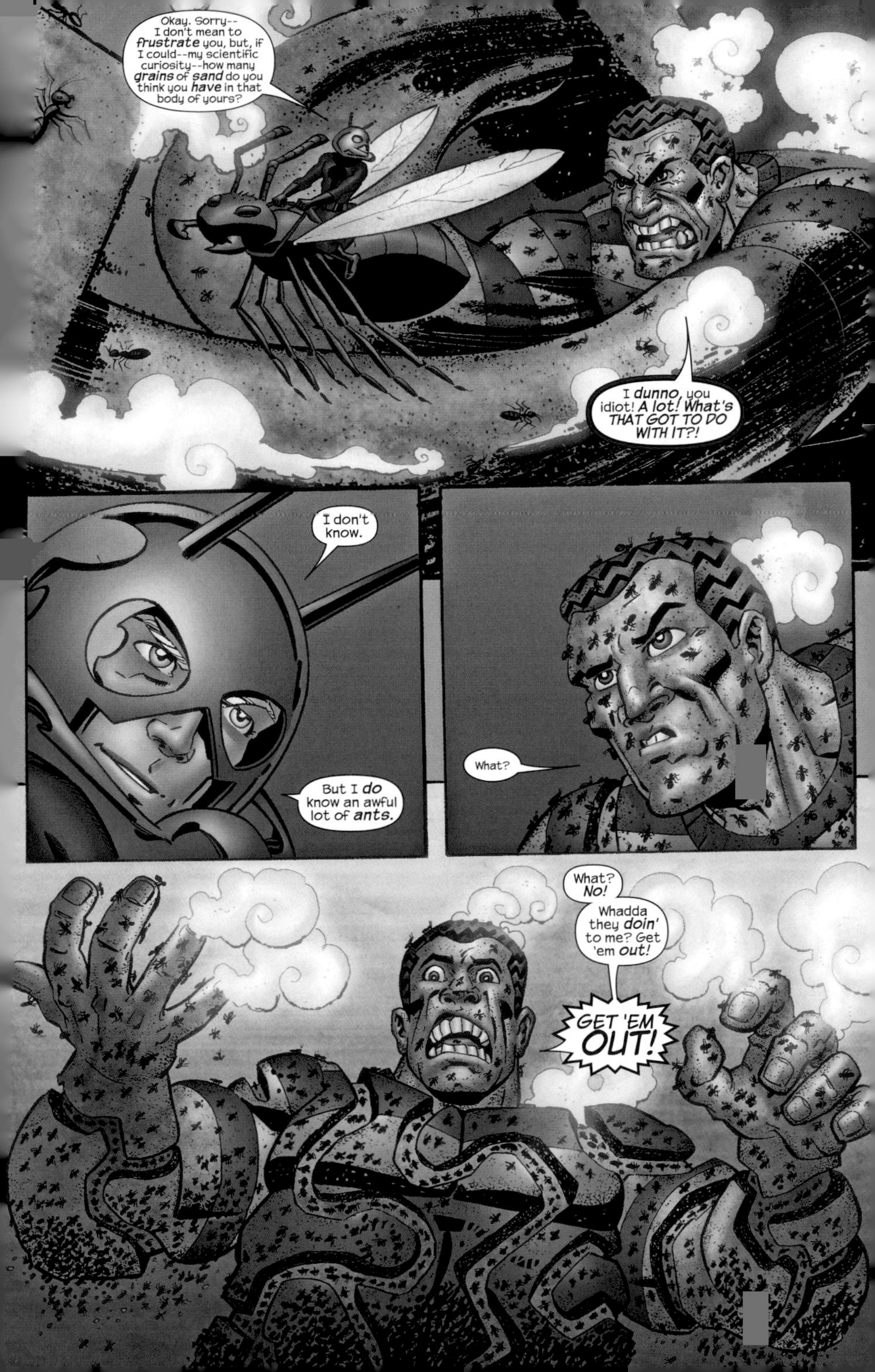
Okay. Sorry-- I don't mean to frustrate you, but, if I could--my scientific curiosity--how many grains of sand do you think you have in that body of yours?
I dunno, you idiot! A lot! What's THAT GOT TO DO WITH IT?!
I don't know.
But I do know an awful lot of ants.
What?
What? No!
Whadda they doin' to me? Get 'em out!
GET 'EM OUT!

NOOOOOOO!

That's it, boys! Just take *each grain* of sand as far away from the *others* as you *can!*

Thank you for rallying the *troops* together, friends.

It took ants from all over the *neighborhoods* to do this. You have my *gratitude.*

And don't forget what you *promised* us, Ant-Man.

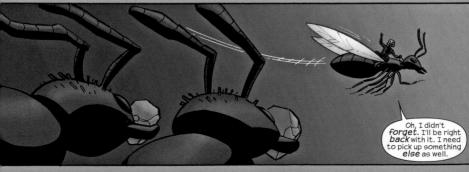

Oh, I didn't *forget.* I'll be right *back* with it. I need to pick up something *else* as well.

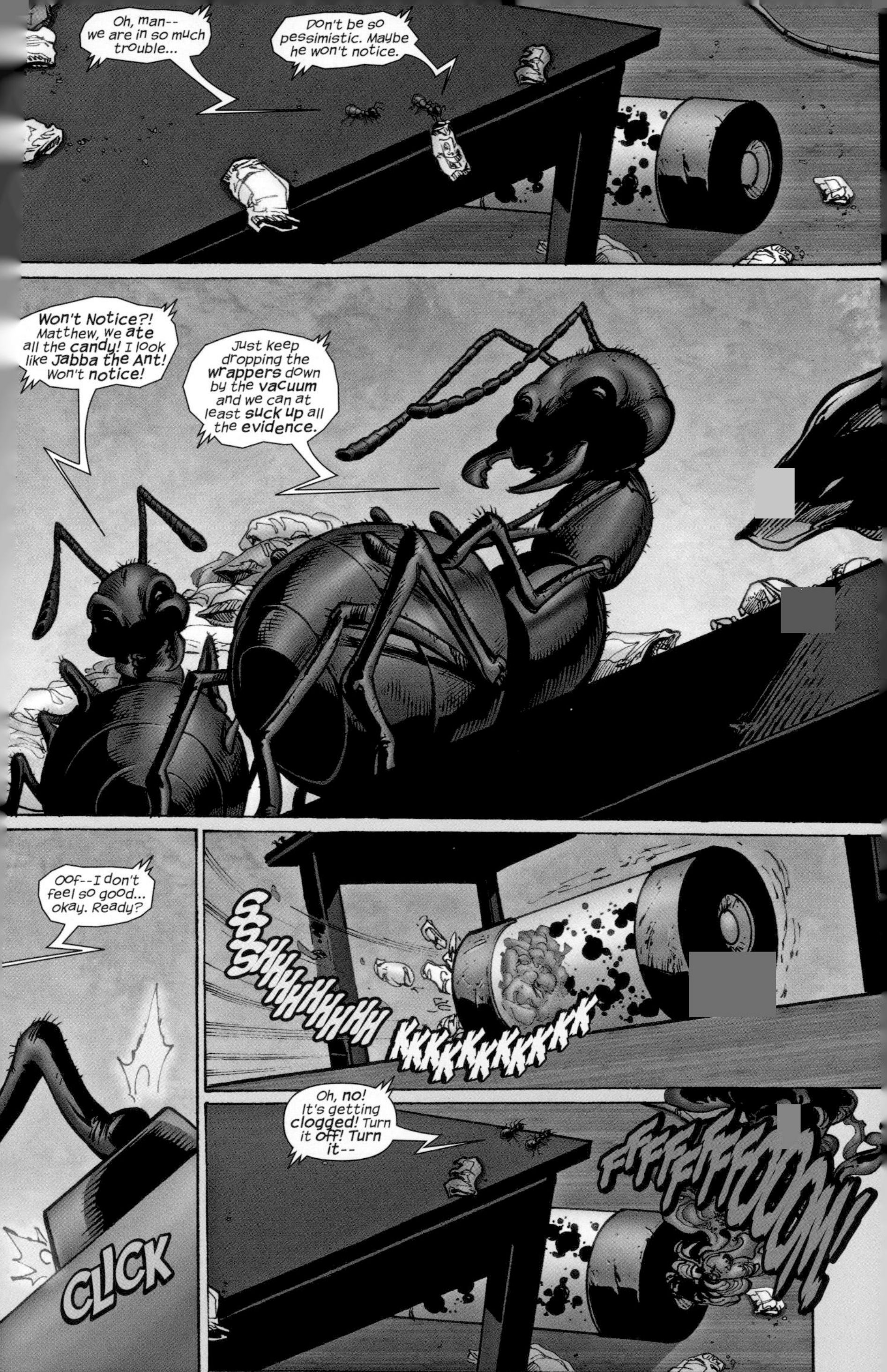
Oh, man-- we are in so much trouble...
Don't be so pessimistic. Maybe he won't notice.
Won't Notice?! Matthew, we ate all the candy! I look like Jabba the Ant! Won't notice!
Just keep dropping the wrappers down by the vacuum and we can at least suck up all the evidence.
Oof--I don't feel so good... okay. Ready?
CLICK
SSSHHHHHHHHHH
KKKKKKKKKKKK
Oh, no! It's getting clogged! Turn it off! Turn it--
FFFFFOOOM!!

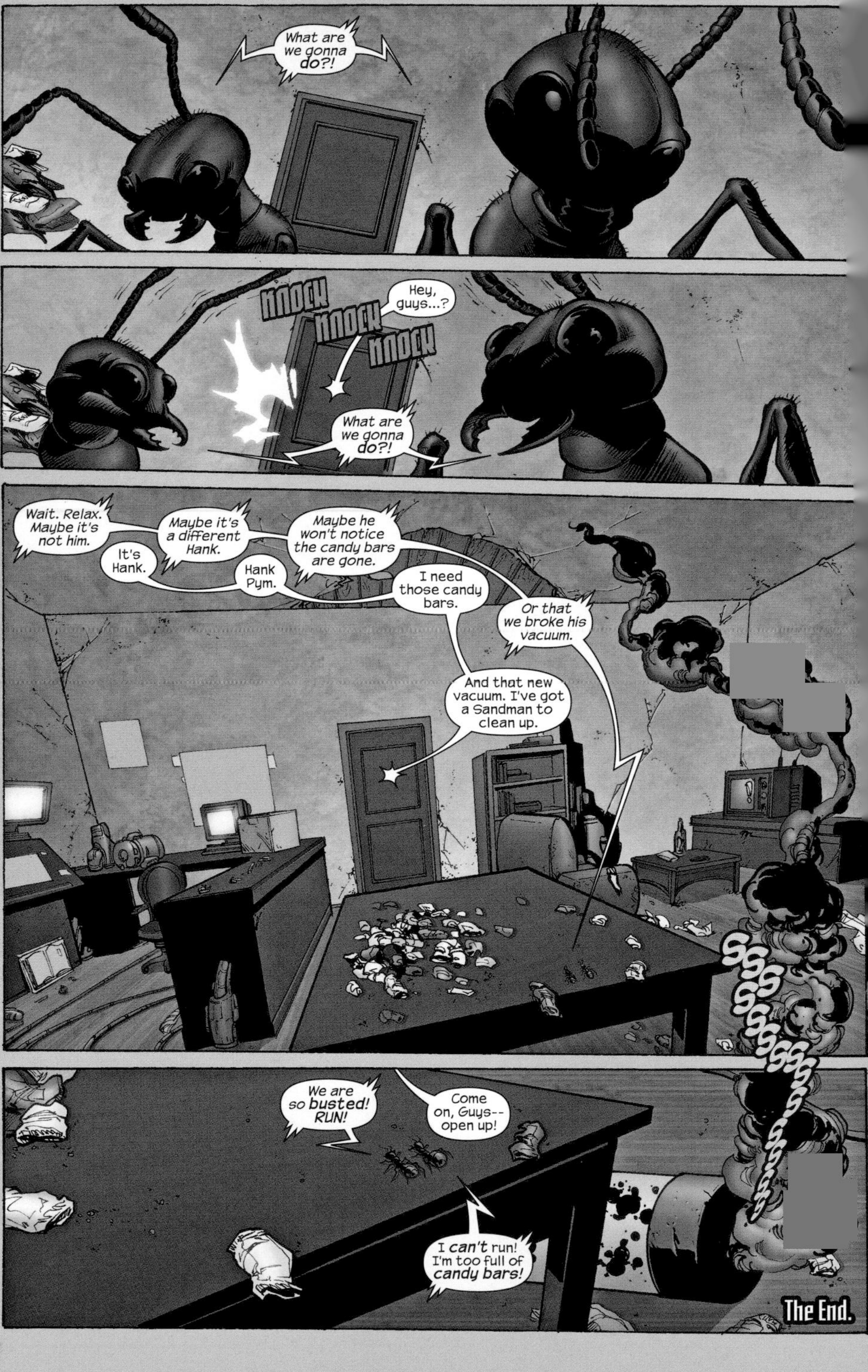

What are we gonna do?!
KNOCK
KNOCK
KNOCK
Hey, guys...?
What are we gonna do?!
Wait. Relax. Maybe it's not him.
It's Hank.
Maybe it's a different Hank.
Hank Pym.
Maybe he won't notice the candy bars are gone.
I need those candy bars.
Or that we broke his vacuum.
And that new vacuum. I've got a Sandman to clean up.
We are so busted! RUN!
Come on, Guys-- open up!
I can't run! I'm too full of candy bars!
The End.

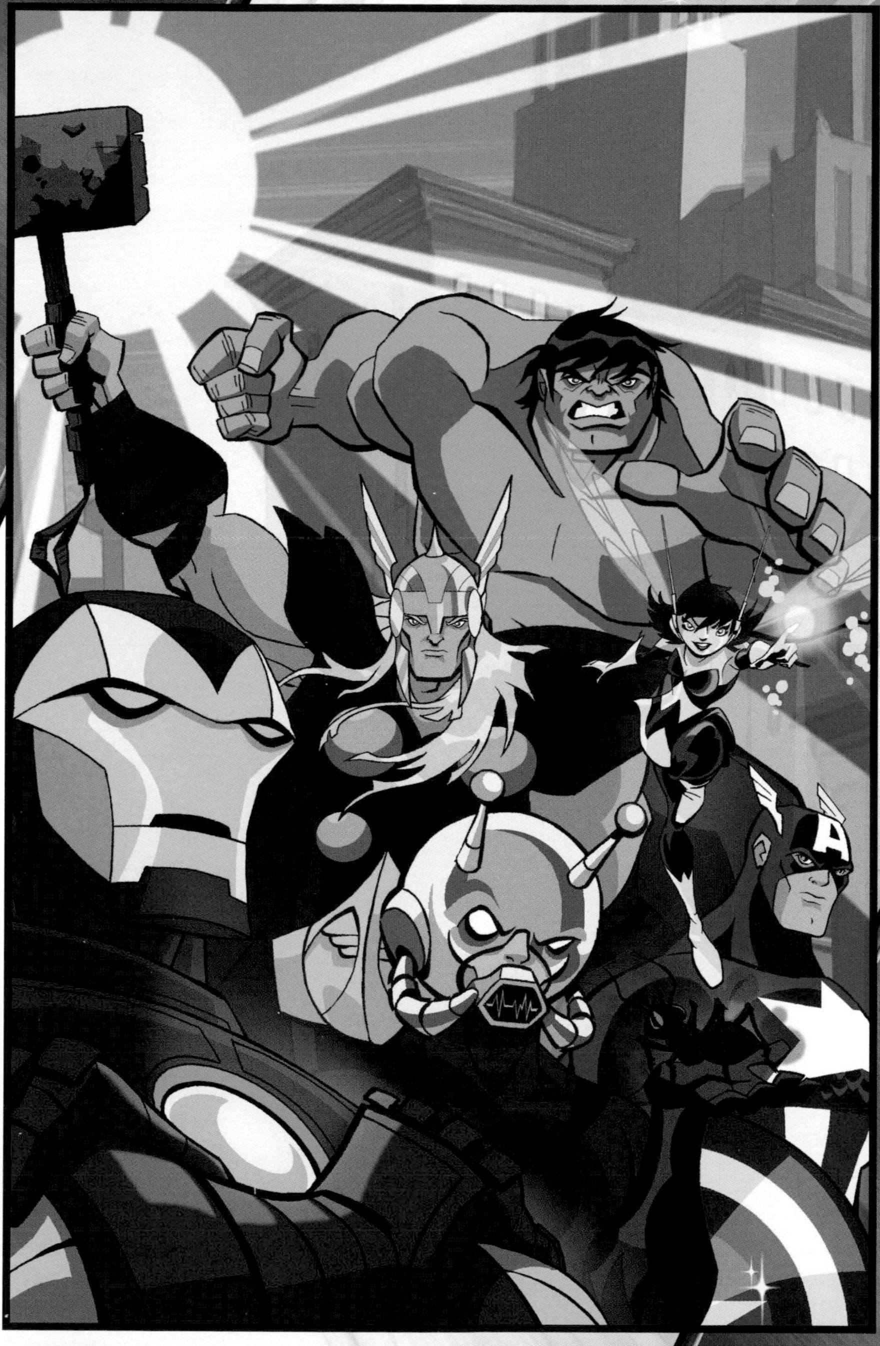

#2 AVENGERS: EARTH'S MIGHTIEST HEROES

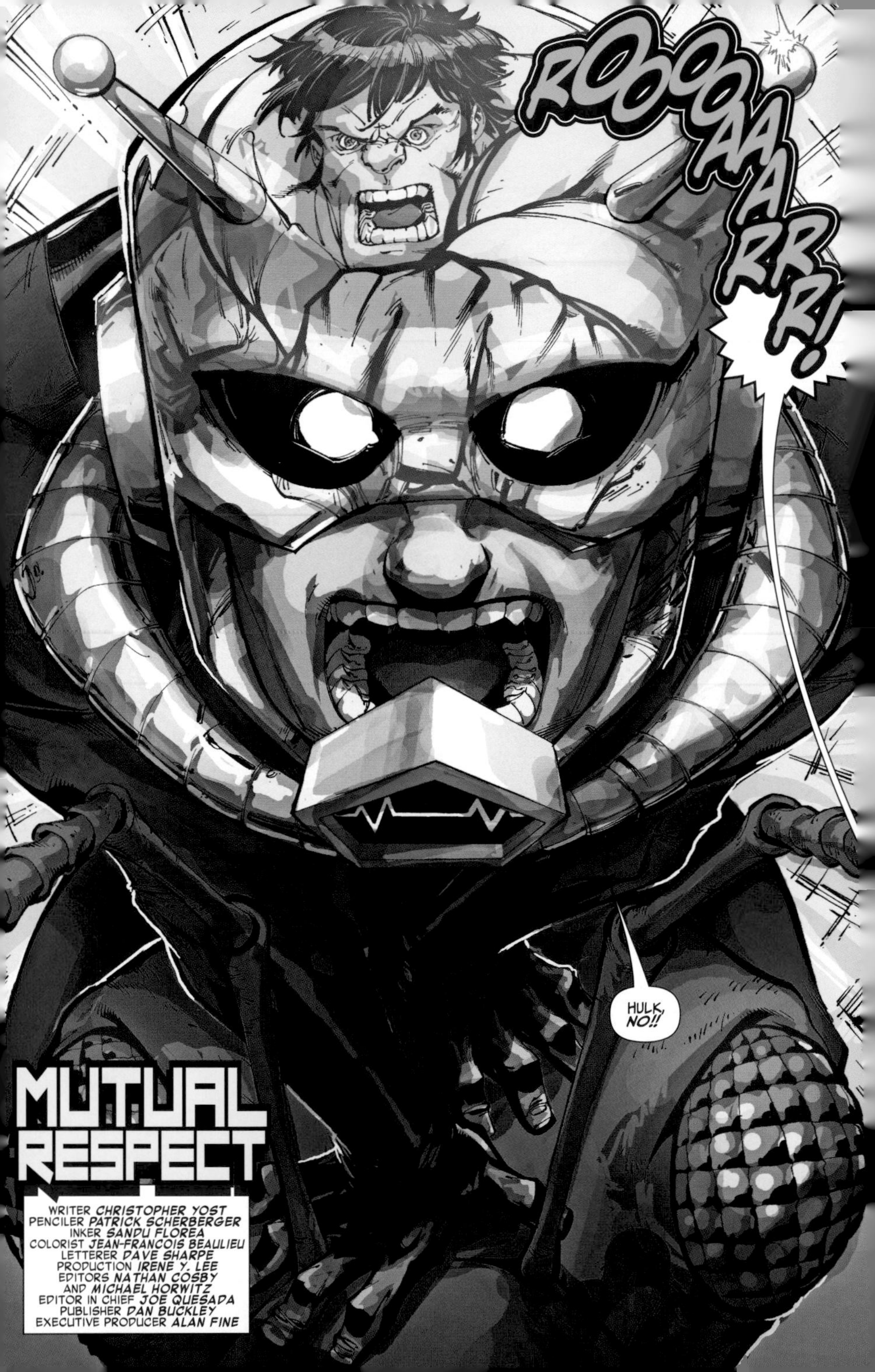

ROOOOAAARRR!
HULK, NO!!
MUTUAL RESPECT
WRITER CHRISTOPHER YOST
PENCILER PATRICK SCHERBERGER
INKER SANDU FLOREA
COLORIST JEAN-FRANCOIS BEAULIEU
LETTERER DAVE SHARPE
PRODUCTION IRENE Y. LEE
EDITORS NATHAN COSBY
AND MICHAEL HORWITZ
EDITOR IN CHIEF JOE QUESADA
PUBLISHER DAN BUCKLEY
EXECUTIVE PRODUCER ALAN FINE

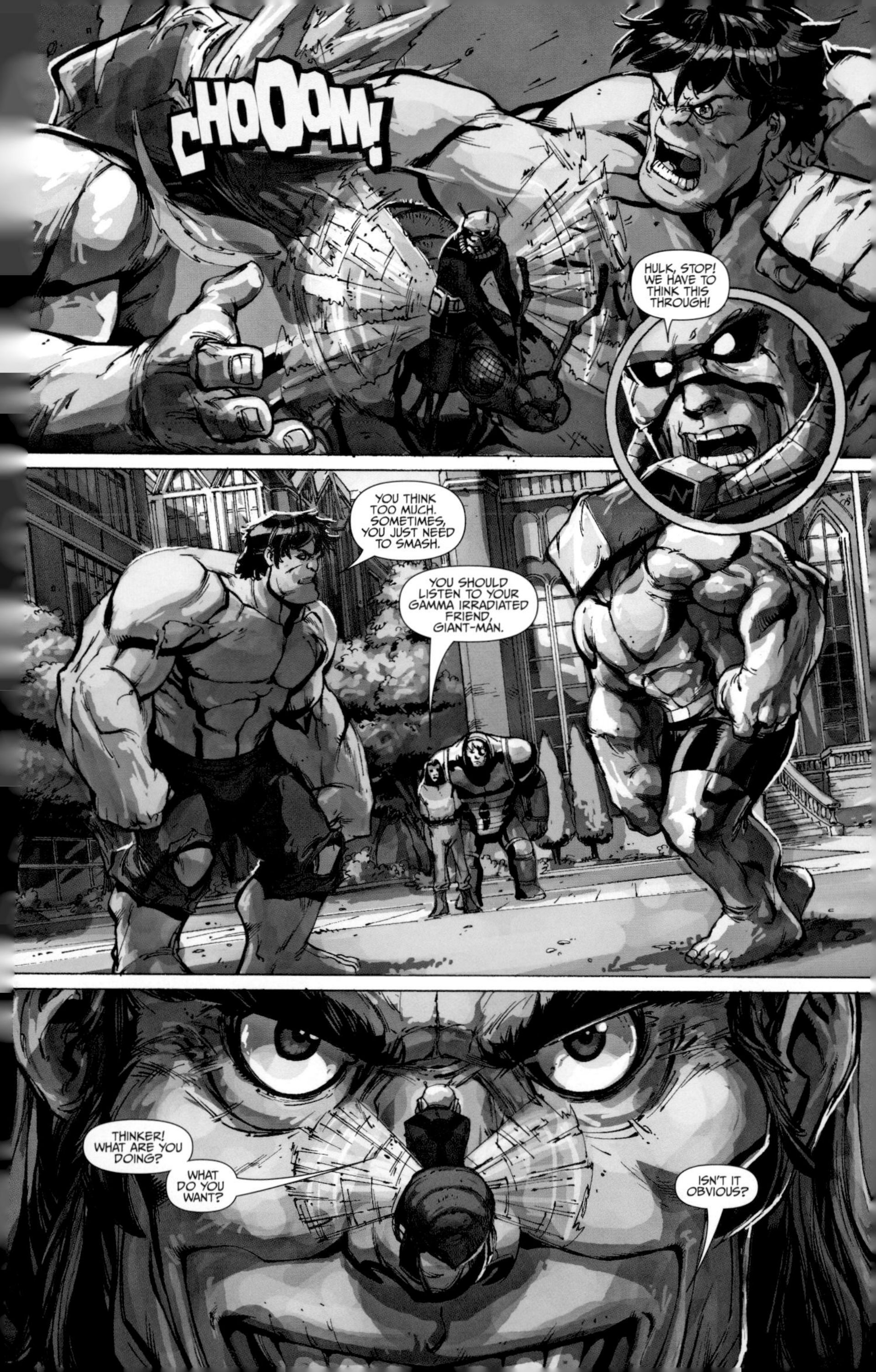
CHOOOM!
HULK, STOP! WE HAVE TO THINK THIS THROUGH!
YOU THINK TOO MUCH. SOMETIMES, YOU JUST NEED TO SMASH.
YOU SHOULD LISTEN TO YOUR GAMMA IRRADIATED FRIEND, GIANT-MAN.
THINKER! WHAT ARE YOU DOING?
WHAT DO YOU WANT?
ISN'T IT OBVIOUS?

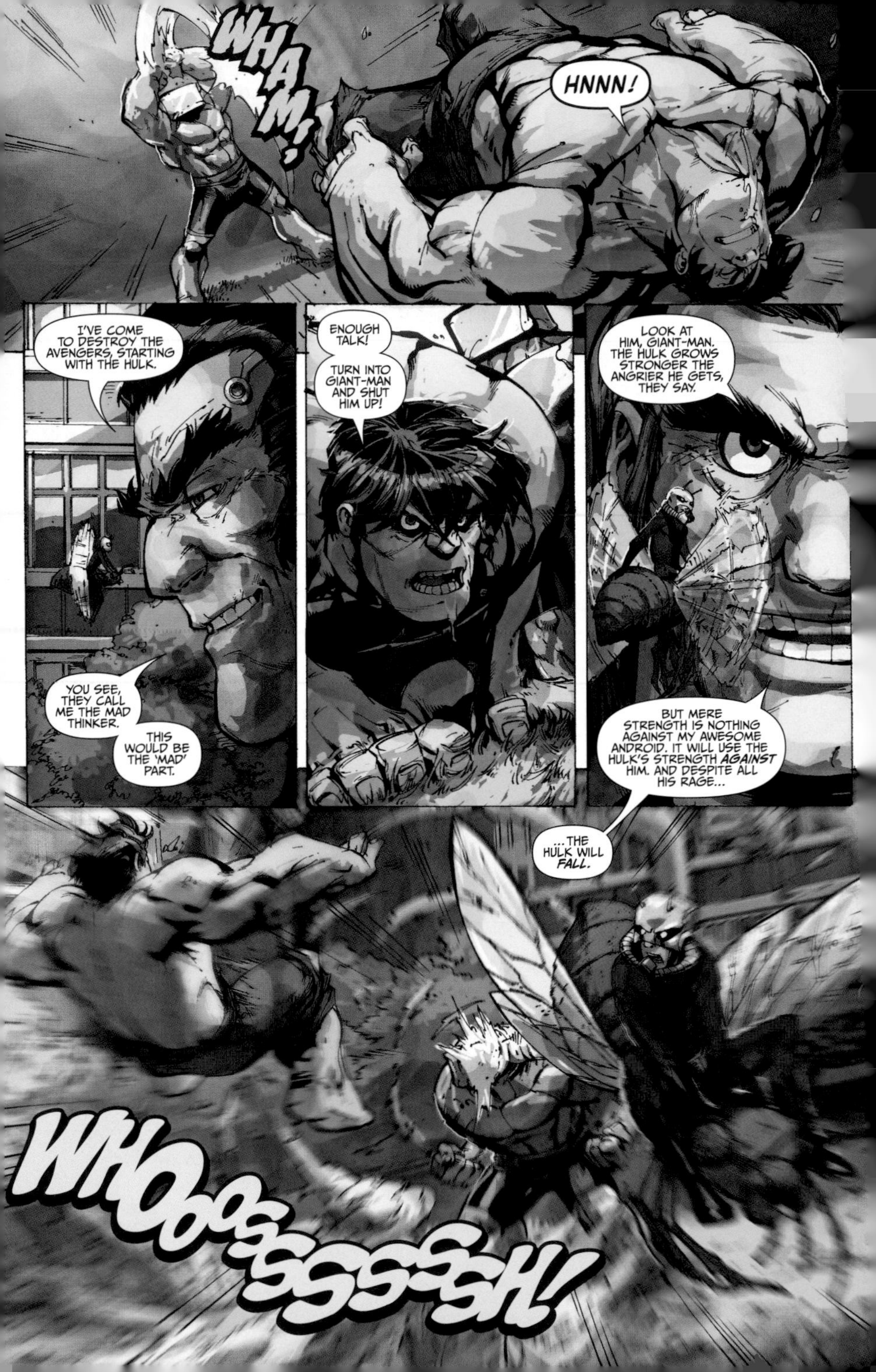
WHAM!
HNNN!
I'VE COME TO DESTROY THE AVENGERS, STARTING WITH THE HULK.
YOU SEE, THEY CALL ME THE MAD THINKER.
THIS WOULD BE THE 'MAD' PART.
ENOUGH TALK!
TURN INTO GIANT-MAN AND SHUT HIM UP!
LOOK AT HIM, GIANT-MAN. THE HULK GROWS STRONGER THE ANGRIER HE GETS, THEY SAY.
BUT MERE STRENGTH IS NOTHING AGAINST MY AWESOME ANDROID. IT WILL USE THE HULK'S STRENGTH AGAINST HIM. AND DESPITE ALL HIS RAGE...
...THE HULK WILL FALL.
WHOOOSSSSSH!

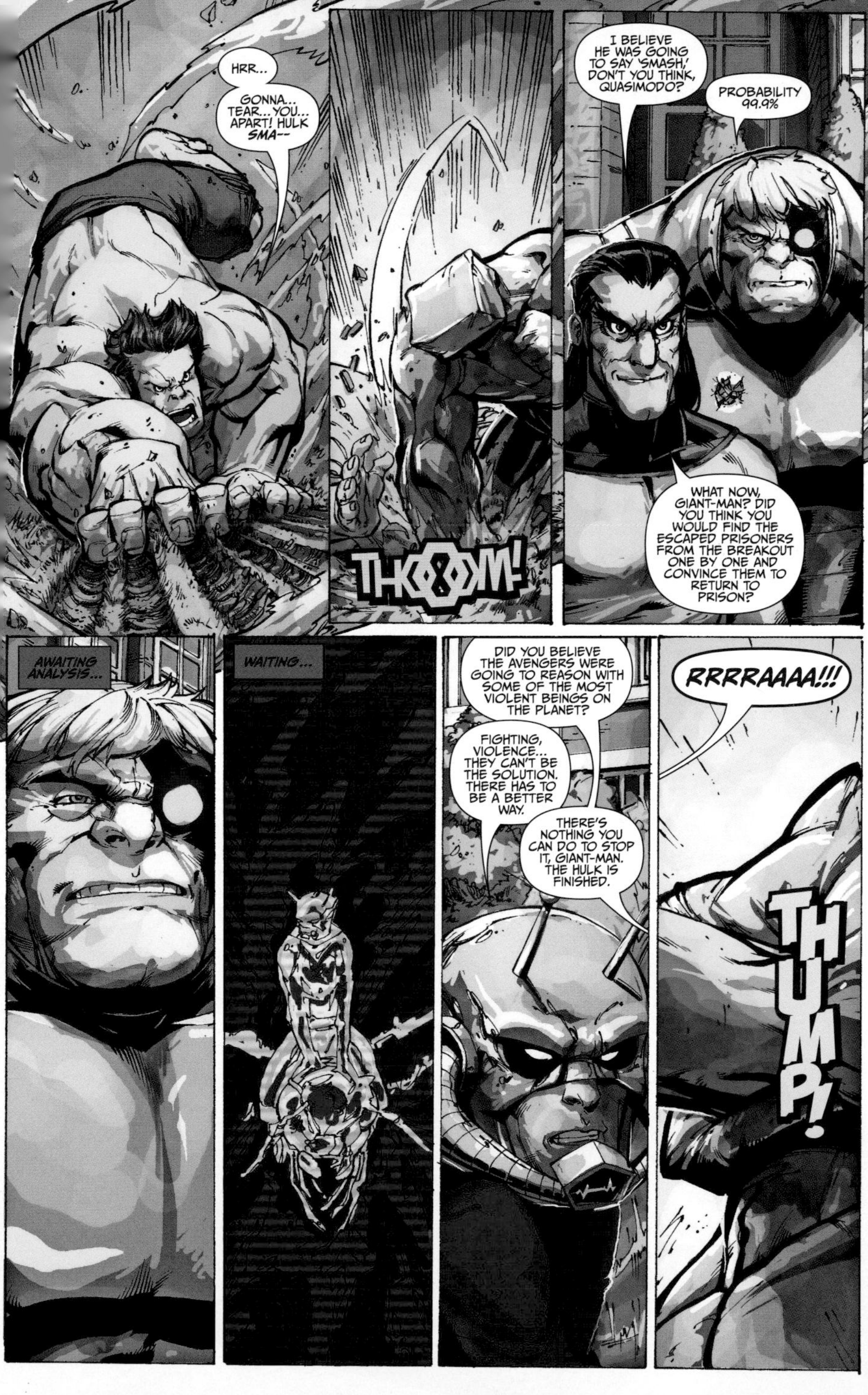

HRR...
GONNA... TEAR... YOU... APART! HULK SMA--
THOOM!
I BELIEVE HE WAS GOING TO SAY 'SMASH,' DON'T YOU THINK, QUASIMODO?
PROBABILITY 99.9%
WHAT NOW, GIANT-MAN? DID YOU THINK YOU WOULD FIND THE ESCAPED PRISONERS FROM THE BREAKOUT ONE BY ONE AND CONVINCE THEM TO RETURN TO PRISON?
AWAITING ANALYSIS...
WAITING...
DID YOU BELIEVE THE AVENGERS WERE GOING TO REASON WITH SOME OF THE MOST VIOLENT BEINGS ON THE PLANET?
FIGHTING, VIOLENCE... THEY CAN'T BE THE SOLUTION. THERE HAS TO BE A BETTER WAY.
THERE'S NOTHING YOU CAN DO TO STOP IT, GIANT-MAN. THE HULK IS FINISHED.
RRRRAAAA!!!
THUMP!

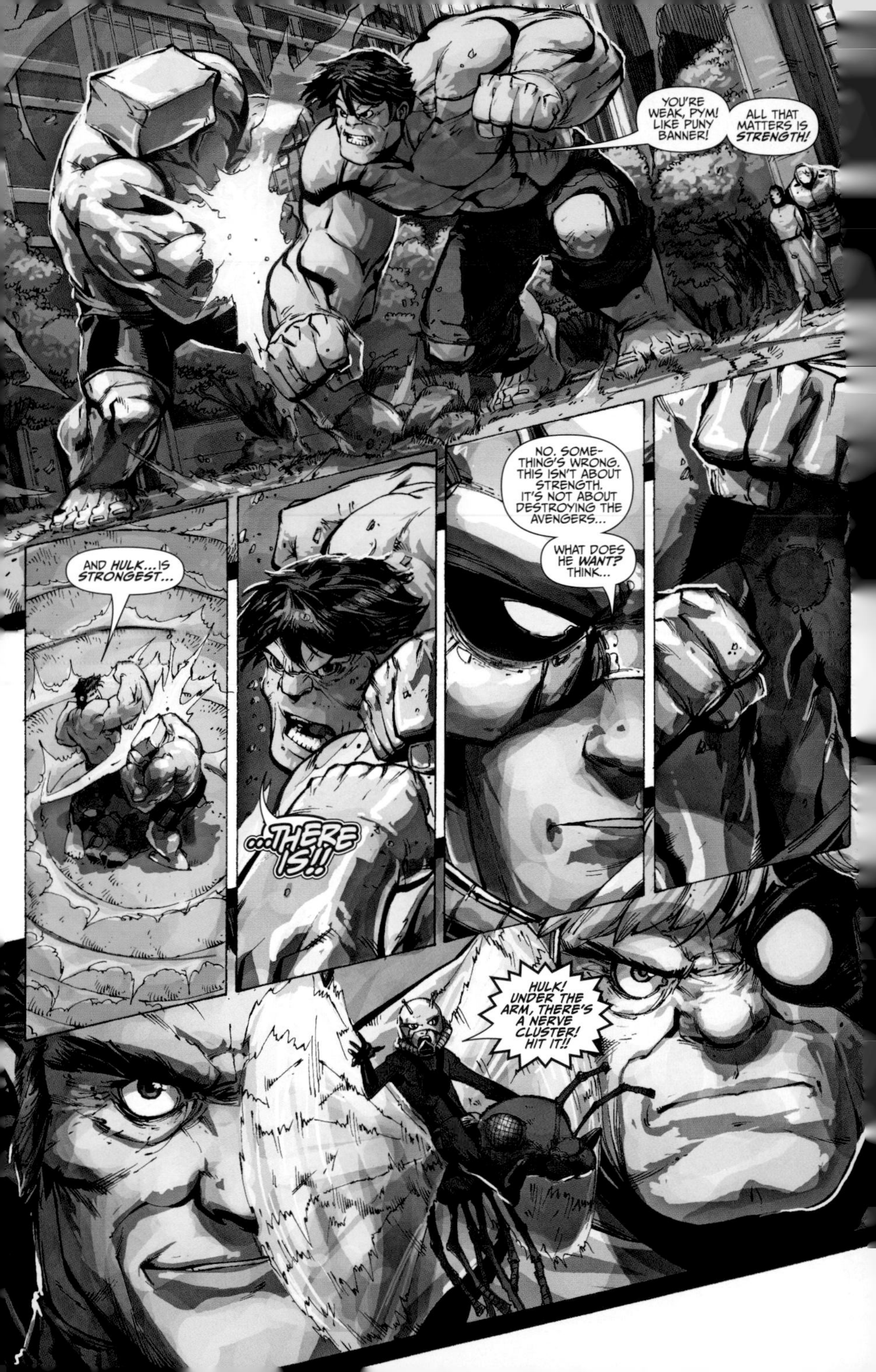

YOU'RE WEAK, PYM! LIKE PUNY BANNER!
ALL THAT MATTERS IS STRENGTH!
AND HULK...IS STRONGEST...
...THERE IS!!
NO. SOMETHING'S WRONG. THIS ISN'T ABOUT STRENGTH. IT'S NOT ABOUT DESTROYING THE AVENGERS...
WHAT DOES HE WANT? THINK...
HULK! UNDER THE ARM, THERE'S A NERVE CLUSTER! HIT IT!!

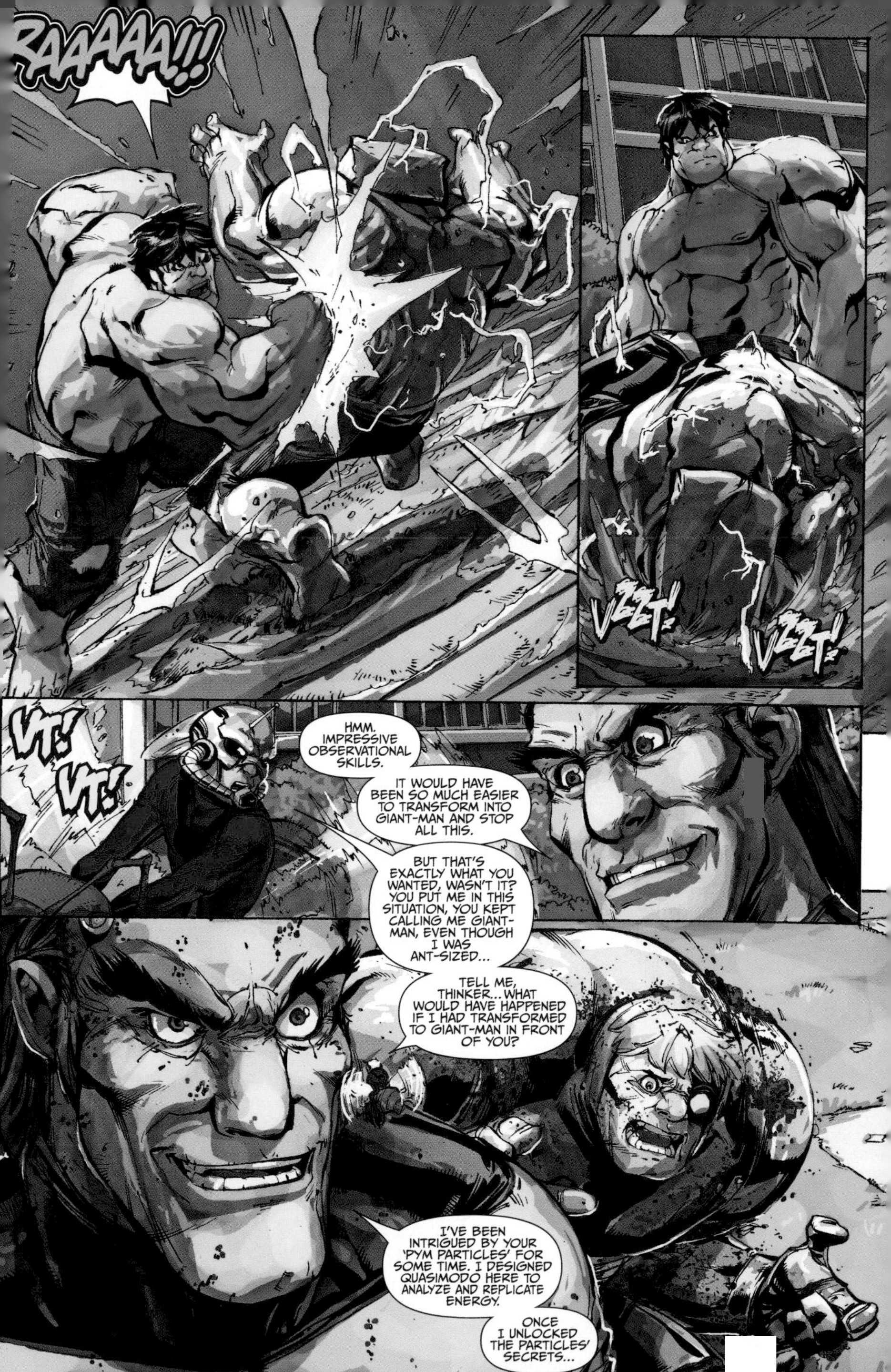
RAAAAA!!!
VZZT!
VZZT!
VT!
VT!
HMM. IMPRESSIVE OBSERVATIONAL SKILLS.
IT WOULD HAVE BEEN SO MUCH EASIER TO TRANSFORM INTO GIANT-MAN AND STOP ALL THIS.
BUT THAT'S EXACTLY WHAT YOU WANTED, WASN'T IT? YOU PUT ME IN THIS SITUATION, YOU KEPT CALLING ME GIANT-MAN, EVEN THOUGH I WAS ANT-SIZED...
TELL ME, THINKER... WHAT WOULD HAVE HAPPENED IF I HAD TRANSFORMED TO GIANT-MAN IN FRONT OF YOU?
I'VE BEEN INTRIGUED BY YOUR 'PYM PARTICLES' FOR SOME TIME. I DESIGNED QUASIMODO HERE TO ANALYZE AND REPLICATE ENERGY.
ONCE I UNLOCKED THE PARTICLES' SECRETS...

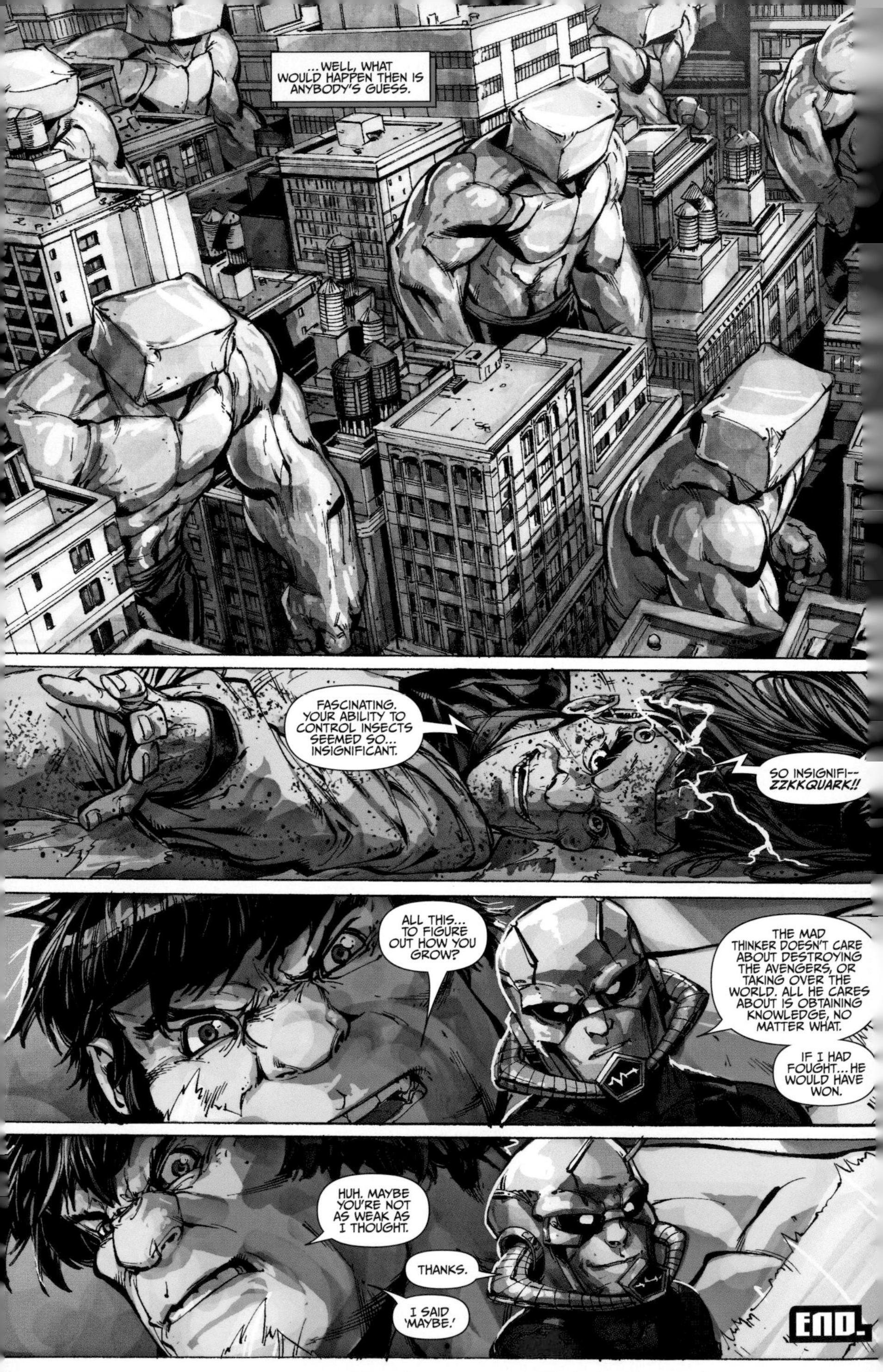
...WELL, WHAT WOULD HAPPEN THEN IS ANYBODY'S GUESS.
FASCINATING. YOUR ABILITY TO CONTROL INSECTS SEEMED SO... INSIGNIFICANT.
SO INSIGNIFI-- ZZKKQUARK!!
ALL THIS... TO FIGURE OUT HOW YOU GROW?
THE MAD THINKER DOESN'T CARE ABOUT DESTROYING THE AVENGERS, OR TAKING OVER THE WORLD. ALL HE CARES ABOUT IS OBTAINING KNOWLEDGE, NO MATTER WHAT.
IF I HAD FOUGHT... HE WOULD HAVE WON.
HUH. MAYBE YOU'RE NOT AS WEAK AS I THOUGHT.
THANKS.
I SAID 'MAYBE.'
END.

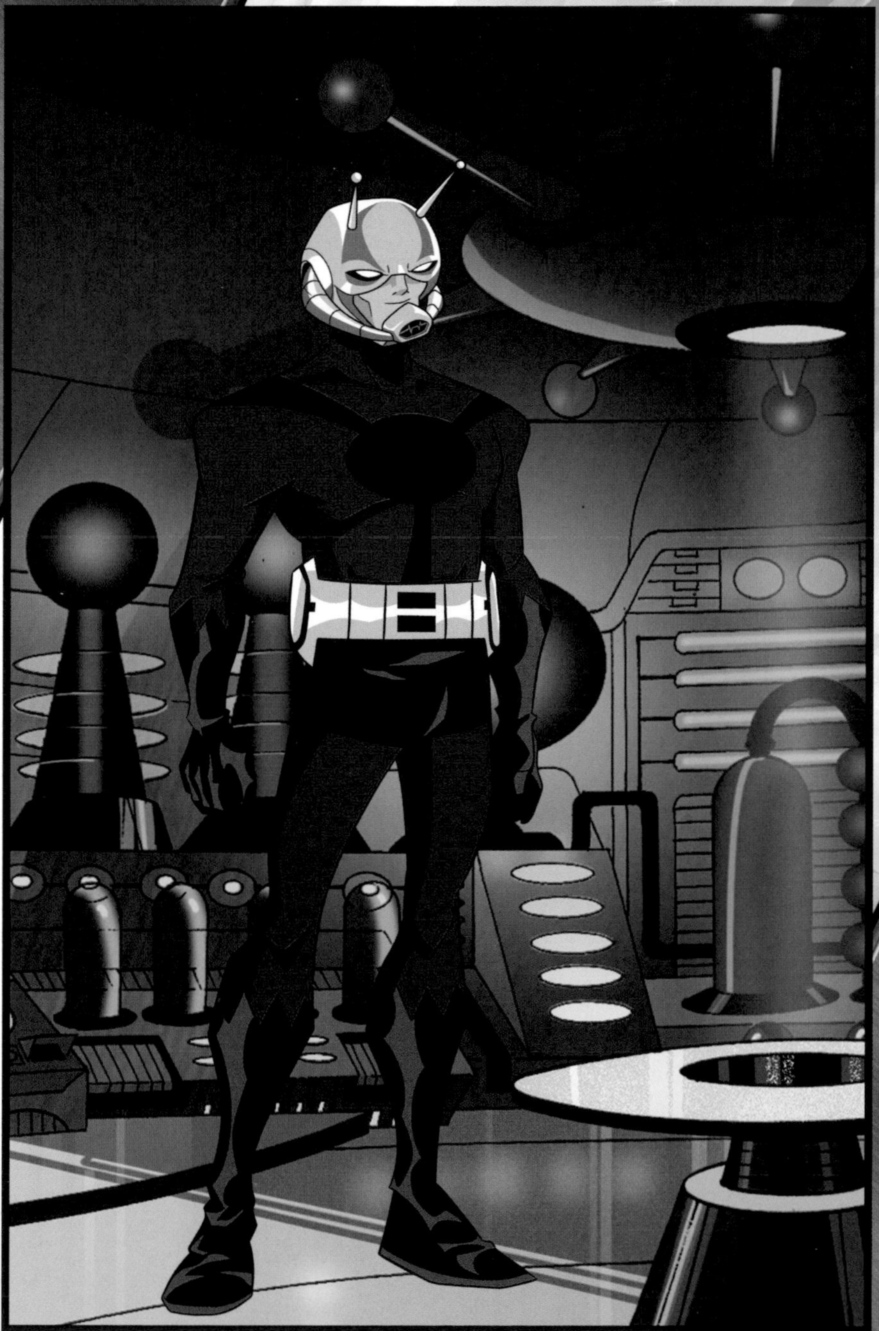

#19 MARVEL ADVENTURES SUPER HEROES

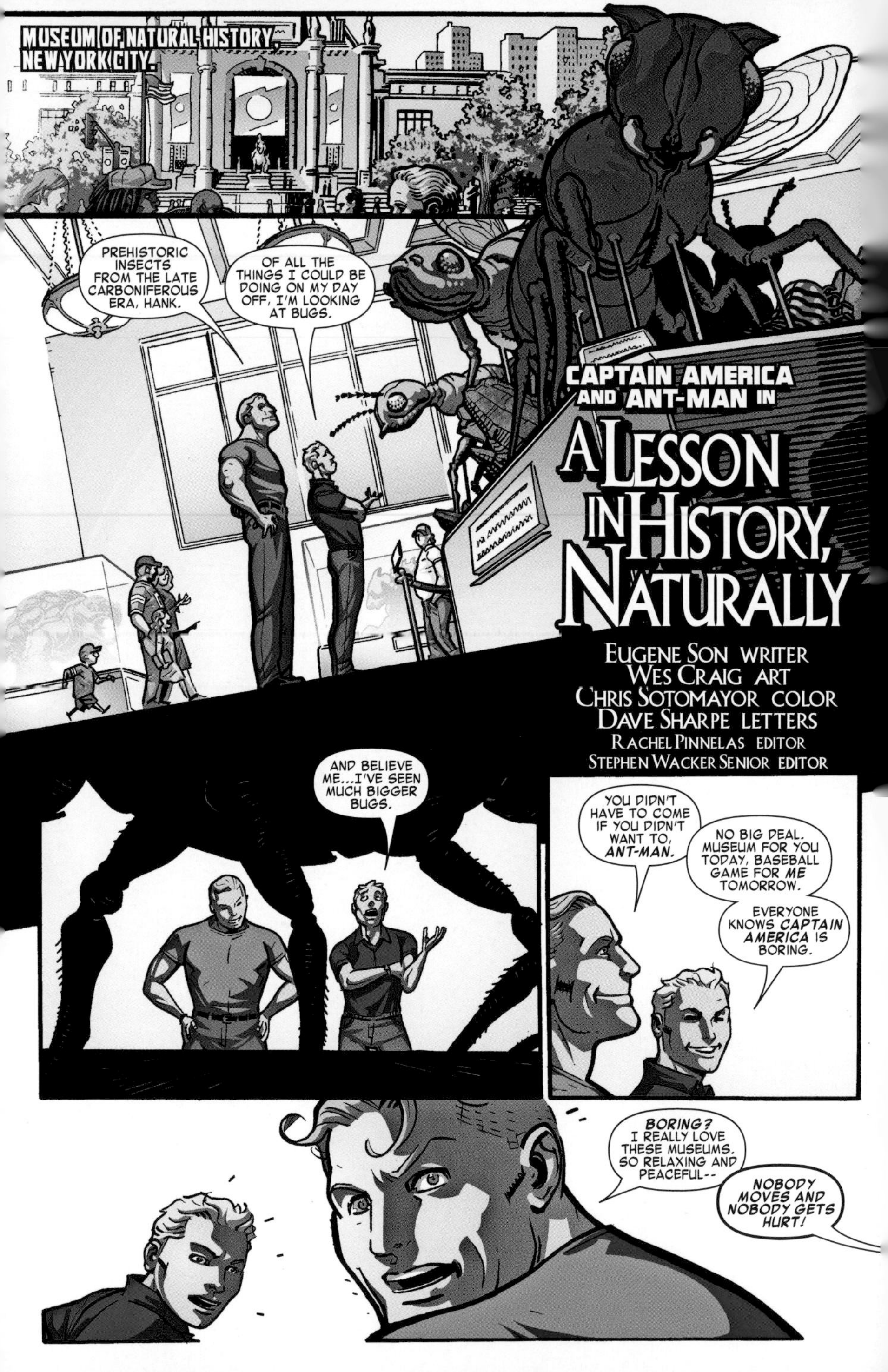
MUSEUM OF NATURAL HISTORY, NEW YORK CITY.
PREHISTORIC INSECTS FROM THE LATE CARBONIFEROUS ERA, HANK.
OF ALL THE THINGS I COULD BE DOING ON MY DAY OFF, I'M LOOKING AT BUGS.
CAPTAIN AMERICA AND ANT-MAN IN
A LESSON IN HISTORY, NATURALLY
EUGENE SON WRITER
WES CRAIG ART
CHRIS SOTOMAYOR COLOR
DAVE SHARPE LETTERS
RACHEL PINNELAS EDITOR
STEPHEN WACKER SENIOR EDITOR
AND BELIEVE ME...I'VE SEEN MUCH BIGGER BUGS.
YOU DIDN'T HAVE TO COME IF YOU DIDN'T WANT TO, ANT-MAN.
NO BIG DEAL. MUSEUM FOR YOU TODAY, BASEBALL GAME FOR ME TOMORROW.
EVERYONE KNOWS CAPTAIN AMERICA IS BORING.
BORING? I REALLY LOVE THESE MUSEUMS. SO RELAXING AND PEACEFUL--
NOBODY MOVES AND NOBODY GETS HURT!

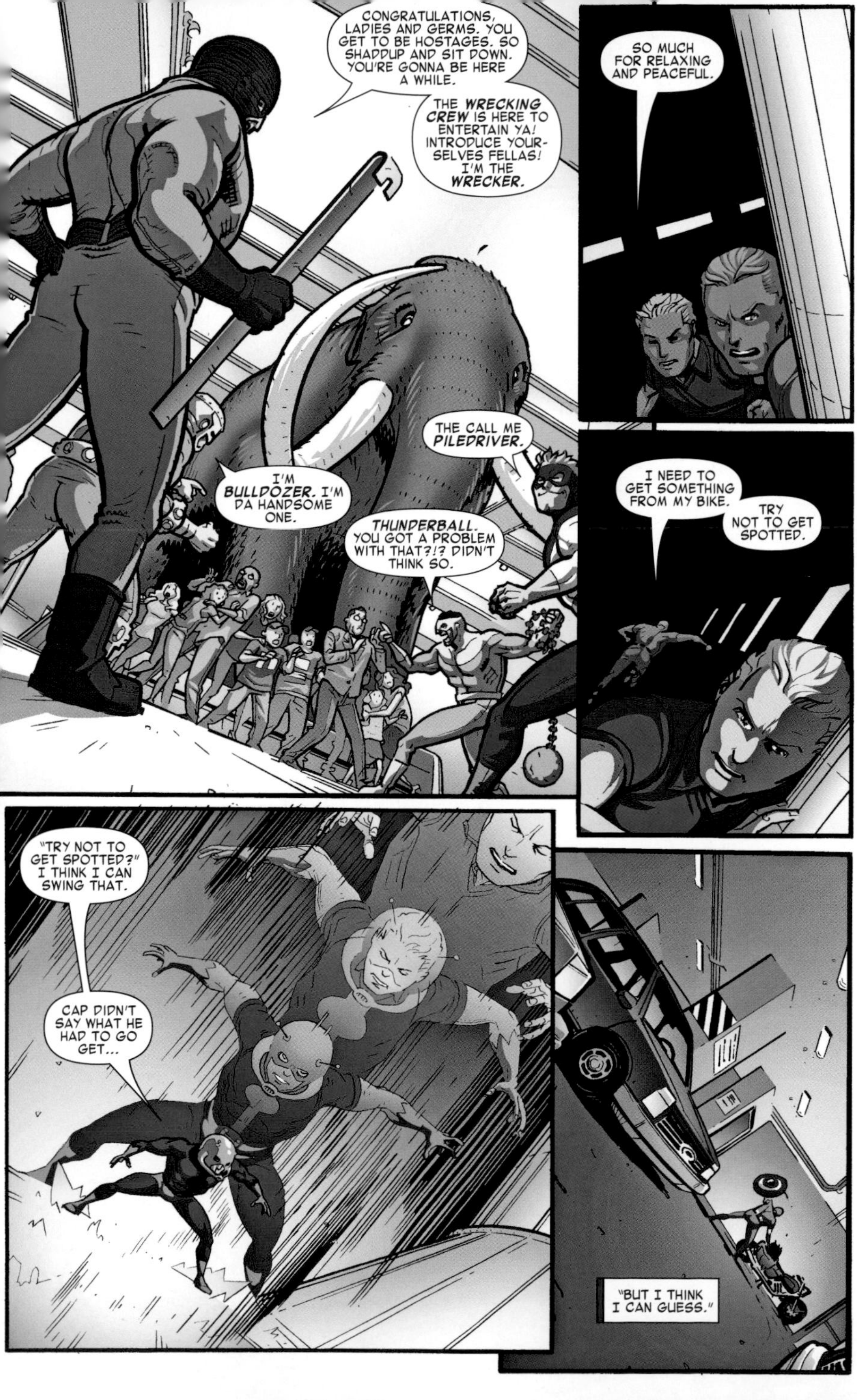
CONGRATULATIONS, LADIES AND GERMS. YOU GET TO BE HOSTAGES. SO SHADDUP AND SIT DOWN. YOU'RE GONNA BE HERE A WHILE.
THE WRECKING CREW IS HERE TO ENTERTAIN YA! INTRODUCE YOUR-SELVES FELLAS! I'M THE WRECKER.
THE CALL ME PILEDRIVER.
I'M BULLDOZER. I'M DA HANDSOME ONE.
THUNDERBALL. YOU GOT A PROBLEM WITH THAT?!? DIDN'T THINK SO.
SO MUCH FOR RELAXING AND PEACEFUL.
I NEED TO GET SOMETHING FROM MY BIKE.
TRY NOT TO GET SPOTTED.
"TRY NOT TO GET SPOTTED?" I THINK I CAN SWING THAT.
CAP DIDN'T SAY WHAT HE HAD TO GO GET...
"BUT I THINK I CAN GUESS."

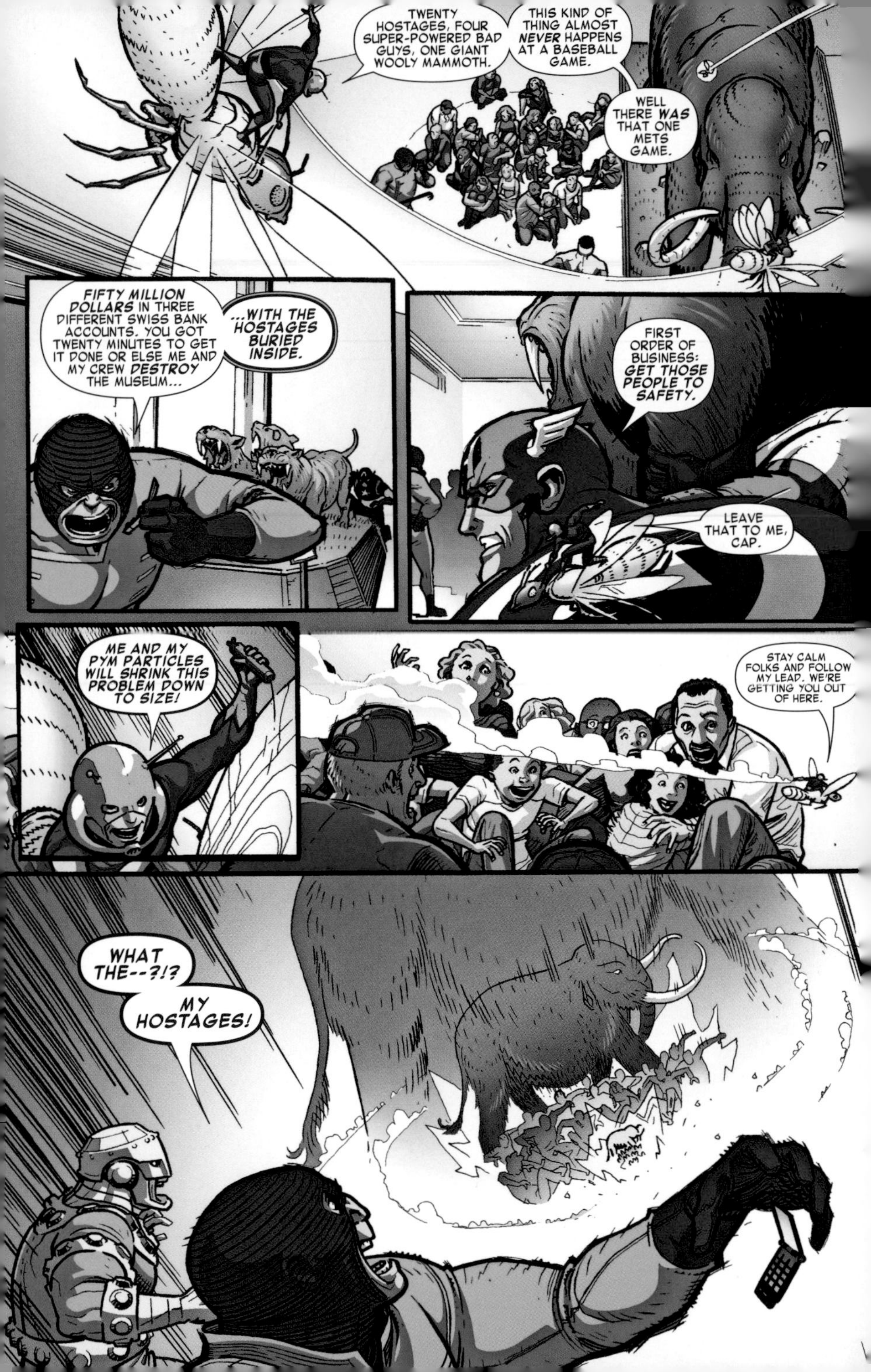
TWENTY HOSTAGES, FOUR SUPER-POWERED BAD GUYS, ONE GIANT WOOLY MAMMOTH.
THIS KIND OF THING ALMOST NEVER HAPPENS AT A BASEBALL GAME.
WELL THERE WAS THAT ONE METS GAME.
FIFTY MILLION DOLLARS IN THREE DIFFERENT SWISS BANK ACCOUNTS. YOU GOT TWENTY MINUTES TO GET IT DONE OR ELSE ME AND MY CREW DESTROY THE MUSEUM...
...WITH THE HOSTAGES BURIED INSIDE.
FIRST ORDER OF BUSINESS: GET THOSE PEOPLE TO SAFETY.
LEAVE THAT TO ME, CAP.
ME AND MY PYM PARTICLES WILL SHRINK THIS PROBLEM DOWN TO SIZE!
STAY CALM FOLKS AND FOLLOW MY LEAD. WE'RE GETTING YOU OUT OF HERE.
WHAT THE--?!?
MY HOSTAGES!

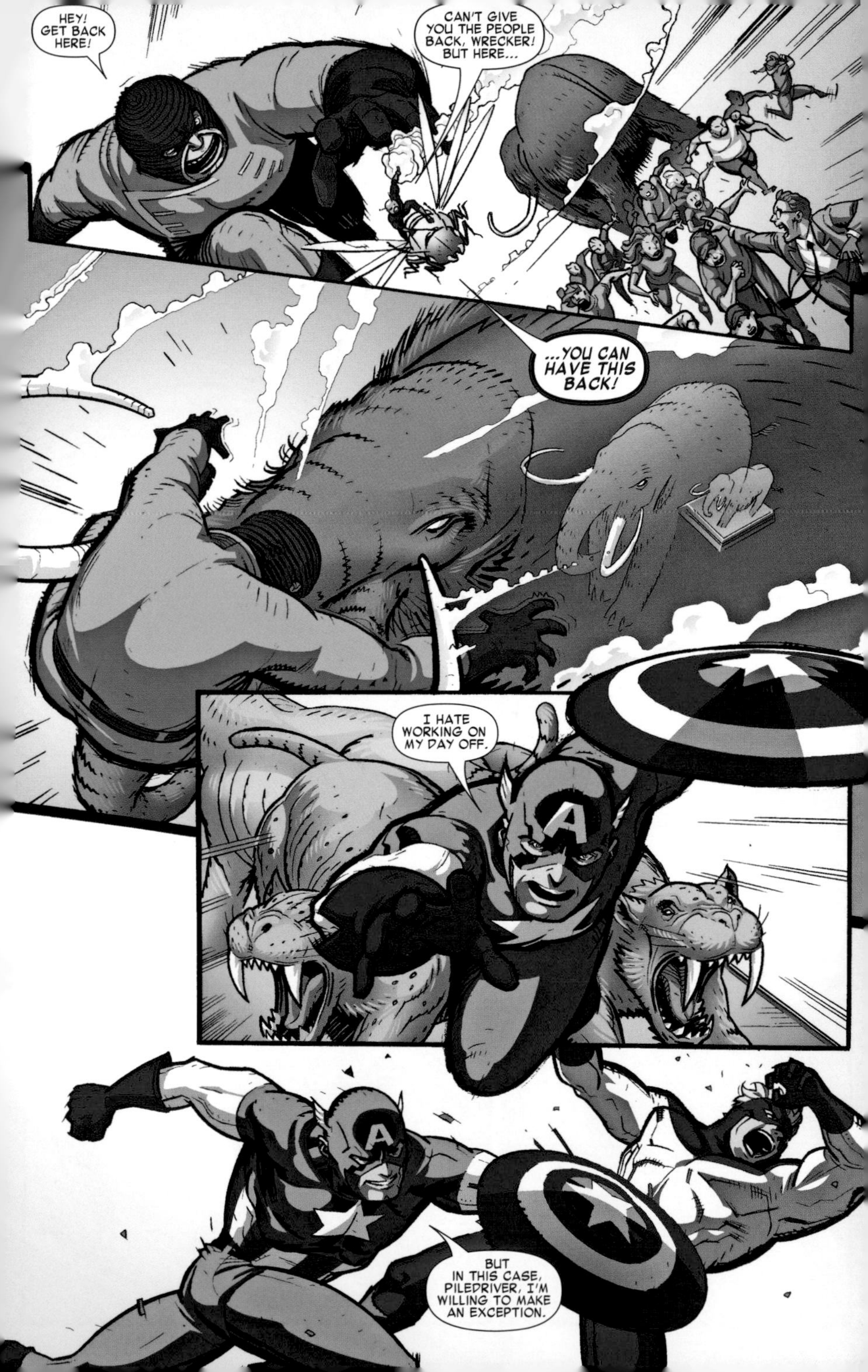
HEY! GET BACK HERE!
CAN'T GIVE YOU THE PEOPLE BACK, WRECKER! BUT HERE...
...YOU CAN HAVE THIS BACK!
I HATE WORKING ON MY DAY OFF.
BUT IN THIS CASE, PILEDRIVER, I'M WILLING TO MAKE AN EXCEPTION.

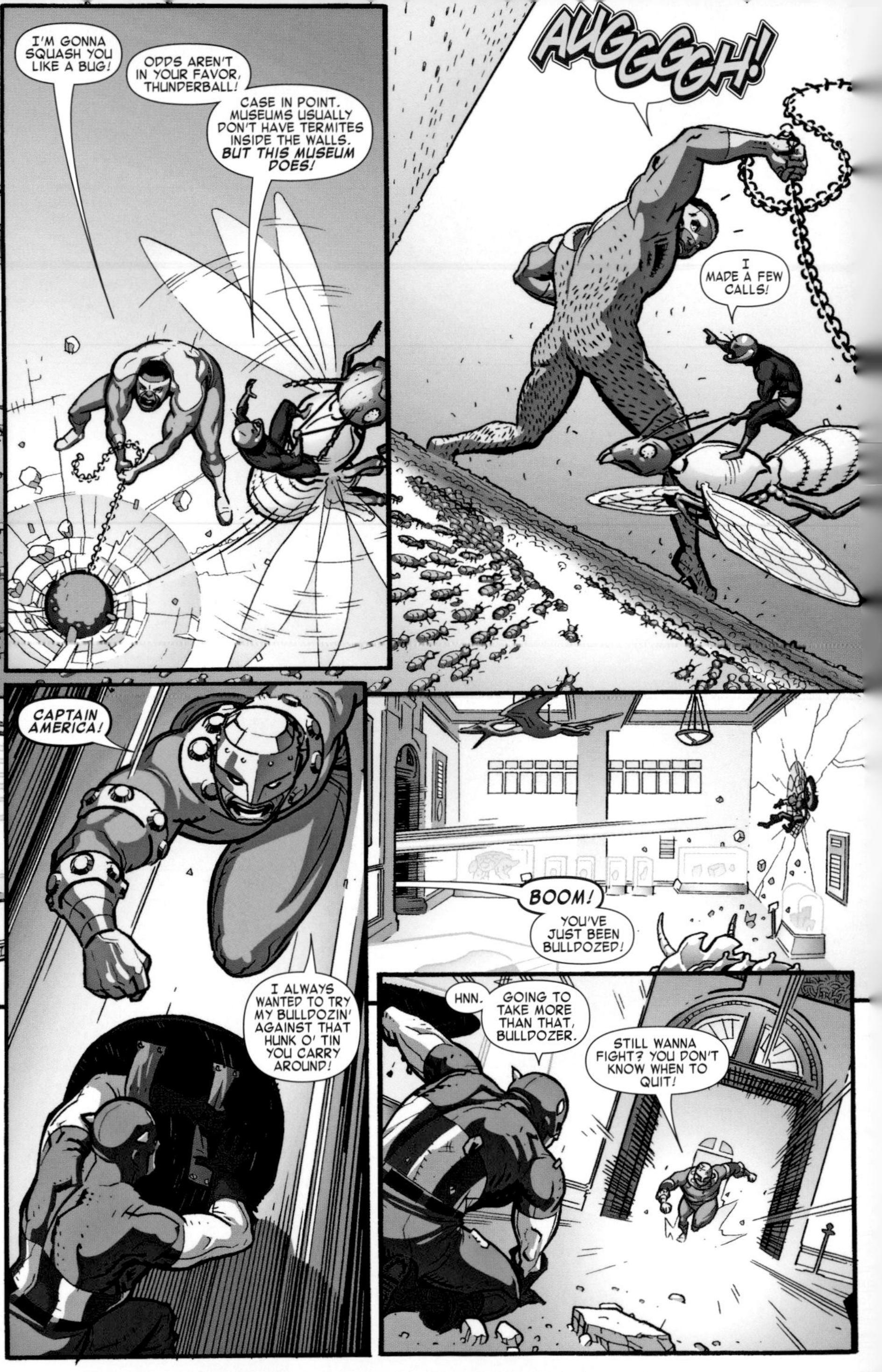
I'M GONNA SQUASH YOU LIKE A BUG!
ODDS AREN'T IN YOUR FAVOR, THUNDERBALL!
CASE IN POINT. MUSEUMS USUALLY DON'T HAVE TERMITES INSIDE THE WALLS. BUT THIS MUSEUM DOES!
AUGGGGH!
I MADE A FEW CALLS!
CAPTAIN AMERICA!
BOOM!
YOU'VE JUST BEEN BULLDOZED!
I ALWAYS WANTED TO TRY MY BULLDOZIN' AGAINST THAT HUNK O' TIN YOU CARRY AROUND!
HNN.
GOING TO TAKE MORE THAN THAT, BULLDOZER.
STILL WANNA FIGHT? YOU DON'T KNOW WHEN TO QUIT!

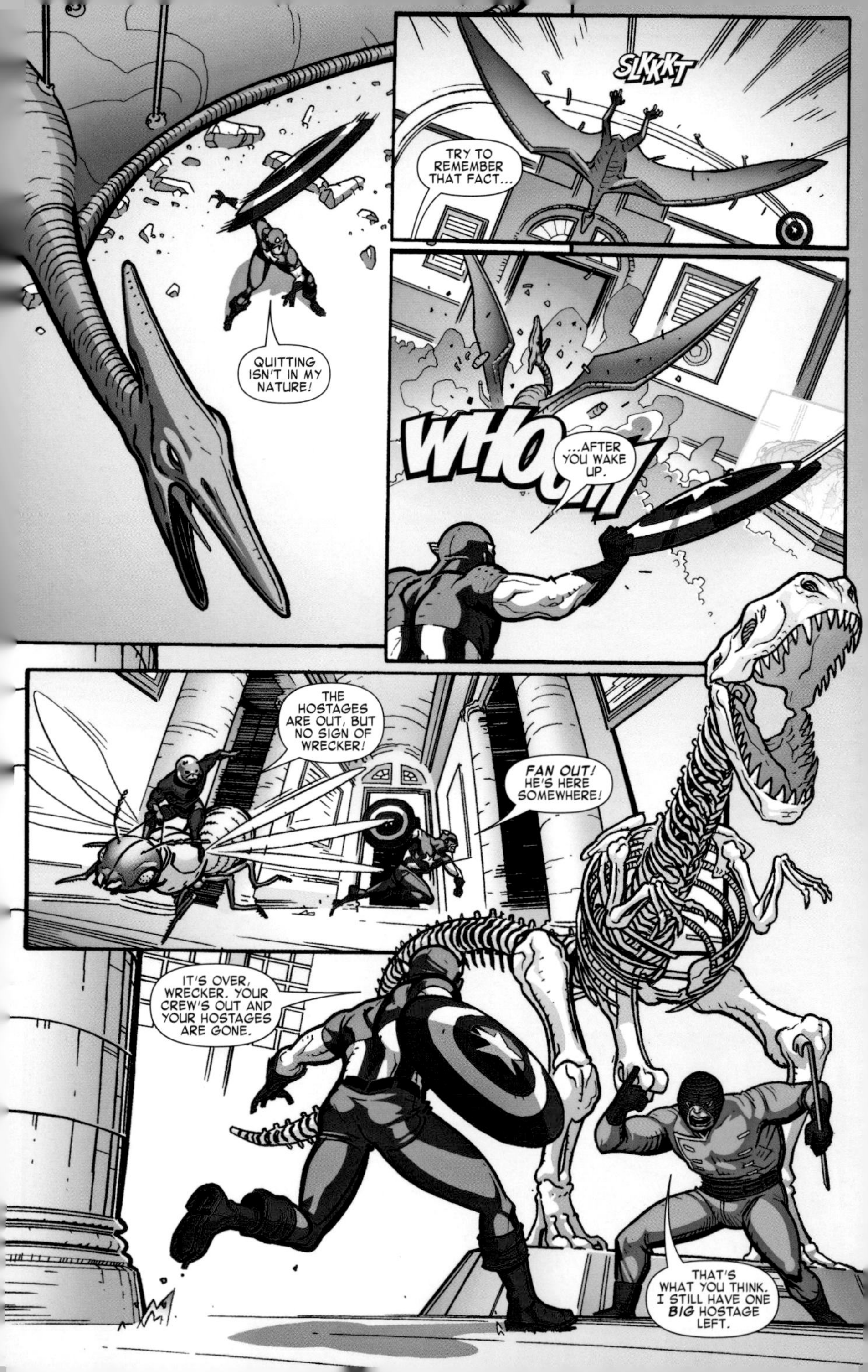
QUITTING ISN'T IN MY NATURE!
SLKKKT
TRY TO REMEMBER THAT FACT...
WHOOM
...AFTER YOU WAKE UP.
THE HOSTAGES ARE OUT, BUT NO SIGN OF WRECKER!
FAN OUT! HE'S HERE SOMEWHERE!
IT'S OVER, WRECKER. YOUR CREW'S OUT AND YOUR HOSTAGES ARE GONE.
THAT'S WHAT YOU THINK. I STILL HAVE ONE BIG HOSTAGE LEFT.

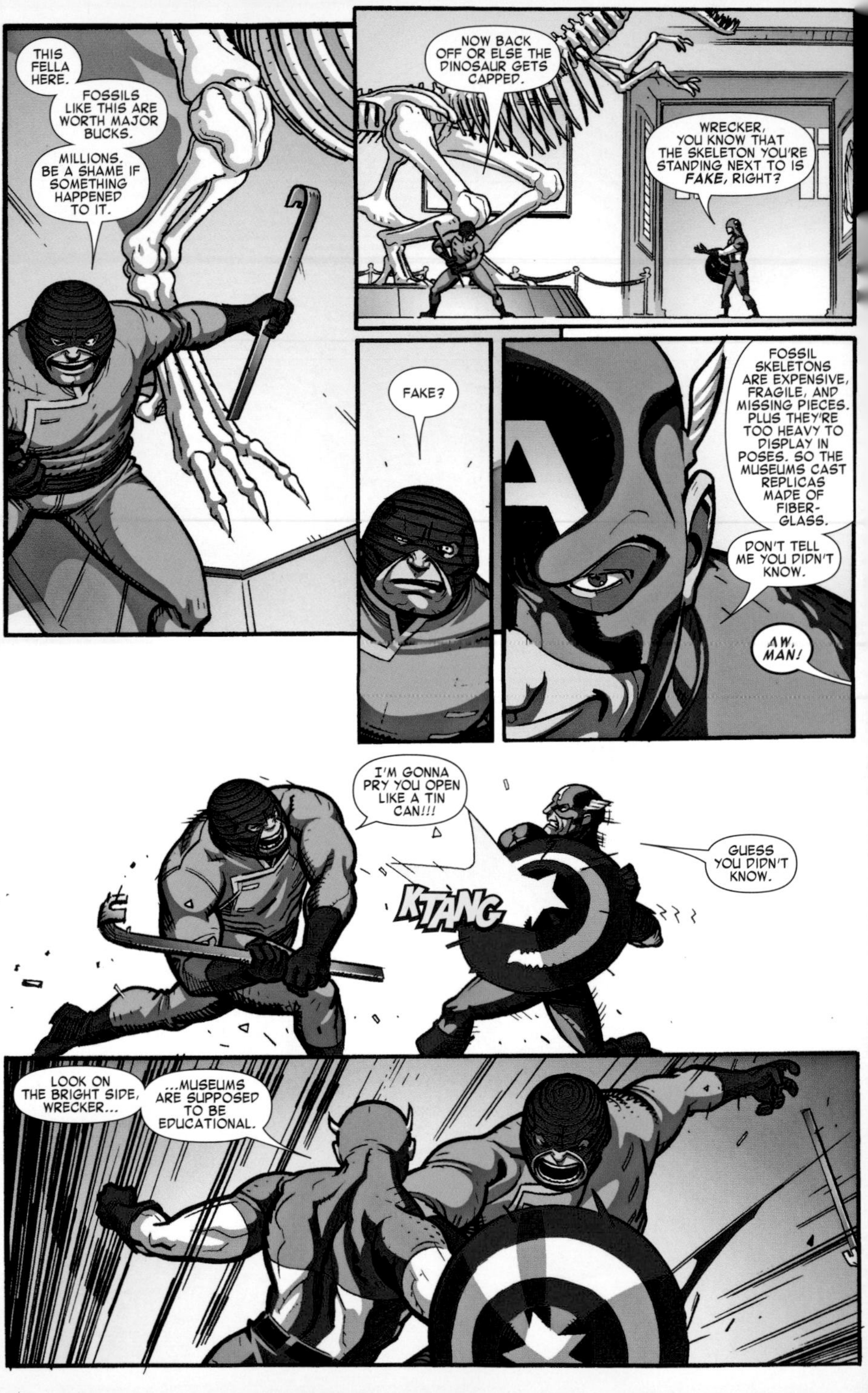

THIS FELLA HERE.
FOSSILS LIKE THIS ARE WORTH MAJOR BUCKS.
MILLIONS. BE A SHAME IF SOMETHING HAPPENED TO IT.
NOW BACK OFF OR ELSE THE DINOSAUR GETS CAPPED.
WRECKER, YOU KNOW THAT THE SKELETON YOU'RE STANDING NEXT TO IS *FAKE*, RIGHT?
FAKE?
FOSSIL SKELETONS ARE EXPENSIVE, FRAGILE, AND MISSING PIECES. PLUS THEY'RE TOO HEAVY TO DISPLAY IN POSES. SO THE MUSEUMS CAST REPLICAS MADE OF FIBER-GLASS.
DON'T TELL ME YOU DIDN'T KNOW.
AW, MAN!
I'M GONNA PRY YOU OPEN LIKE A TIN CAN!!!
GUESS YOU DIDN'T KNOW.
KTANG
LOOK ON THE BRIGHT SIDE, WRECKER...
...MUSEUMS ARE SUPPOSED TO BE EDUCATIONAL.

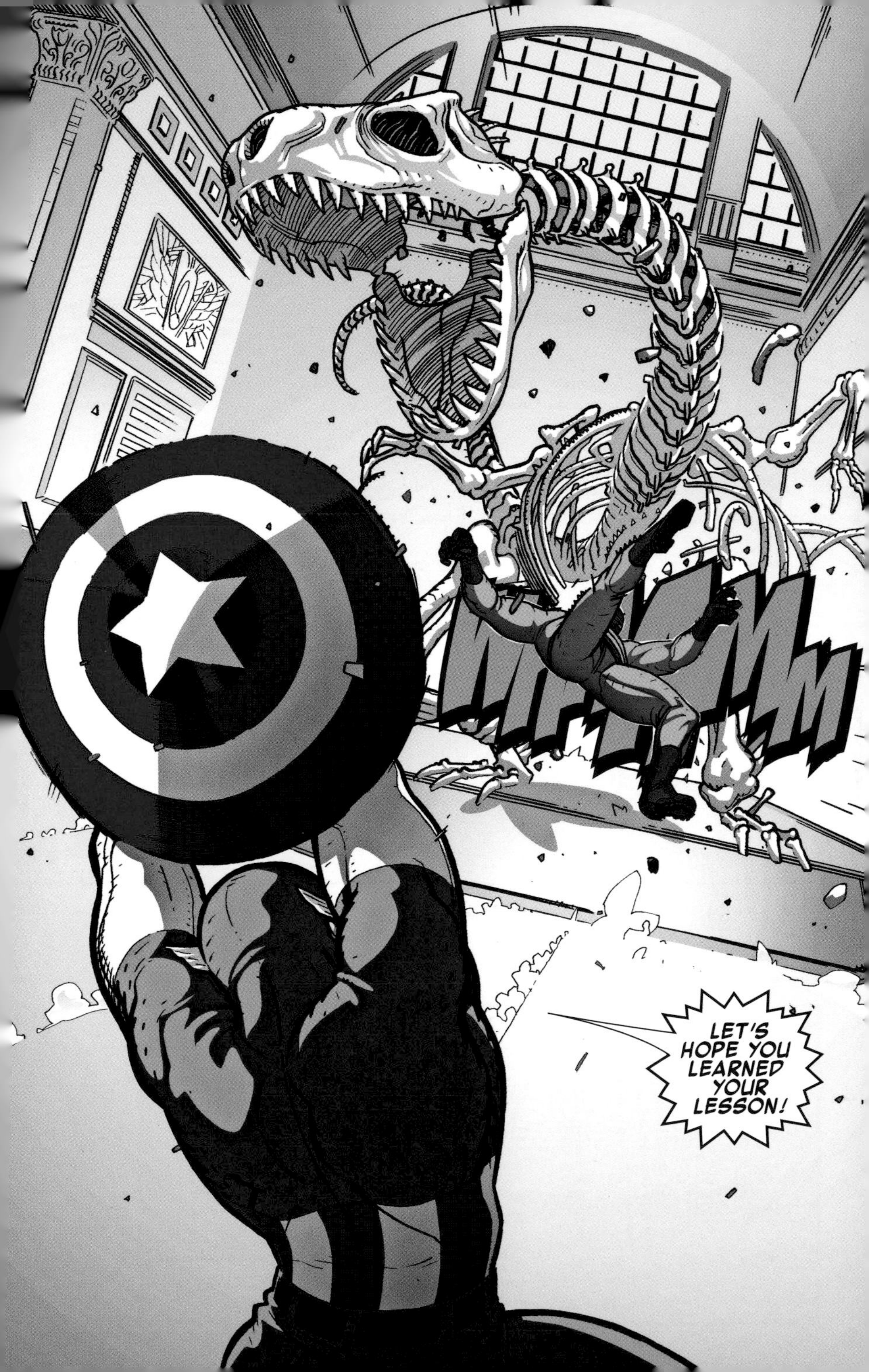
LET'S HOPE YOU LEARNED YOUR LESSON!

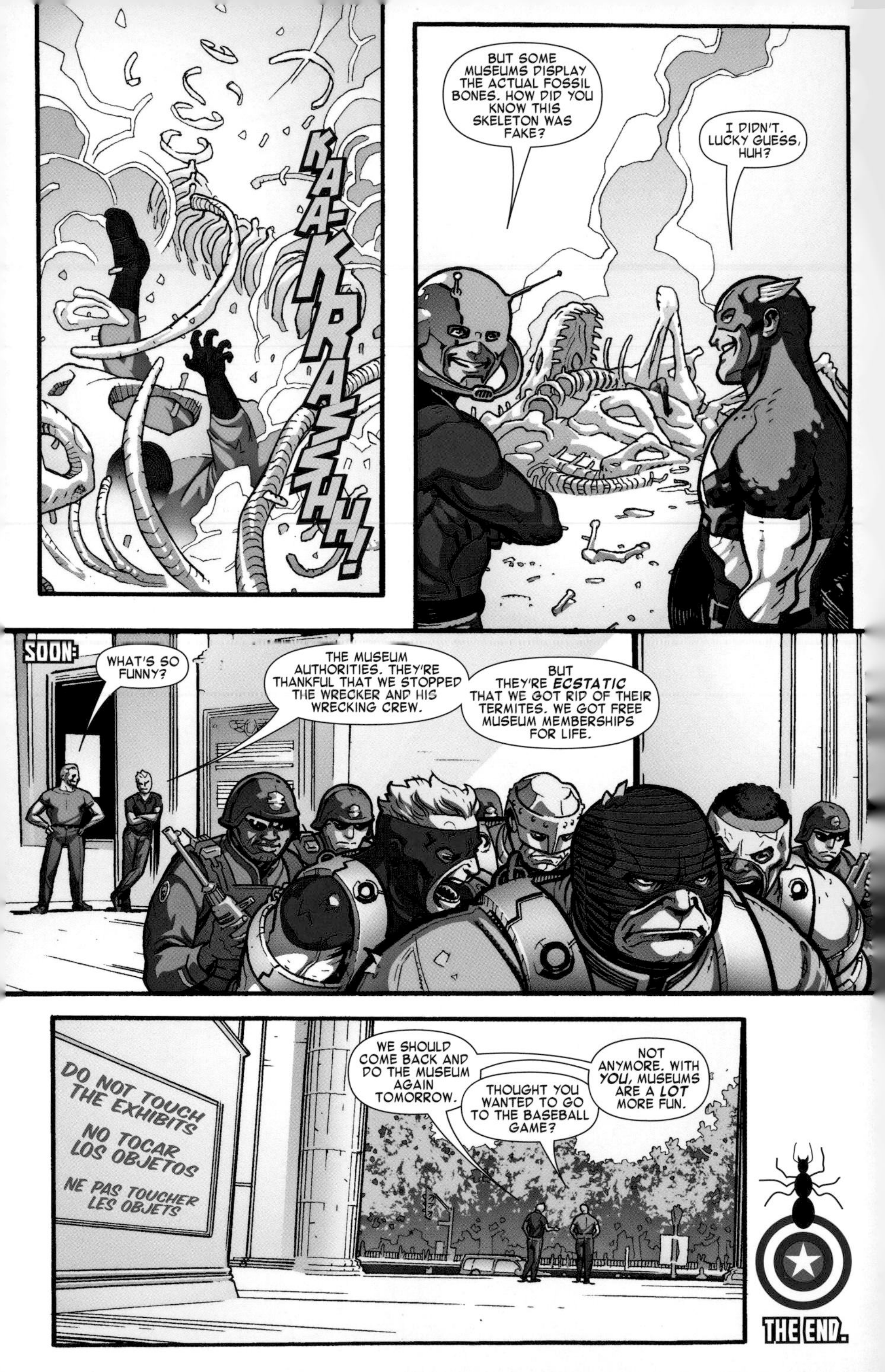
KA-A-KRASSHH!
BUT SOME MUSEUMS DISPLAY THE ACTUAL FOSSIL BONES. HOW DID YOU KNOW THIS SKELETON WAS FAKE?
I DIDN'T. LUCKY GUESS, HUH?
SOON:
WHAT'S SO FUNNY?
THE MUSEUM AUTHORITIES. THEY'RE THANKFUL THAT WE STOPPED THE WRECKER AND HIS WRECKING CREW.
BUT THEY'RE ECSTATIC THAT WE GOT RID OF THEIR TERMITES. WE GOT FREE MUSEUM MEMBERSHIPS FOR LIFE.
DO NOT TOUCH THE EXHIBITS
NO TOCAR LOS OBJETOS
NE PAS TOUCHER LES OBJETS
WE SHOULD COME BACK AND DO THE MUSEUM AGAIN TOMORROW.
THOUGHT YOU WANTED TO GO TO THE BASEBALL GAME?
NOT ANYMORE. WITH YOU, MUSEUMS ARE A LOT MORE FUN.
THE END.

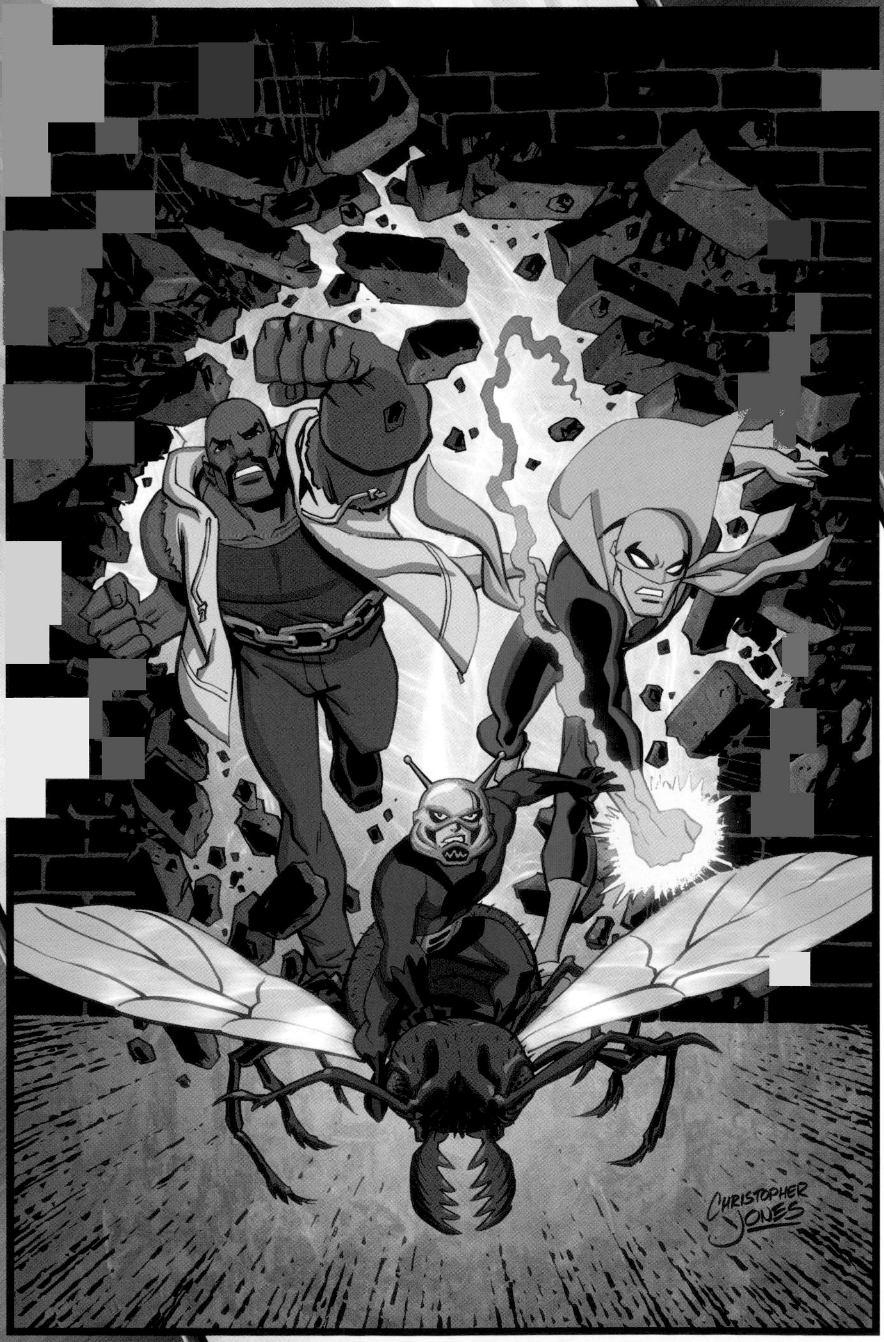
CHRISTOPHER JONES

#17 MARVEL UNIVERSE AVENGERS EARTH'S MIGHTIEST HEROES

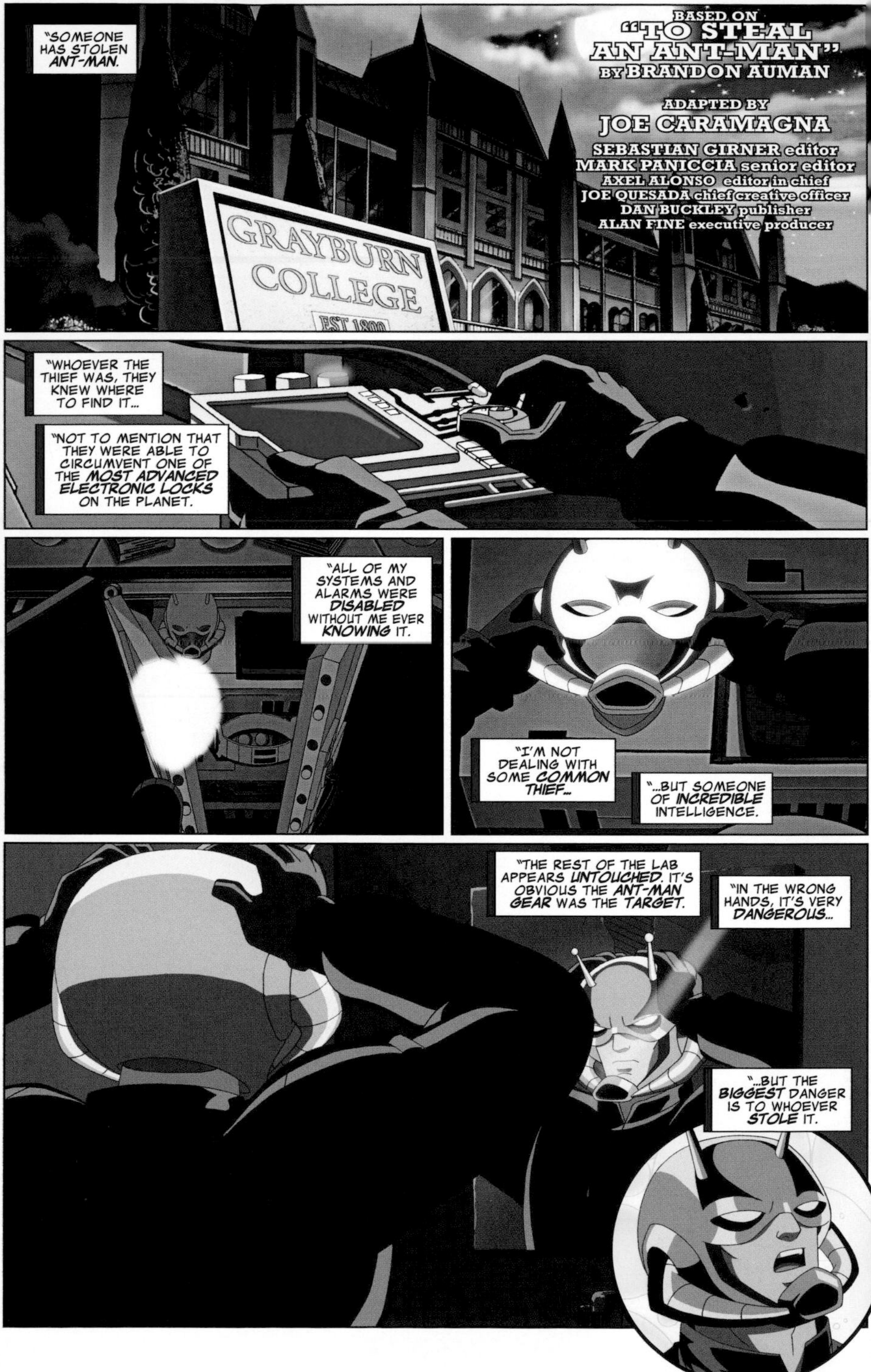
"SOMEONE HAS STOLEN ANT-MAN.
BASED ON "TO STEAL AN ANT-MAN" BY BRANDON AUMAN
ADAPTED BY JOE CARAMAGNA
SEBASTIAN GIRNER editor
MARK PANICCIA senior editor
AXEL ALONSO editor in chief
JOE QUESADA chief creative officer
DAN BUCKLEY publisher
ALAN FINE executive producer
GRAYBURN COLLEGE
EST 1800
"WHOEVER THE THIEF WAS, THEY KNEW WHERE TO FIND IT...
"NOT TO MENTION THAT THEY WERE ABLE TO CIRCUMVENT ONE OF THE MOST ADVANCED ELECTRONIC LOCKS ON THE PLANET.
"ALL OF MY SYSTEMS AND ALARMS WERE DISABLED WITHOUT ME EVER KNOWING IT.
"I'M NOT DEALING WITH SOME COMMON THIEF...
"...BUT SOMEONE OF INCREDIBLE INTELLIGENCE.
"THE REST OF THE LAB APPEARS UNTOUCHED. IT'S OBVIOUS THE ANT-MAN GEAR WAS THE TARGET.
"IN THE WRONG HANDS, IT'S VERY DANGEROUS...
"...BUT THE BIGGEST DANGER IS TO WHOEVER STOLE IT.

"IF THE THIEF WERE TO ACTIVATE THE *PYM PARTICLES* IN THE *BELT,* THEY'D FIND THEMSELVES IN WHAT WOULD LOOK LIKE *ANOTHER WORLD*--

"--THINGS LOOK DIFFERENT WHEN YOU'RE AN INCH HIGH."

AH!

"AT THAT SIZE, YOU ENTER A WHOLE *NEW LEVEL* OF THE FOOD CHAIN.

"BUT EVEN AT THAT SIZE, THE PYM PARTICLES WILL MAINTAIN THE THIEF'S STRENGTH AND SPEED RELATIVE TO BEING *FULL-SIZED*--THEY CAN STILL TAKE DOWN FULL-SIZED *HUMANS*...

"...BUT THE INSECT POPULATION HAS *NATURAL DEFENSES* THAT ARE DANGEROUS TO *ANY* INTRUDER."

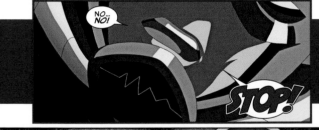

NO... NO!

STOP!

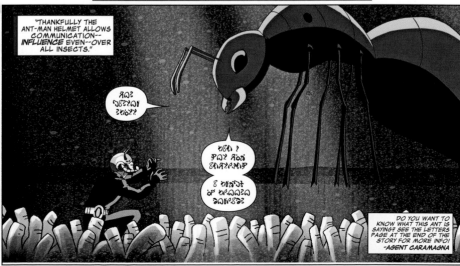

"THANKFULLY THE ANT-MAN HELMET ALLOWS COMMUNICATION-- *INFLUENCE* EVEN--OVER ALL INSECTS."

DO YOU WANT TO KNOW WHAT THIS ANT IS SAYING? SEE THE LETTERS PAGE AT THE END OF THE STORY FOR MORE INFO!
-AGENT CARAMAGNA

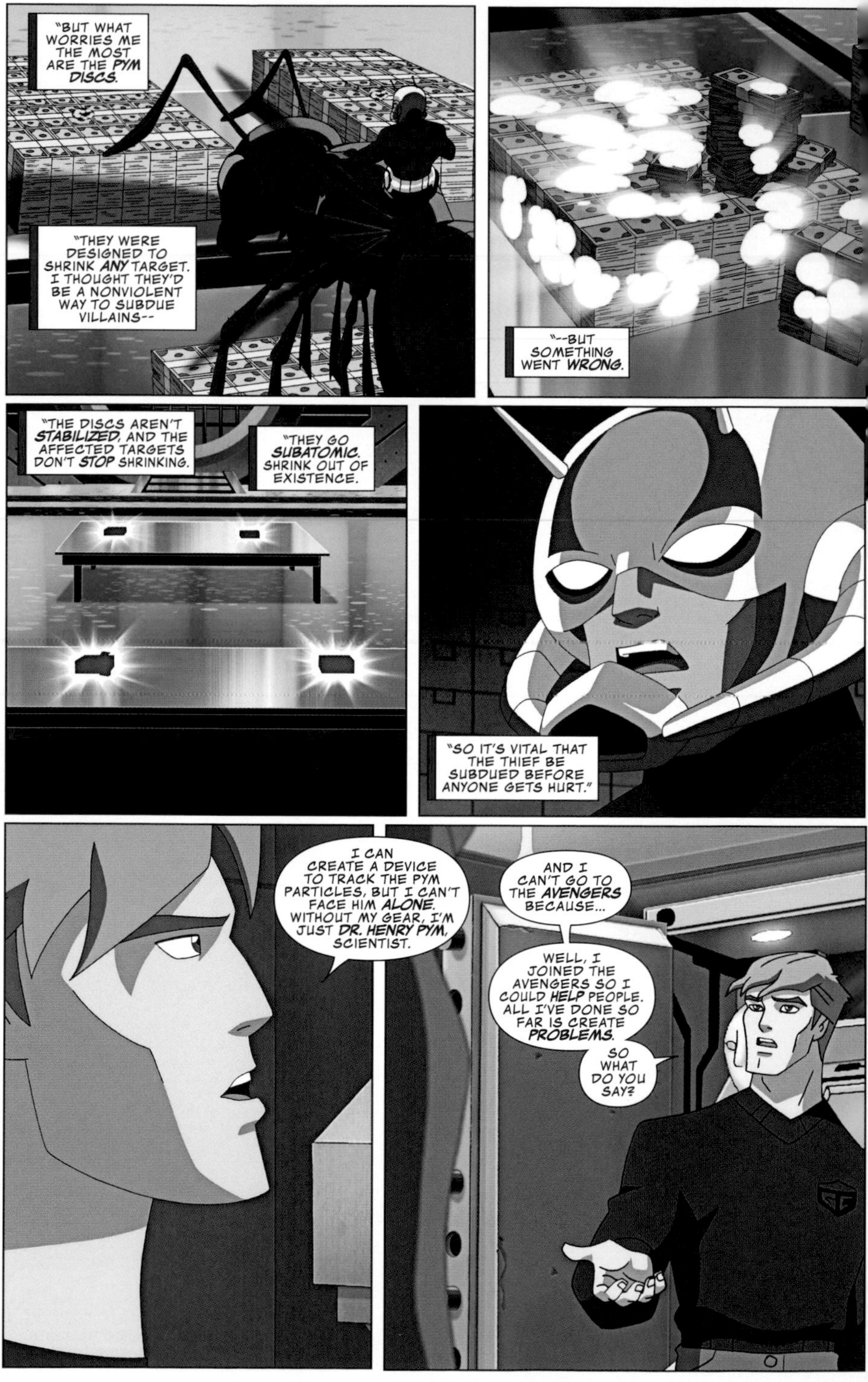
"BUT WHAT WORRIES ME THE MOST ARE THE PYM DISCS.
"THEY WERE DESIGNED TO SHRINK ANY TARGET. I THOUGHT THEY'D BE A NONVIOLENT WAY TO SUBDUE VILLAINS--
"--BUT SOMETHING WENT WRONG.
"THE DISCS AREN'T STABILIZED, AND THE AFFECTED TARGETS DON'T STOP SHRINKING.
"THEY GO SUBATOMIC. SHRINK OUT OF EXISTENCE.
"SO IT'S VITAL THAT THE THIEF BE SUBDUED BEFORE ANYONE GETS HURT."
I CAN CREATE A DEVICE TO TRACK THE PYM PARTICLES, BUT I CAN'T FACE HIM ALONE. WITHOUT MY GEAR, I'M JUST DR. HENRY PYM, SCIENTIST.
AND I CAN'T GO TO THE AVENGERS BECAUSE...
WELL, I JOINED THE AVENGERS SO I COULD HELP PEOPLE. ALL I'VE DONE SO FAR IS CREATE PROBLEMS.
SO WHAT DO YOU SAY?

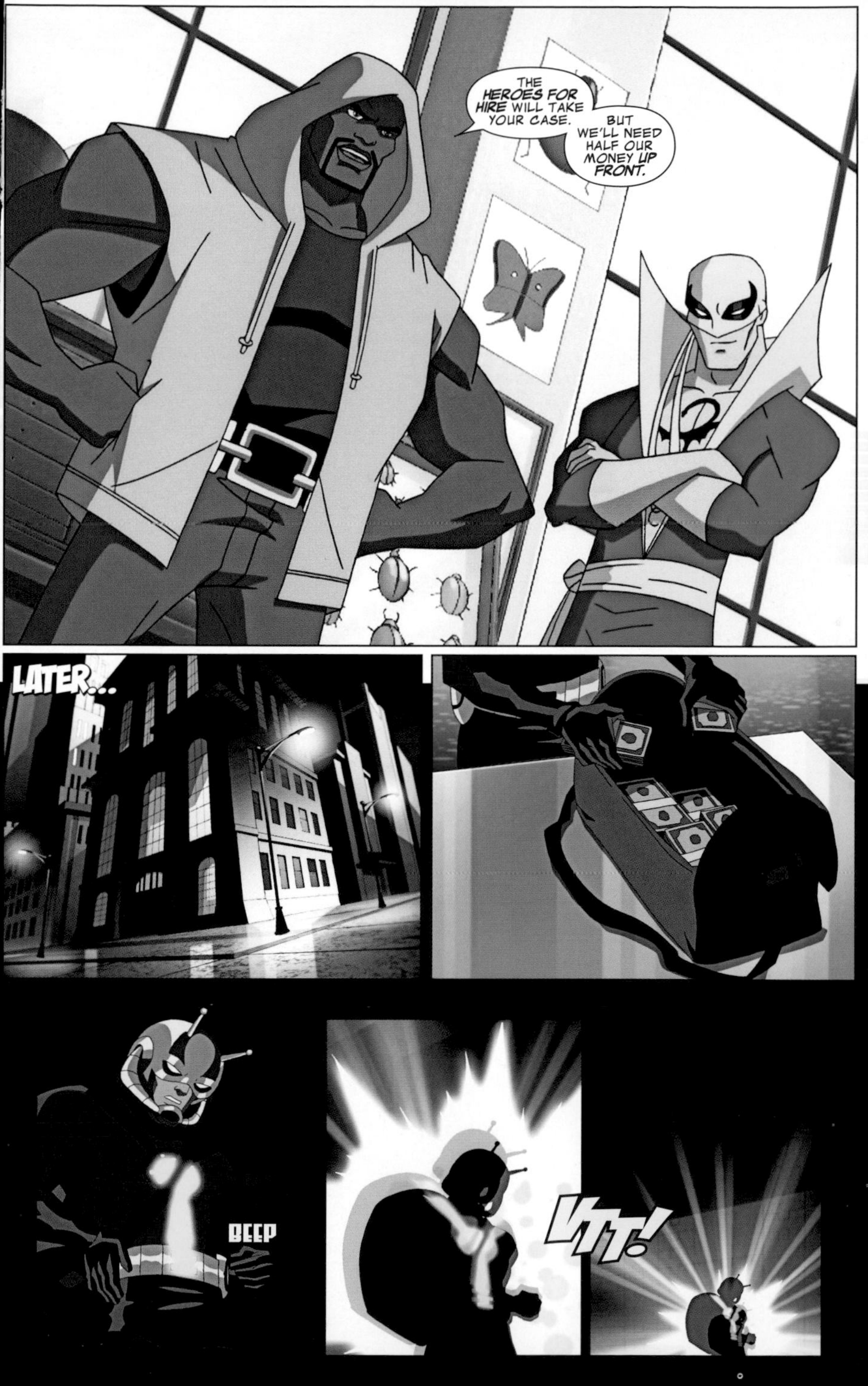
THE HEROES FOR HIRE WILL TAKE YOUR CASE.
BUT WE'LL NEED HALF OUR MONEY UP FRONT.
LATER...
BEEP
VTT!

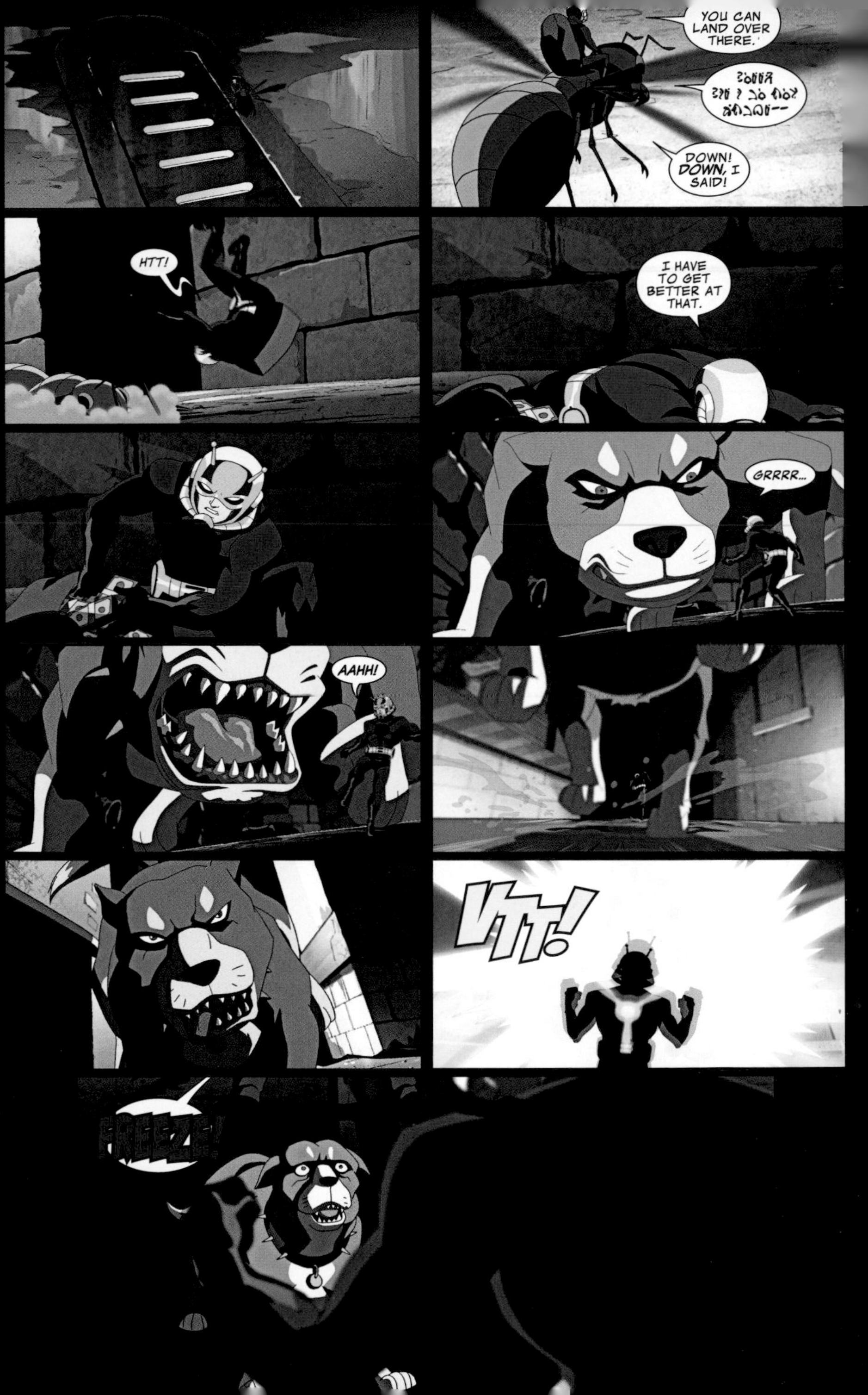

YOU CAN LAND OVER THERE.
DOWN! DOWN, I SAID!
HTT!
I HAVE TO GET BETTER AT THAT.
GRRRR...
AAHH!
VTT!
FREEZE!

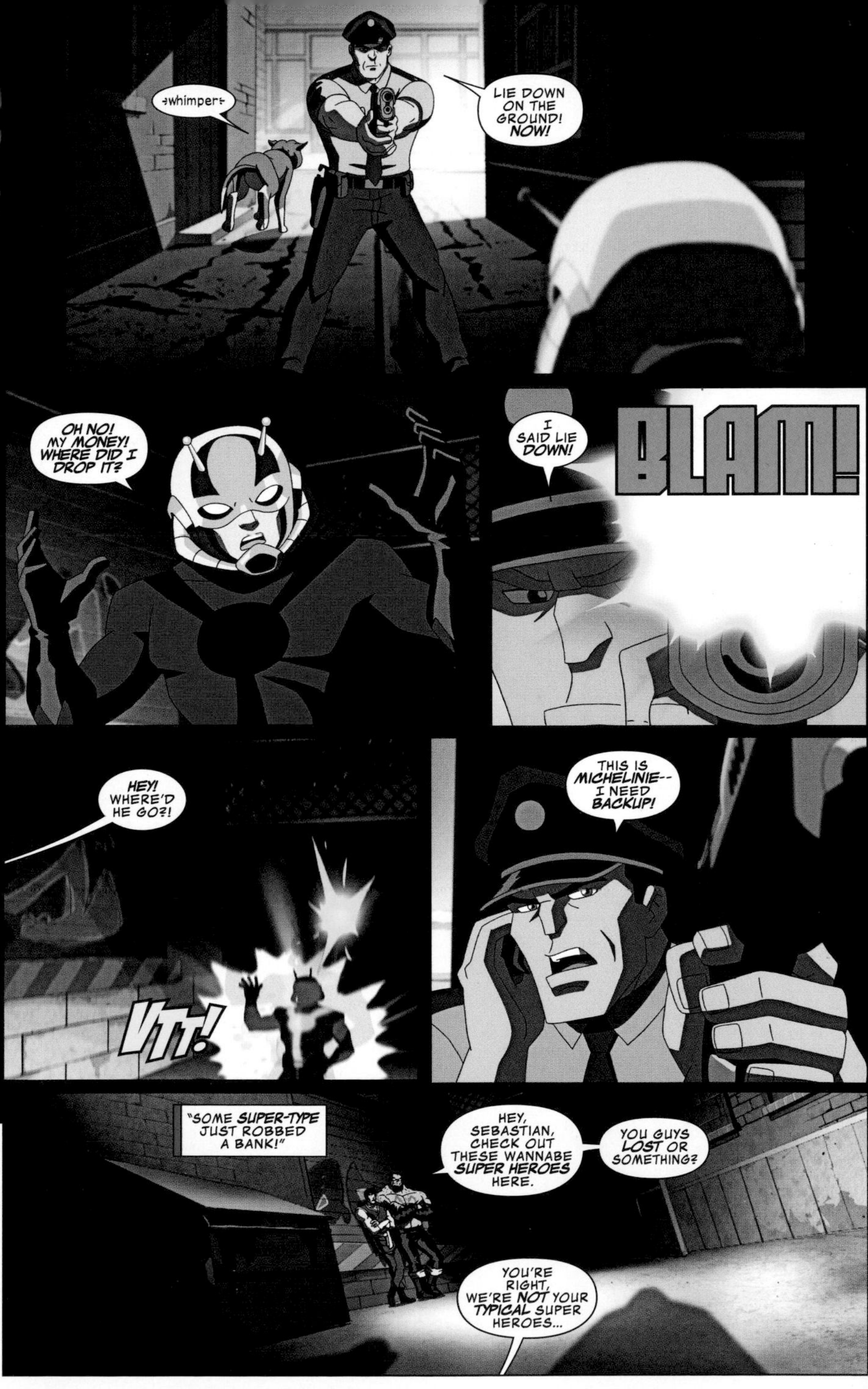

-whimper-
LIE DOWN ON THE GROUND! NOW!
OH NO! MY MONEY! WHERE DID I DROP IT?
I SAID LIE DOWN!
BLAM!
HEY! WHERE'D HE GO?!
VTT!
THIS IS MICHELINIE-- I NEED BACKUP!
"SOME SUPER-TYPE JUST ROBBED A BANK!"
HEY, SEBASTIAN, CHECK OUT THESE WANNABE SUPER HEROES HERE.
YOU GUYS LOST OR SOMETHING?
YOU'RE RIGHT, WE'RE NOT YOUR TYPICAL SUPER HEROES...

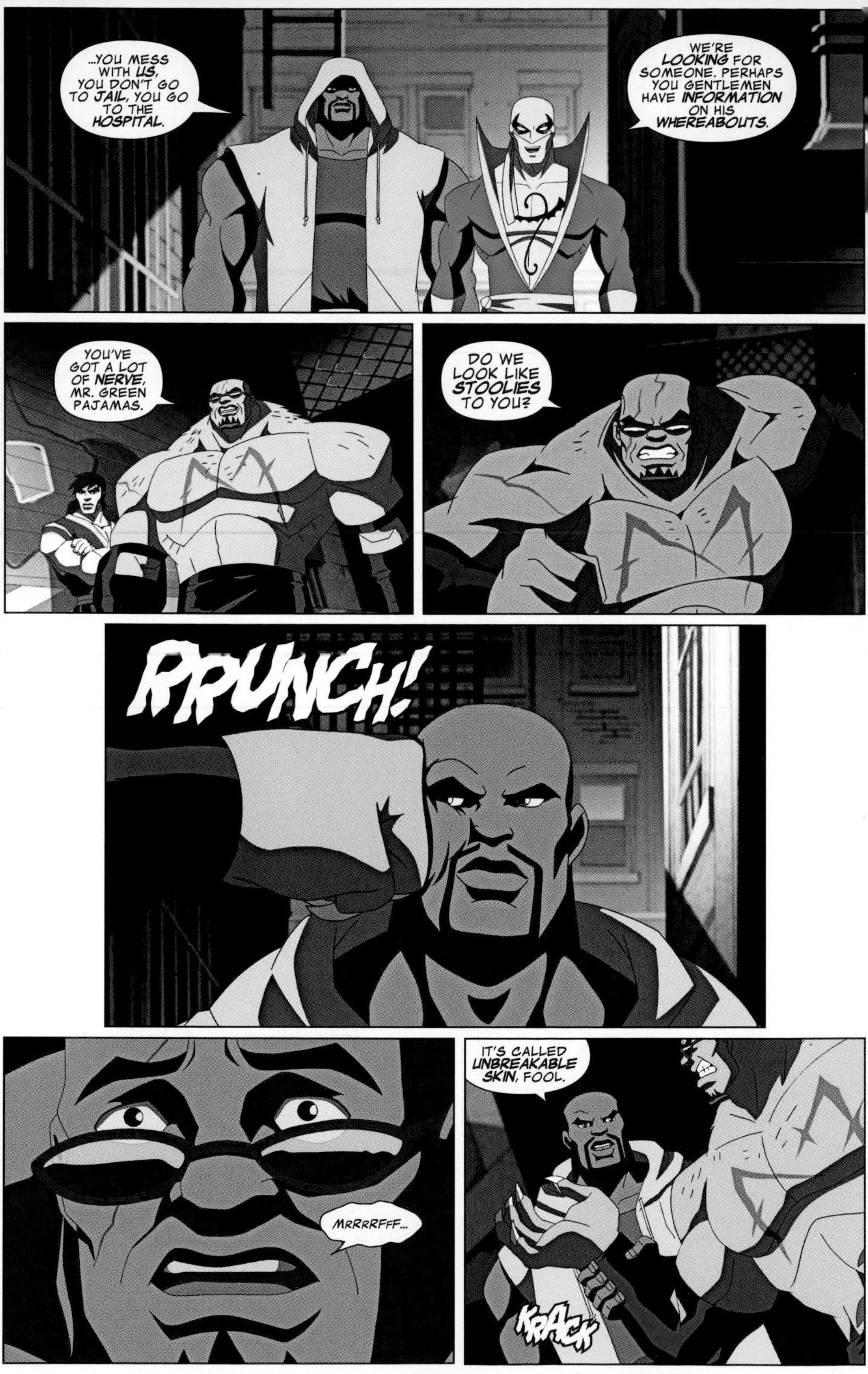
...YOU MESS WITH US, YOU DON'T GO TO JAIL, YOU GO TO THE HOSPITAL.
WE'RE LOOKING FOR SOMEONE. PERHAPS YOU GENTLEMEN HAVE INFORMATION ON HIS WHEREABOUTS.
YOU'VE GOT A LOT OF NERVE, MR. GREEN PAJAMAS.
DO WE LOOK LIKE STOOLIES TO YOU?
RRUNCH!
MRRRRFFF...
IT'S CALLED UNBREAKABLE SKIN, FOOL.
KRACK

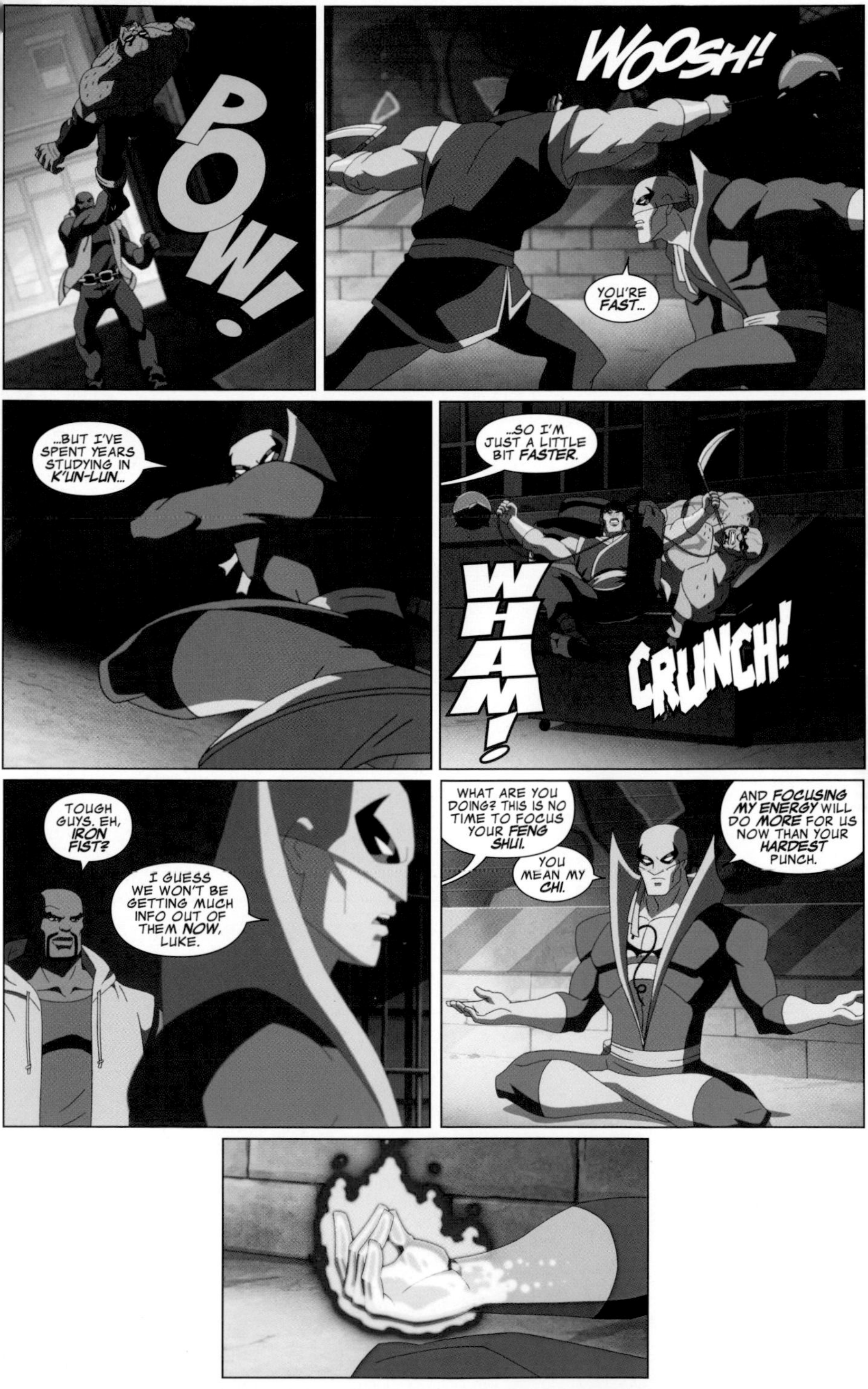
POW!
WOOSH!
YOU'RE FAST...
...BUT I'VE SPENT YEARS STUDYING IN K'UN-LUN...
...SO I'M JUST A LITTLE BIT FASTER.
WHAM!
CRUNCH!
TOUGH GUYS. EH, IRON FIST?
I GUESS WE WON'T BE GETTING MUCH INFO OUT OF THEM NOW, LUKE.
WHAT ARE YOU DOING? THIS IS NO TIME TO FOCUS YOUR FENG SHUI.
YOU MEAN MY CHI.
AND FOCUSING MY ENERGY WILL DO MORE FOR US NOW THAN YOUR HARDEST PUNCH.

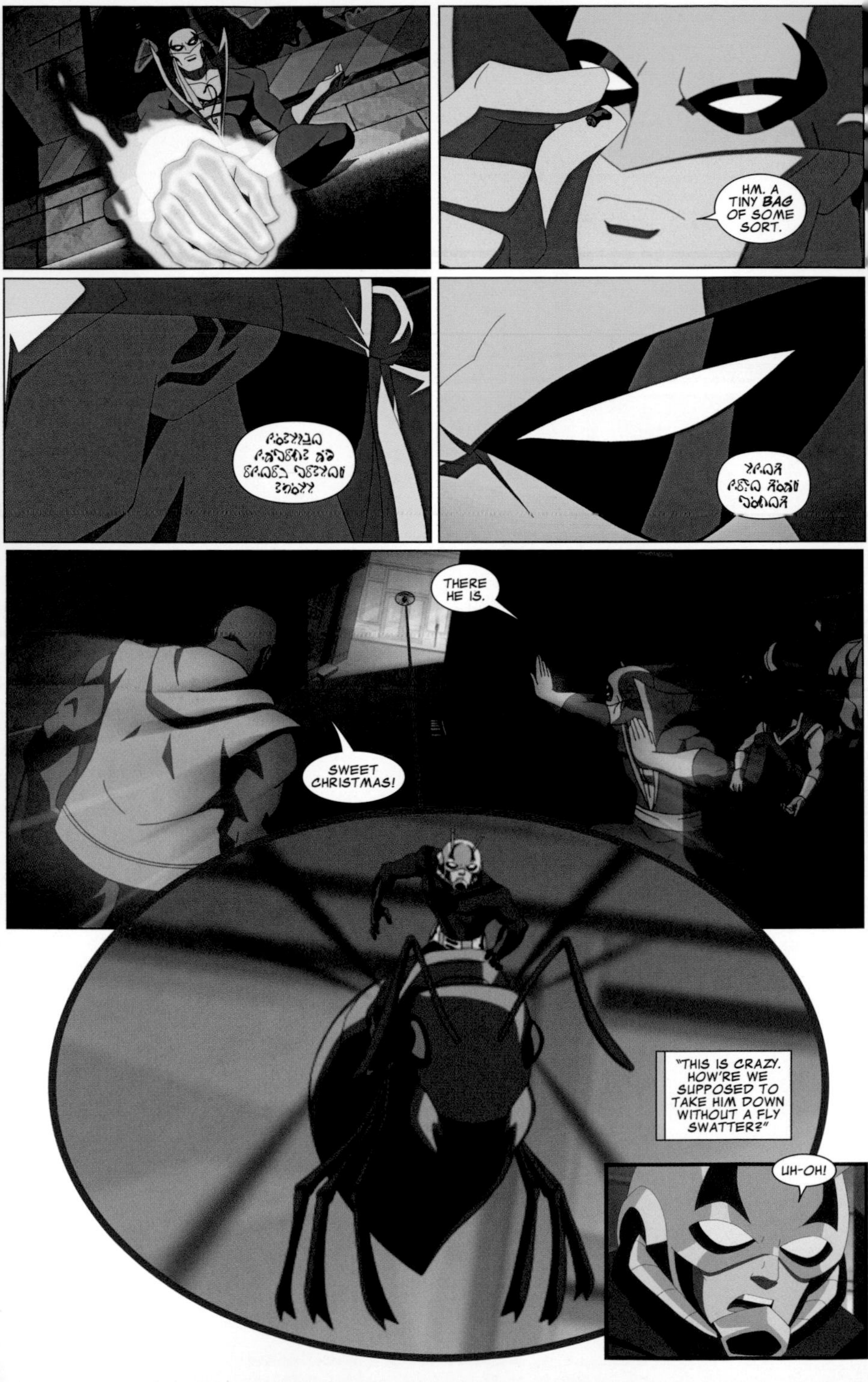
HM. A TINY BAG OF SOME SORT.
THERE HE IS.
SWEET CHRISTMAS!
"THIS IS CRAZY. HOW'RE WE SUPPOSED TO TAKE HIM DOWN WITHOUT A FLY SWATTER?"
UH-OH!

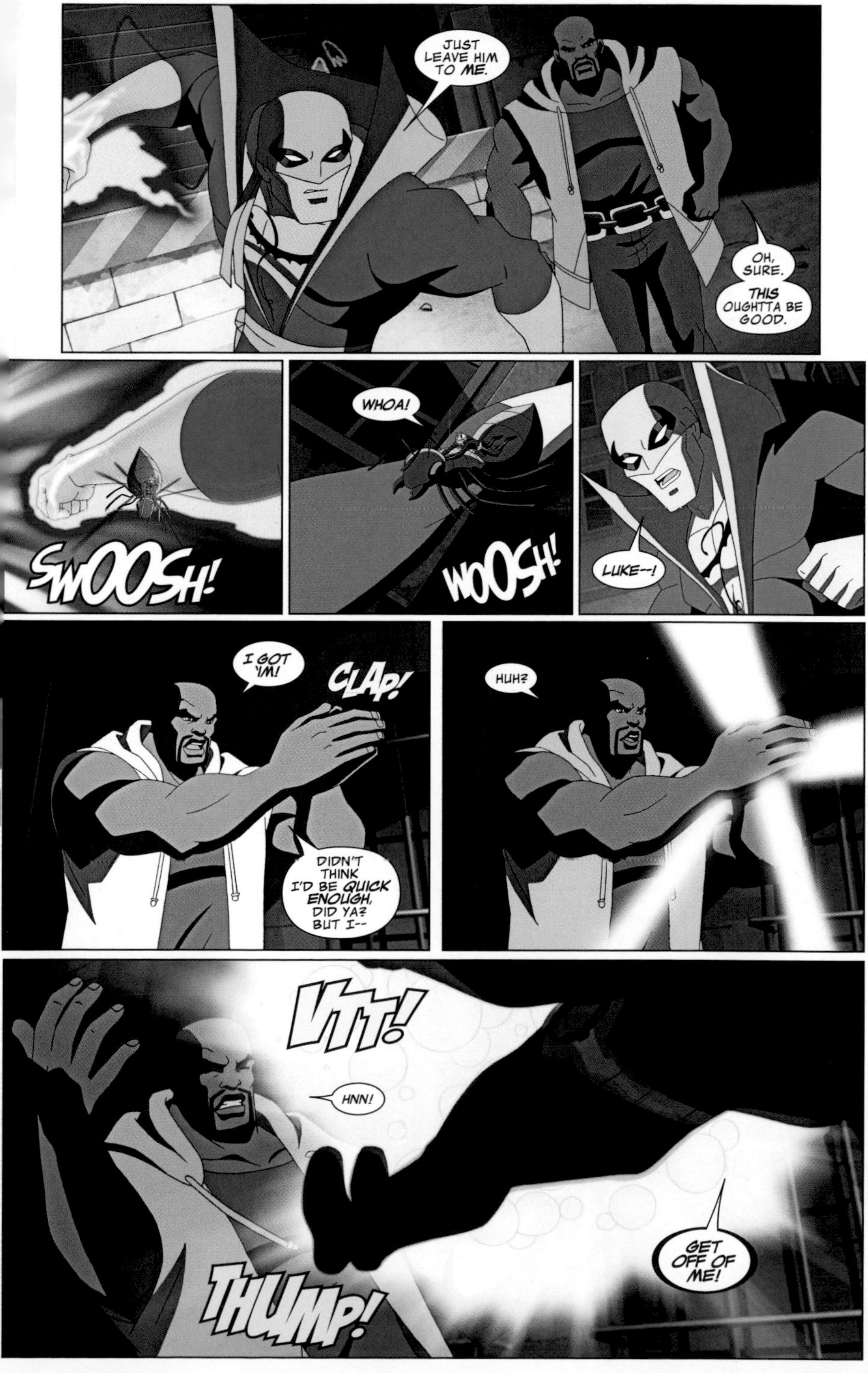
JUST LEAVE HIM TO ME.
OH, SURE. THIS OUGHTTA BE GOOD.
SWOOSH!
WHOA!
WOOSH!
LUKE--!
I GOT 'IM!
CLAP!
DIDN'T THINK I'D BE QUICK ENOUGH, DID YA? BUT I--
HUH?
VTT!
HNN!
GET OFF OF ME!
THUMP!

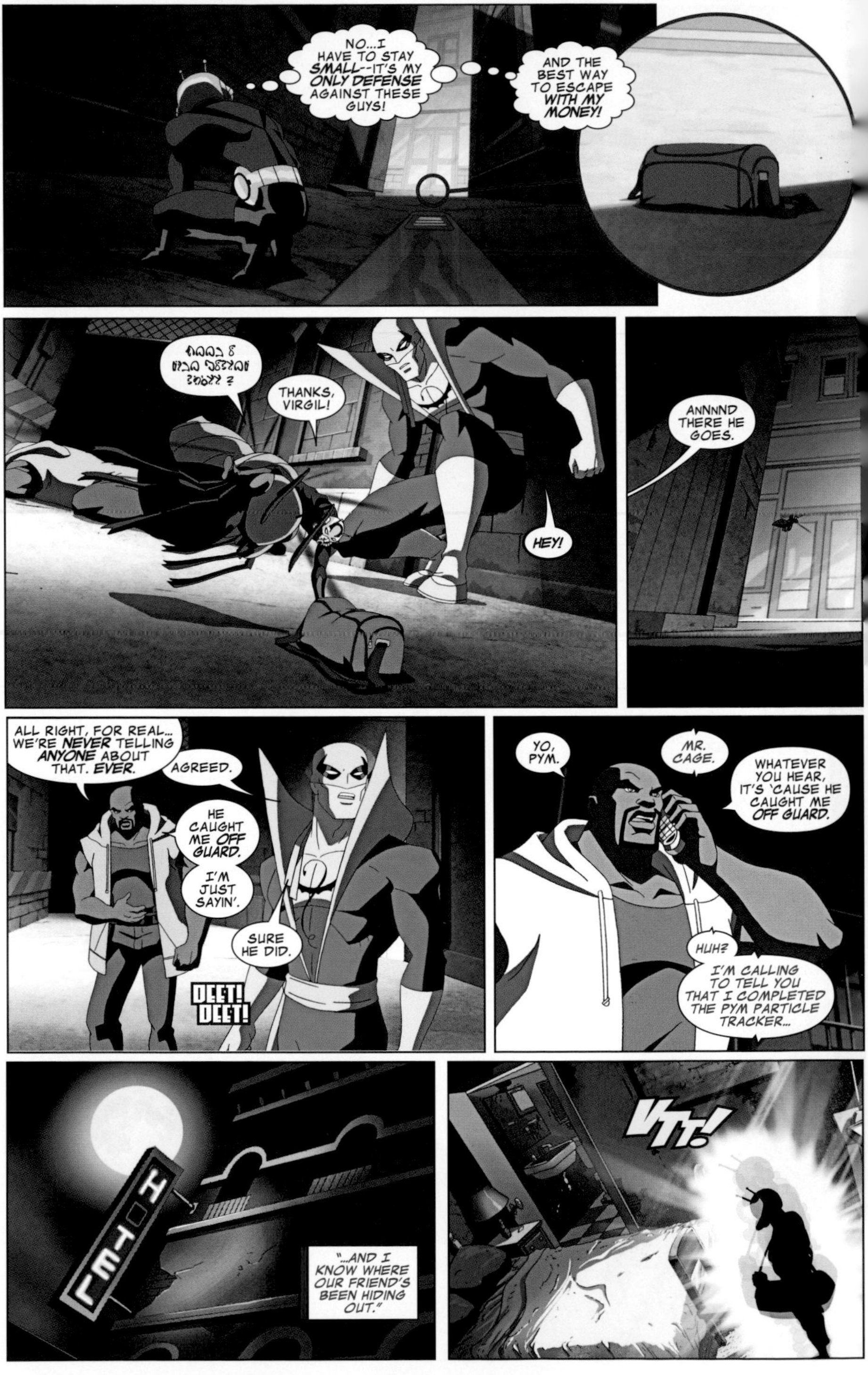
NO...I HAVE TO STAY SMALL--IT'S MY ONLY DEFENSE AGAINST THESE GUYS!
AND THE BEST WAY TO ESCAPE WITH MY MONEY!
THANKS, VIRGIL!
HEY!
ANNNND THERE HE GOES.
ALL RIGHT, FOR REAL... WE'RE NEVER TELLING ANYONE ABOUT THAT. EVER.
AGREED.
HE CAUGHT ME OFF GUARD.
I'M JUST SAYIN'.
SURE HE DID.
DEET! DEET!
YO, PYM.
MR. CAGE.
WHATEVER YOU HEAR, IT'S 'CAUSE HE CAUGHT ME OFF GUARD.
HUH?
I'M CALLING TO TELL YOU THAT I COMPLETED THE PYM PARTICLE TRACKER...
HOTEL
"...AND I KNOW WHERE OUR FRIEND'S BEEN HIDING OUT."
VTT!

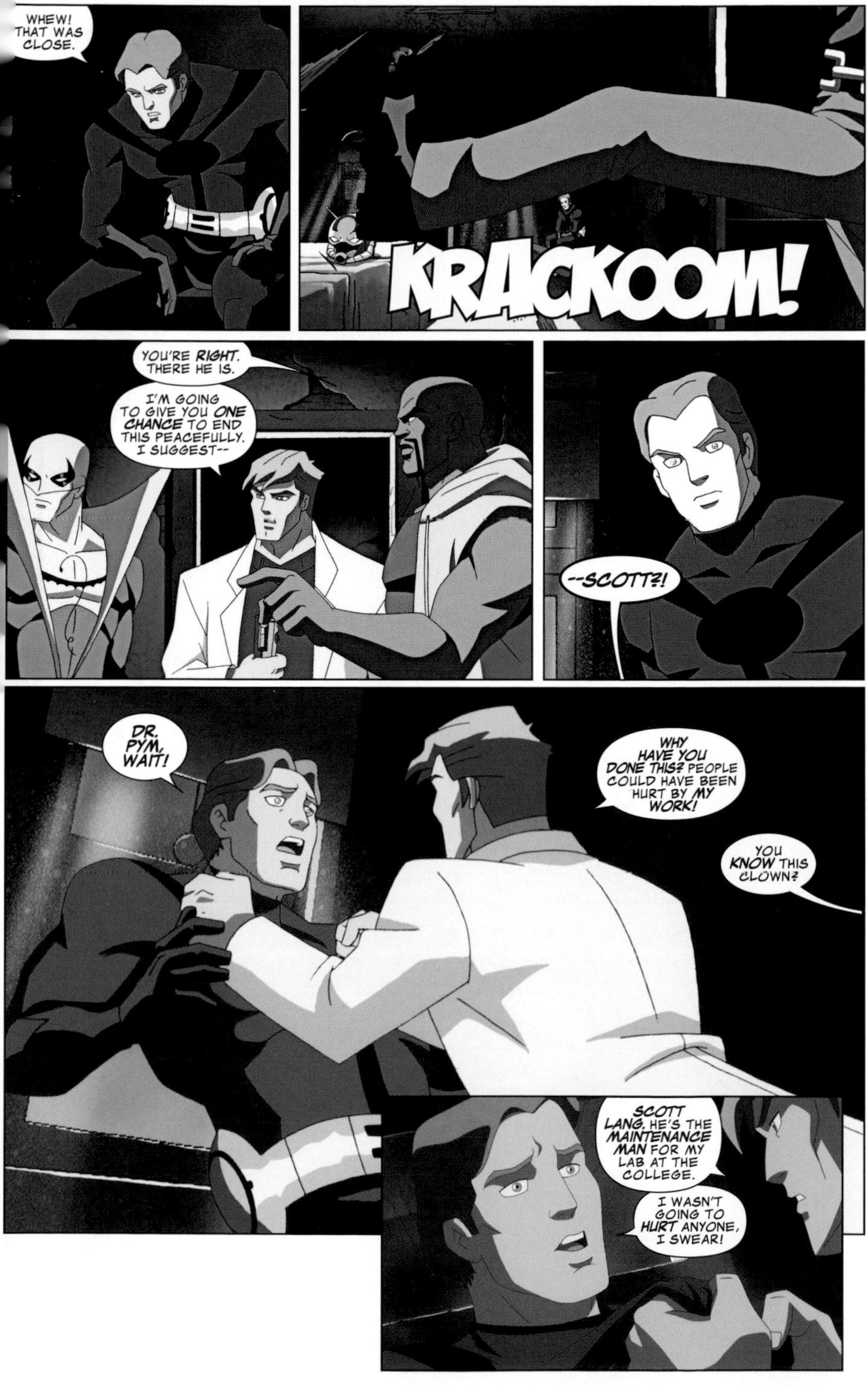
WHEW! THAT WAS CLOSE.
KRACKOOM!
YOU'RE RIGHT. THERE HE IS.
I'M GOING TO GIVE YOU ONE CHANCE TO END THIS PEACEFULLY. I SUGGEST--
--SCOTT?!
DR. PYM, WAIT!
WHY HAVE YOU DONE THIS? PEOPLE COULD HAVE BEEN HURT BY MY WORK!
YOU KNOW THIS CLOWN?
SCOTT LANG. HE'S THE MAINTENANCE MAN FOR MY LAB AT THE COLLEGE.
I WASN'T GOING TO HURT ANYONE, I SWEAR!

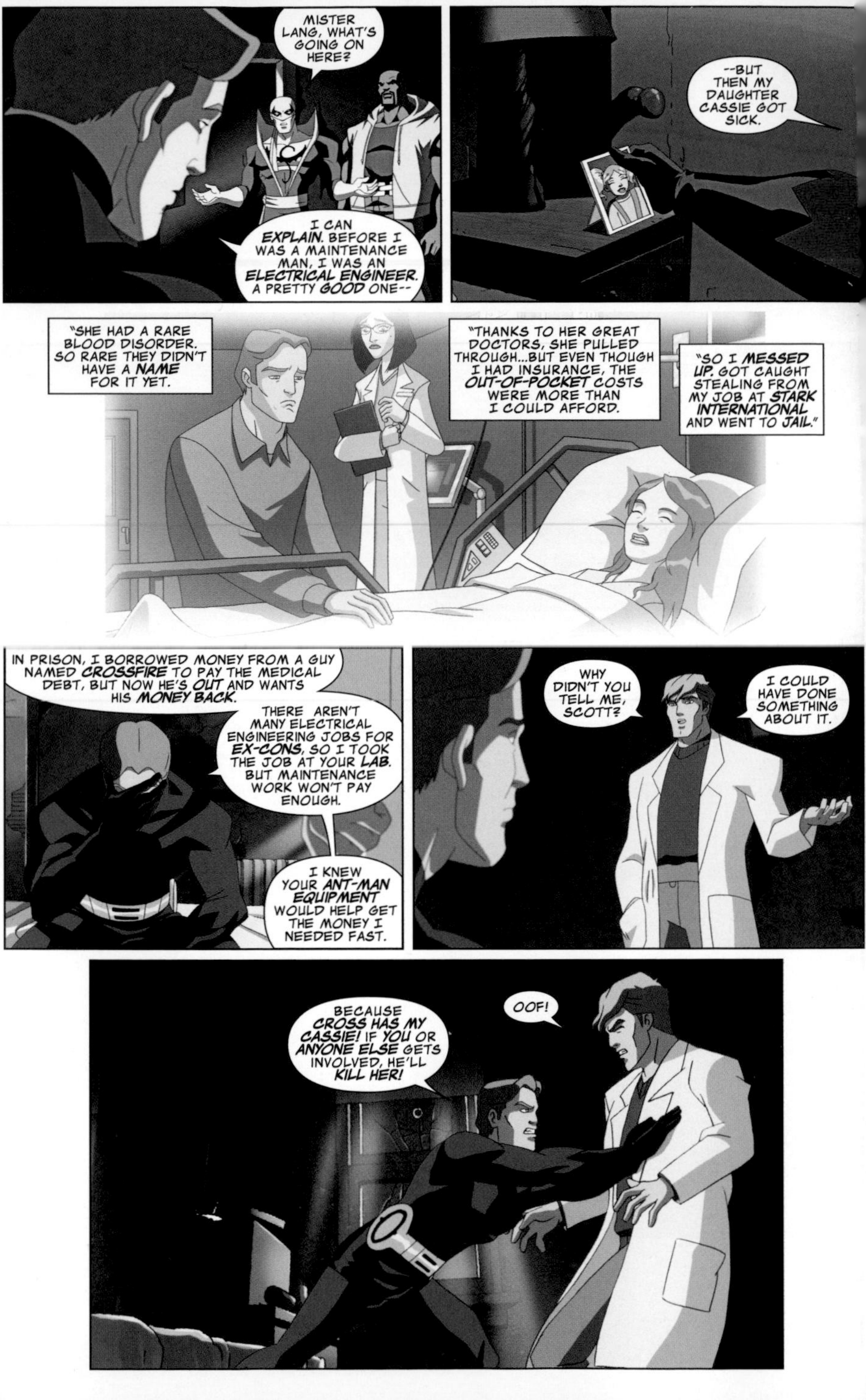
MISTER LANG, WHAT'S GOING ON HERE?
I CAN EXPLAIN. BEFORE I WAS A MAINTENANCE MAN, I WAS AN ELECTRICAL ENGINEER. A PRETTY GOOD ONE--
--BUT THEN MY DAUGHTER CASSIE GOT SICK.
"SHE HAD A RARE BLOOD DISORDER. SO RARE THEY DIDN'T HAVE A NAME FOR IT YET.
"THANKS TO HER GREAT DOCTORS, SHE PULLED THROUGH...BUT EVEN THOUGH I HAD INSURANCE, THE OUT-OF-POCKET COSTS WERE MORE THAN I COULD AFFORD.
"SO I MESSED UP. GOT CAUGHT STEALING FROM MY JOB AT STARK INTERNATIONAL AND WENT TO JAIL."
IN PRISON, I BORROWED MONEY FROM A GUY NAMED CROSSFIRE TO PAY THE MEDICAL DEBT, BUT NOW HE'S OUT AND WANTS HIS MONEY BACK.
THERE AREN'T MANY ELECTRICAL ENGINEERING JOBS FOR EX-CONS, SO I TOOK THE JOB AT YOUR LAB. BUT MAINTENANCE WORK WON'T PAY ENOUGH.
I KNEW YOUR ANT-MAN EQUIPMENT WOULD HELP GET THE MONEY I NEEDED FAST.
WHY DIDN'T YOU TELL ME, SCOTT?
I COULD HAVE DONE SOMETHING ABOUT IT.
BECAUSE CROSS HAS MY CASSIE! IF YOU OR ANYONE ELSE GETS INVOLVED, HE'LL KILL HER!
OOF!

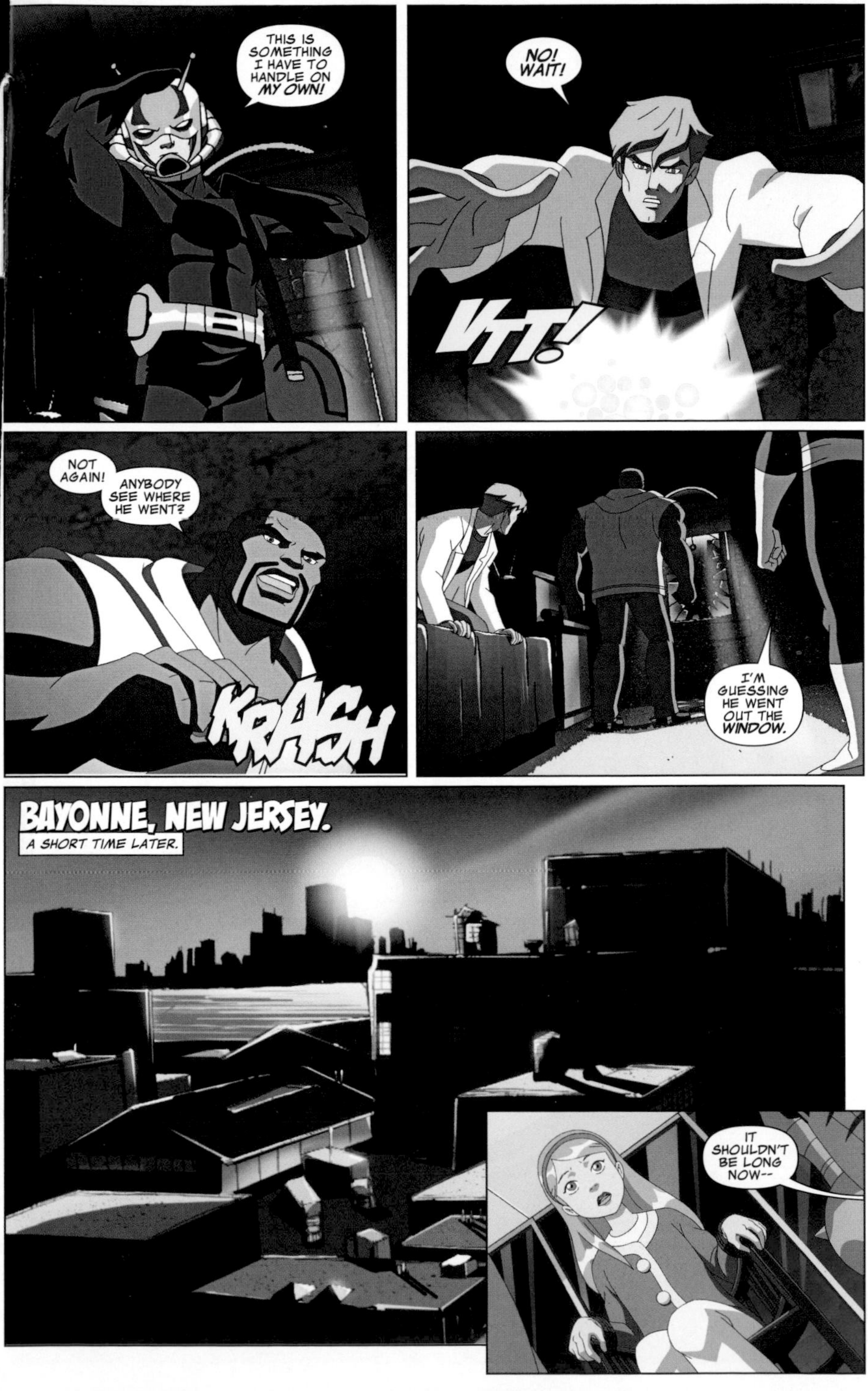
THIS IS SOMETHING I HAVE TO HANDLE ON MY OWN!
NO! WAIT!
VTT!
NOT AGAIN!
ANYBODY SEE WHERE HE WENT?
KRASH
I'M GUESSING HE WENT OUT THE WINDOW.
BAYONNE, NEW JERSEY.
A SHORT TIME LATER.
IT SHOULDN'T BE LONG NOW--

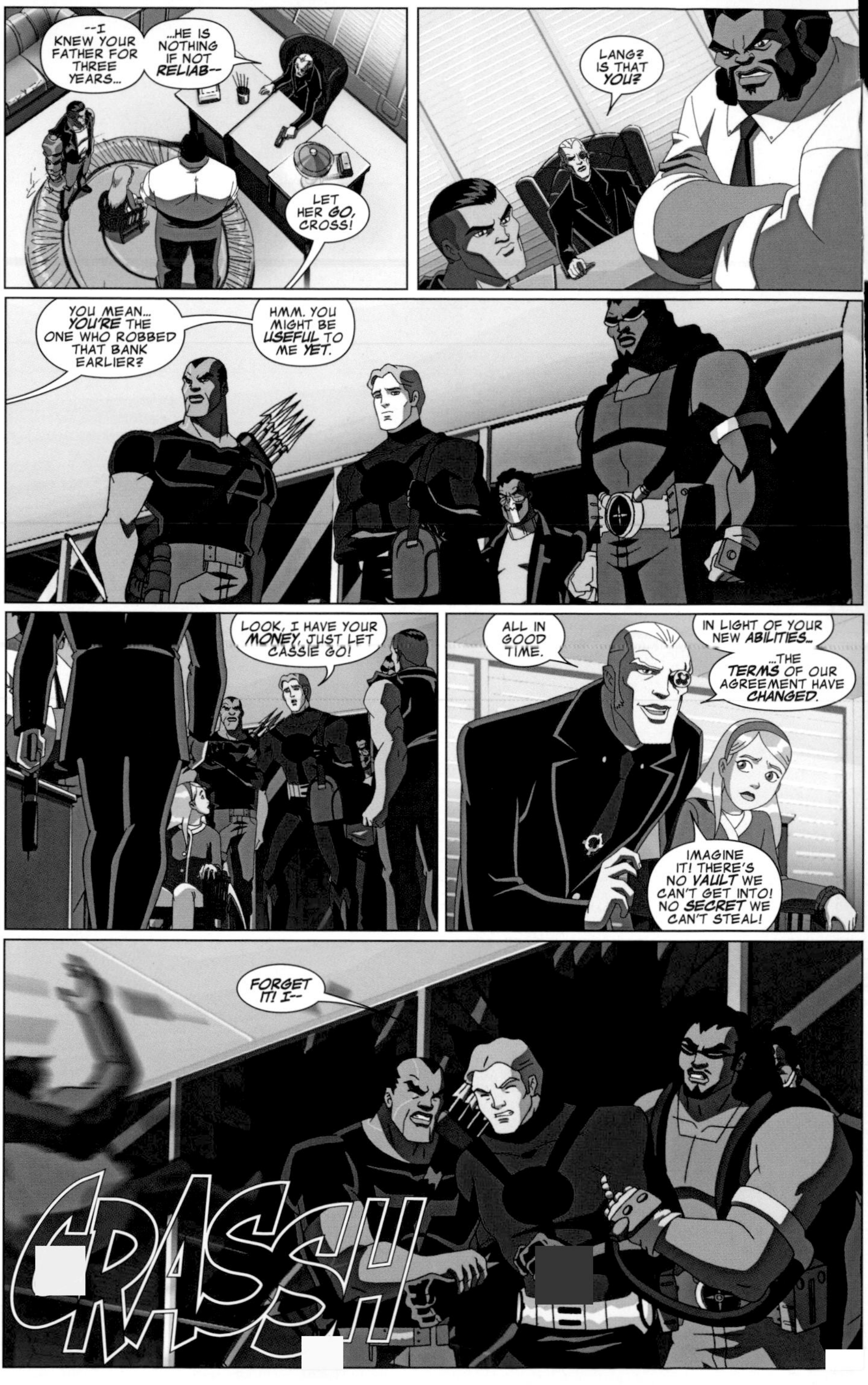
--I KNEW YOUR FATHER FOR THREE YEARS...
...HE IS NOTHING IF NOT RELIAB--
LET HER GO, CROSS!
LANG? IS THAT YOU?
YOU MEAN... YOU'RE THE ONE WHO ROBBED THAT BANK EARLIER?
HMM. YOU MIGHT BE USEFUL TO ME YET.
LOOK, I HAVE YOUR MONEY, JUST LET CASSIE GO!
ALL IN GOOD TIME.
IN LIGHT OF YOUR NEW ABILITIES...
...THE TERMS OF OUR AGREEMENT HAVE CHANGED.
IMAGINE IT! THERE'S NO VAULT WE CAN'T GET INTO! NO SECRET WE CAN'T STEAL!
FORGET IT! I--
CRASSH

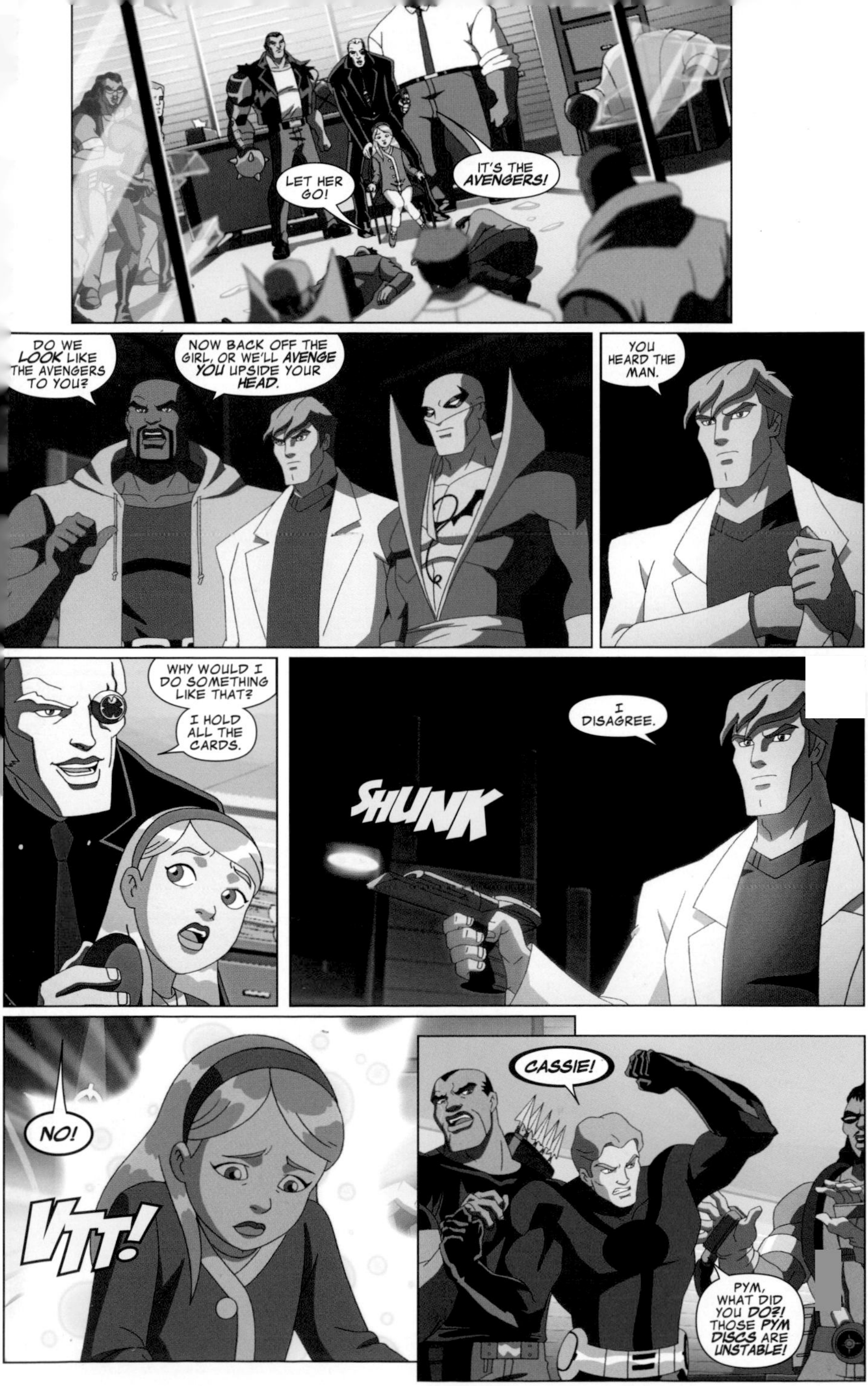

LET HER GO!
IT'S THE AVENGERS!
DO WE LOOK LIKE THE AVENGERS TO YOU?
NOW BACK OFF THE GIRL, OR WE'LL AVENGE YOU UPSIDE YOUR HEAD.
YOU HEARD THE MAN.
WHY WOULD I DO SOMETHING LIKE THAT?
I HOLD ALL THE CARDS.
I DISAGREE.
SHUNK
NO!
VTT!
CASSIE!
PYM, WHAT DID YOU DO?! THOSE PYM DISCS ARE UNSTABLE!

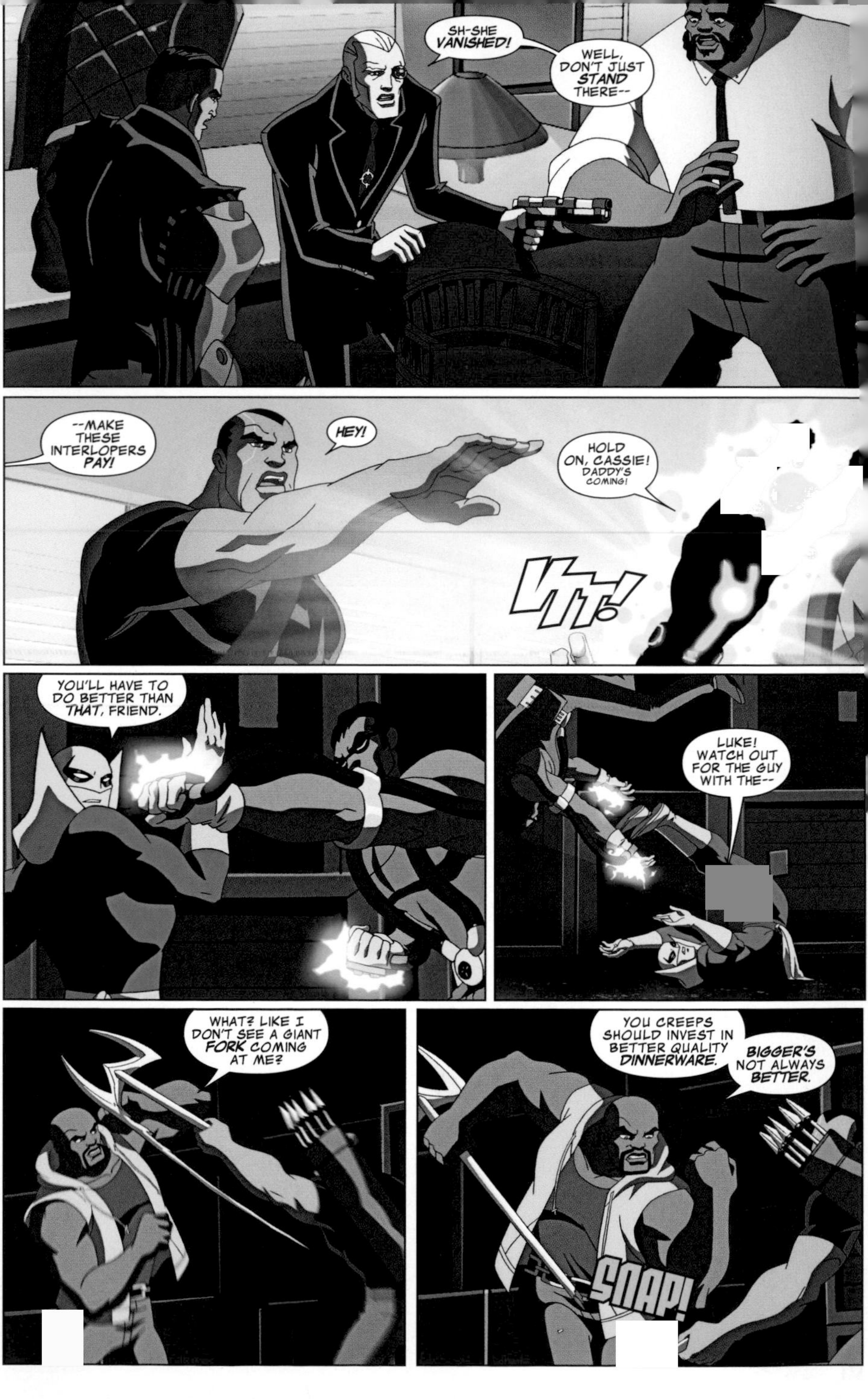

SH-SHE VANISHED!
WELL, DON'T JUST STAND THERE--
--MAKE THESE INTERLOPERS PAY!
HEY!
HOLD ON, CASSIE! DADDY'S COMING!
YOU'LL HAVE TO DO BETTER THAN THAT, FRIEND.
LUKE! WATCH OUT FOR THE GUY WITH THE--
WHAT? LIKE I DON'T SEE A GIANT FORK COMING AT ME?
YOU CREEPS SHOULD INVEST IN BETTER QUALITY DINNERWARE.
BIGGER'S NOT ALWAYS BETTER.
SNAP!

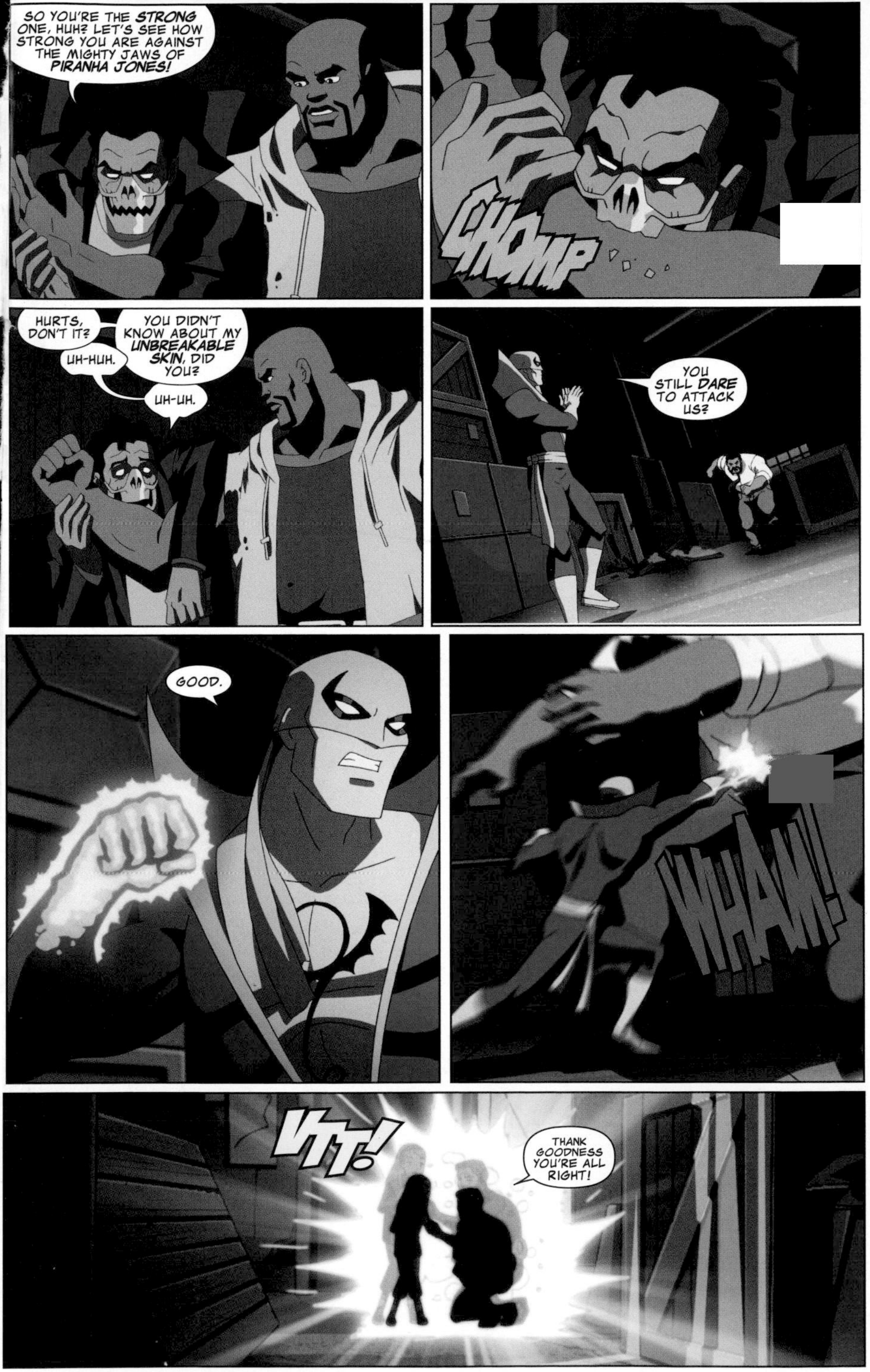
SO YOU'RE THE STRONG ONE, HUH? LET'S SEE HOW STRONG YOU ARE AGAINST THE MIGHTY JAWS OF PIRANHA JONES!
CHOMP
HURTS, DON'T IT?
UH-HUH.
YOU DIDN'T KNOW ABOUT MY UNBREAKABLE SKIN, DID YOU?
UH-UH.
YOU STILL DARE TO ATTACK US?
GOOD.
WHAM!
VTT!
THANK GOODNESS YOU'RE ALL RIGHT!

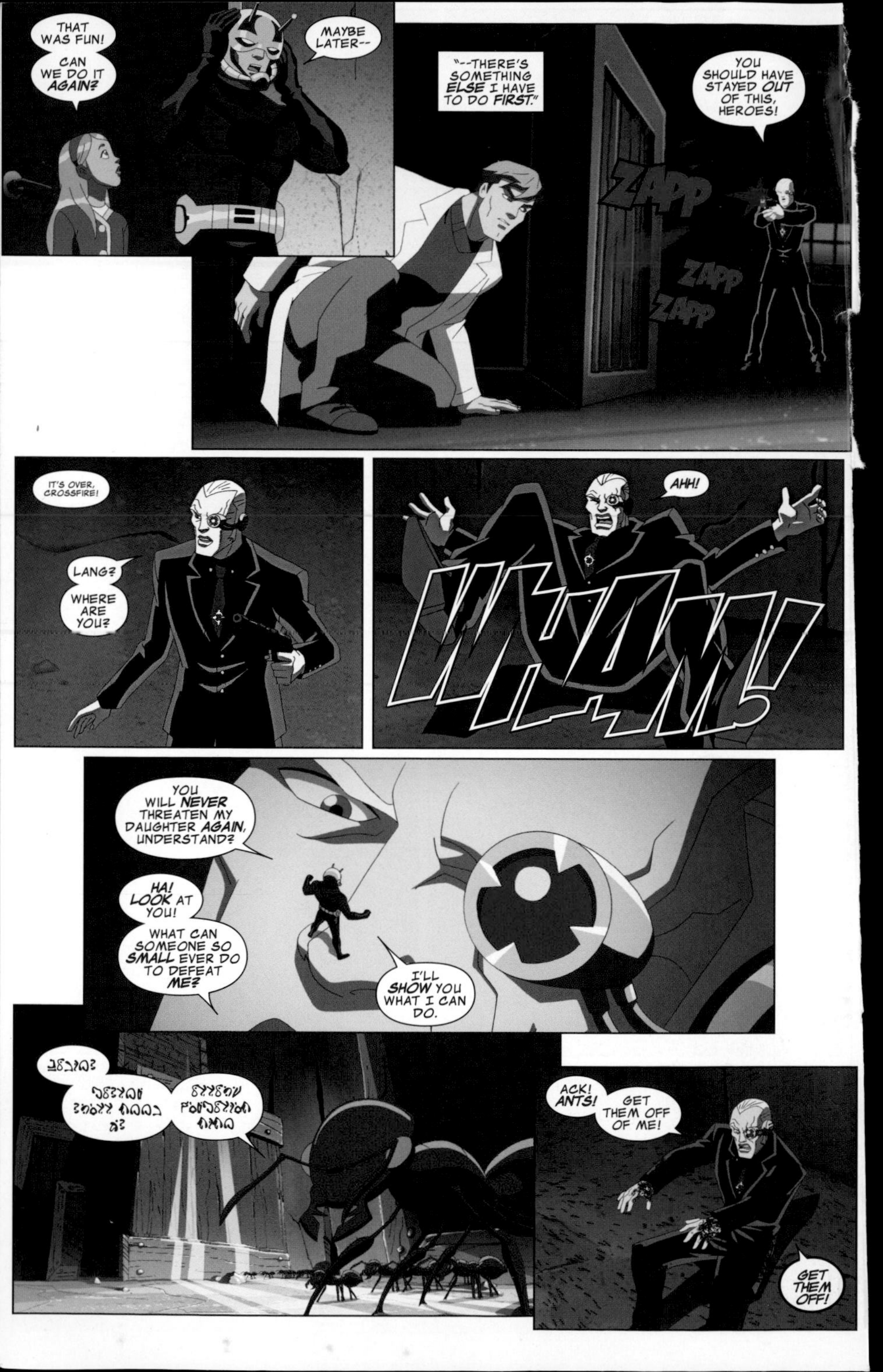
THAT WAS FUN!
CAN WE DO IT AGAIN?
MAYBE LATER--
"--THERE'S SOMETHING ELSE I HAVE TO DO FIRST."
YOU SHOULD HAVE STAYED OUT OF THIS, HEROES!
ZAPP
ZAPP
ZAPP
IT'S OVER, CROSSFIRE!
LANG?
WHERE ARE YOU?
AHH!
YOU WILL NEVER THREATEN MY DAUGHTER AGAIN, UNDERSTAND?
HA! LOOK AT YOU!
WHAT CAN SOMEONE SO SMALL EVER DO TO DEFEAT ME?
I'LL SHOW YOU WHAT I CAN DO.
ACK! ANTS!
GET THEM OFF OF ME!
GET THEM OFF!

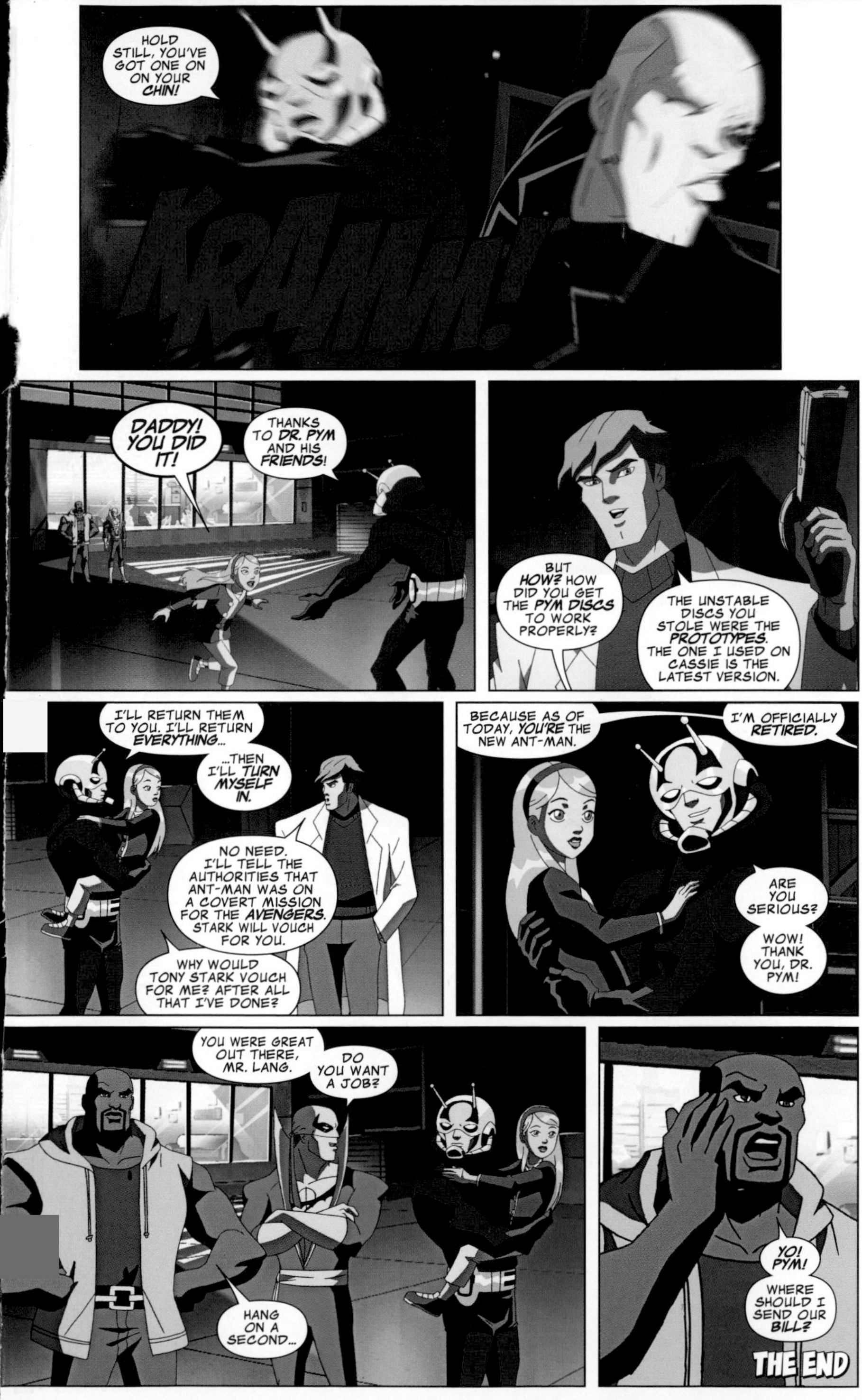
HOLD STILL, YOU'VE GOT ONE ON ON YOUR CHIN!
KRAAAM!
DADDY! YOU DID IT!
THANKS TO DR. PYM AND HIS FRIENDS!
BUT HOW? HOW DID YOU GET THE PYM DISCS TO WORK PROPERLY?
THE UNSTABLE DISCS YOU STOLE WERE THE PROTOTYPES. THE ONE I USED ON CASSIE IS THE LATEST VERSION.
I'LL RETURN THEM TO YOU. I'LL RETURN EVERYTHING...
...THEN I'LL TURN MYSELF IN.
NO NEED. I'LL TELL THE AUTHORITIES THAT ANT-MAN WAS ON A COVERT MISSION FOR THE AVENGERS. STARK WILL VOUCH FOR YOU.
WHY WOULD TONY STARK VOUCH FOR ME? AFTER ALL THAT I'VE DONE?
BECAUSE AS OF TODAY, YOU'RE THE NEW ANT-MAN.
I'M OFFICIALLY RETIRED.
ARE YOU SERIOUS?
WOW! THANK YOU, DR. PYM!
YOU WERE GREAT OUT THERE, MR. LANG.
DO YOU WANT A JOB?
HANG ON A SECOND...
YO! PYM!
WHERE SHOULD I SEND OUR BILL?
THE END

USE THIS CHART TO DECODE WHAT THE ANTS SAY IN *MARVEL UNIVERSE AVENGERS EARTH'S MIGHTIEST HEROES #17*

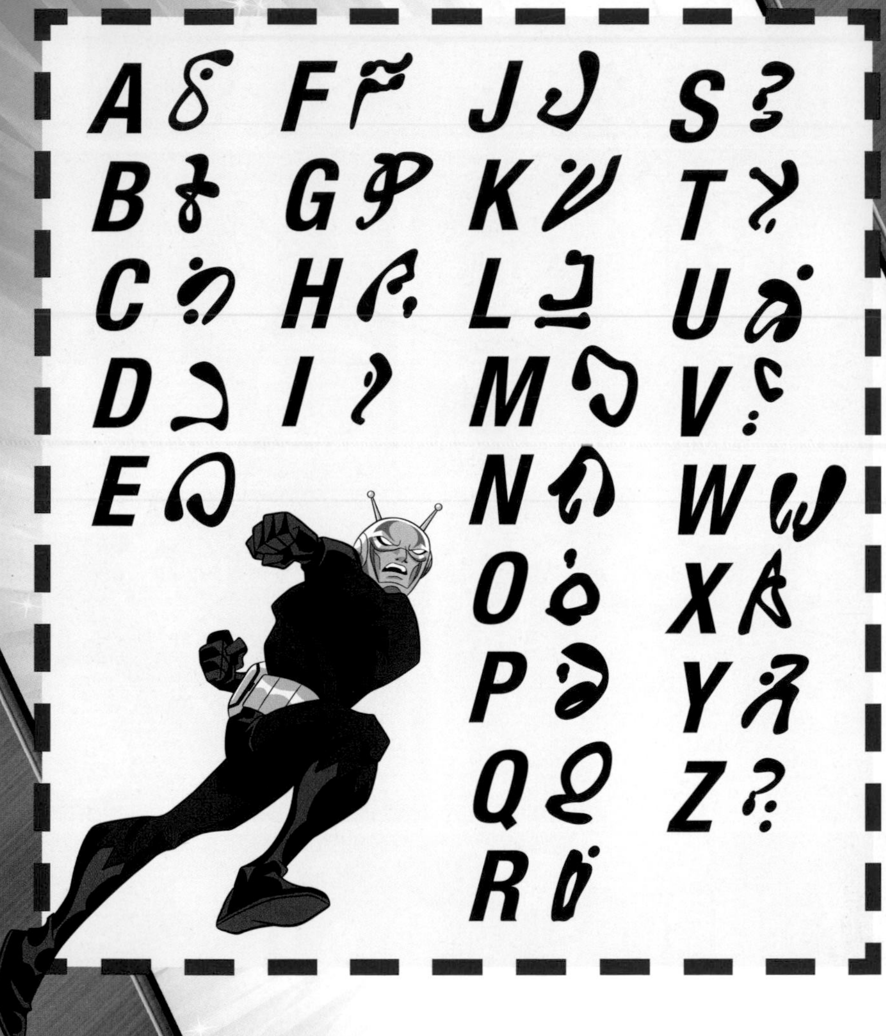
A
B
C
D
E
F
G
H
I
J
K
L
M
N
O
P
Q
R
S
T
U
V
W
X
Y
Z